ALSO AVAILABLE IN T
SERIE$

Undercurre

Drowned Voices

JOIN MY 'KEEP IN TOUCH' LIST!

If you'd like to be kept in the know about my new books and special offers, join my 'keep in touch list' by visiting www. mariafrankland.co.uk You'll receive a free novella as a thank you for joining!

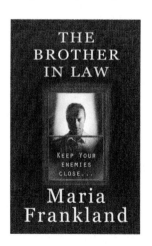

PROLOGUE

THE VAN'S on its roof, I'm sure of it. I must be lying on it. The seat's above my head, and there's a broken concrete post sitting next to it. It looks to have missed me by inches. I feel as sick as a pig, but at least I'm alive.

Letting my eyes close, I try to recall the impact, my head hurting more with the effort. It must have been substantial – the post has skewered the window and forced the steel door. As I open my eyes, I hoist myself onto my elbows, surveying my surroundings. There should be voices, sirens, footsteps. Instead, there's nothing apart from eerie silence. I complete a brief recce of myself. Although I'm sore, everything seems to bend and move as it should.

Possibilities cascade through my mind as I twist my body through the gap in the doorframe of my cage, my laboured breath loud in the stillness. When I get to the other side, I pause. And listen. The driver's cab is silent, as is the accompanying officer who was travelling back here with me. As my eyes adjust to the darkness, I pick his shape out, slumped beside the luggage racks. The angle of his neck suggests he's just taken his last journey.

I straighten myself into a sitting position, waiting for pain. Surely something must be broken, mangled, dismembered... but no. As I roll my shoulders, then my neck, I wince, but I'm clearly made of tougher stuff than these two fairies were. Other than the bang to the back of my head and what could be whiplash, I'm unscathed.

My gaze falls on two large polythene bags emblazoned with the HM Prison Service logo. My stuff. Bloody hell. This could be it here. I'd be an idiot not to take this chance. I crawl through the debris and drag the bags towards me. With shaking hands, I eventually rip them apart. One contains the effects from twelve long years of incarceration – sachets of soup, hot chocolate, dog-eared photographs. The other has my belongings from when I was arrested, most of which were not worth keeping after being dredged from the river, but they've been kept anyway. I grapple in the bag for my wallet, praying it's still stuffed with the twenty-pound notes I withdrew when I took Heidi on the run. It is. It bloody is. I let a long breath out. Then I rummage for the bag containing the clothes I wore for my trial. No matter how battered and bruised I feel, I'll have to get changed. I won't get far in what I'm currently wearing.

I hardly dare to believe I can get out of this and away from here. But who in their right mind wouldn't grab this opportunity with both hands?

Normally I'd be up an embankment like this in two seconds flat, but it feels like five inches forward, ten inches back. Getting to the top takes an age, but eventually I'm here, peering around in the darkness, in the hope there'll be a road sign not too far away. I don't have a clue where I am. Nor do I know what time it is. The battery will have long ago run out on my watch in the property bag. It's disorientating enough travelling backwards in a transfer van. But I could have been unconscious for hours for all I know. And as for what day it is – well for all these years, they've just meshed into each other. I really don't know what's going to happen from here, or how far I'll get. But I know exactly where I'm heading.

PART I

HEIDI

1

HEIDI

I SIGH at the usual trail of destruction as I open the door to our flat. No wonder Uncle Mark relented and allowed Alysha to move in with me before she turned eighteen. At least they don't have all this to put up with anymore. Clothes, make up, plates, wrappers... and that's just the lounge. I close the door to her bedroom as I pass it, knowing I'll get even more peeved if I look in there.

I do love my cousin most of the time, I'm just not sure I want to live with her anymore. Now we're older, we'd probably be better off in our own places. Alysha and I used to be so close, especially with all we've been through together, but at times she really does my head in. Like when I come home after a long day of lectures, followed by a shift at the restaurant and have to face this. Before she moved in, Auntie Claire would sometimes stay through the week – I'd never come home to a massive mess and an empty fridge. And I had fun with Auntie Claire too – pamper nights, films and long chats. Alysha only ever seems to look down her nose at me.

Where is she anyway? It's only Wednesday so she wouldn't normally be having a night out, but I can't think where else she might be this late. She certainly has a better social life than me. Despite my irritation, I know I'll ring her shortly – make sure she's alright. I'm only two years older than her but can't help feeling a sense of responsibility. I know better than anyone, what dangers can lurk in the darkness. But then again, so does Alysha. She just chooses to ignore them.

I clear space on the sofa amongst her clutter and sink back into the cushions. I detest this time of year when the clocks are turned back. It never fails to force the memories back into my mind of what happened, no matter how much I try to get rid of them. Though it's been nearly twelve years, there isn't a day that passes when I don't sense echoes of the past, especially at night when I'm here on my own. I've had everything from counselling to group work to art therapy and still the ghosts follow me around. I thought I'd like the art therapy, after all, art is what I do. It started off OK, but all too soon, I was given some pencils and asked to 'recreate' that night. Another time, I was 'invited' to draw him as I remembered him. When I couldn't bring myself to do that, I was asked to choose colours and use pencil strokes to show how I was feeling. I ended up stabbing through the paper with a thick black pencil point.

As I point the remote at the TV, I shiver. I don't care what's on, I just need background noise to drown out the silence. Some distraction. I stare out of the uncurtained window, and into the inky blackness of the North Sea. It's high tide and even the theme tune to the drama that's ending can't drown the crash of the waves against the sea wall.

We were unbelievably lucky to be allowed to live in this place. Well, it belongs to Uncle Mark really. He could make a fortune if he rented it out, but instead he lets us live here rent free, so long as we pay the bills. He got a massive pay-out after Auntie Lauren died back when I was seven. The money was there to be of benefit to us all, he said, especially Alysha who lost her mother at such a young age. Another reason why I couldn't exactly say no to sharing the flat with her.

Living in Filey is like being on a long holiday in the summer. I like it when it's full of sunshine and families on holiday. It feels lonely and bleak in the winter months when everything is shuttered up. Like I need extra help to feel lonely and bleak in the winter months.

The opening music of News at Ten reverberates through the lounge, something else that brings unwanted memories flooding back. I'll never forget crowding around the TV back in Alderton with Mum, Uncle Mark, Auntie Claire and Alysha's grandma, Brenda, all needing to find out what was happening with him, and also with scary Granny, as me and Alysha have always called her. She's dead now and I'm happy she is. She had a stroke in prison when I was fourteen. Whenever my friends' grandmothers have died over the years, they've all been upset. But no way could I be. Mum told me the truth about what she did and the horrendous lies she told. It's partly her fault that Will Potts, (I can't call him Dad anymore,) turned out like he did. But the worst thing was how she covered for him. She suspected all along what he was doing to women in the River Alder. Whatever her suspicions were, she turned a blind eye and let him get on with it. God knows why. Only she could explain that. She was as warped as he is.

Mum and Uncle Mark have always been honest with me about everything, but I guess they had to be, after all, I lived it. Thank God I 'lived' it too, for if Will Potts had got his way that night, I would never have seen daylight again. I can't go near a river now. In fact, it's left me with a fear of water generally. I might like looking at the sea through our window, but I'll never go down there and paddle in it.

My attention is averted back to the TV as a shot of an

upturned and rather wrecked van flashes up on the screen. It looks like a security van. The picture has been taken at the top of a hill from a road, so the first things visible are the wheels. I'm like most people, my attention's always drawn to the scene of an accident. *Stop rubbernecking,* Mum will say, if we ever drive past one. *How would you like it?*

I catch some of what the reporter says, *driver dead. Accompanying officer dead. Travelling towards Suffolk Prison.* Then *being transferred from secure hospital,* and then *escaped prisoner.*

Oh. My. God. It's the words *secure hospital* and *escaped prisoner.* Dread pools in my stomach. Mum's always said I have a sixth sense about things. I know who the escaped prisoner is before they even name him. My breath still catches in my throat when they do, as I know, with more certainty than I've ever felt in my life, precisely where he'll be heading.

I tug my phone from my bag and google Suffolk Prison. I don't know how far away the van was from the prison when it skidded off the road, but I need to know how far away the crash happened from here. Two hundred and sixty miles. I open 'maps.' Over five hours in a car. Not that he'd be driving. Surely they'll catch him quickly. I search the news headlines for Suffolk. They think the accident was around seven o'clock. That's over three hours ago. He could be nearly here. He could be two hours away. I jump as my phone rings and for a moment I can't bring myself to answer it. What if it's him? It's not. How would he have my number anyway? Or a phone for that matter?

"Uncle Mark, the news, I don't believe it, have you heard?" I'm surprised to realise I have tears streaming down my face. I don't know whether it's shock and fear from hearing the news, or relief at hearing Uncle Mark's voice. Probably a mix of everything.

"Get some stuff together," he says. "Your mum's on her way round to collect you both. You're not staying in that flat tonight.

No way. Not until we've got him. I can't take it in." He barely pauses for breath and I'll be surprised if he hasn't poured himself a brandy. He only drinks when it's Christmas or if he's acutely stressed. I can certainly hear the stress in his voice.

"Me neither. Mum didn't need to come though. I could have driven round myself."

"No arguments Heidi. She wanted to make sure. Get some things together. Both of you."

"But Alysha's not even here."

"So where is she?" His voice rises a notch.

"I've no idea." I glance up at the wall calendar to see if she's written anything down. A birthday or something. "You know what she's like."

"Is she driving?"

I rise from the sofa and lurch towards the window. The road below reveals an empty space behind my Fiesta where her little white Fiat normally goes. "Yes."

"I'll ring her now." The line falls silent. Uncle Mark is not usually so abrupt, he'd normally say goodbye, but I guess he just needs to know where Alysha is, although it'll be me that's more at risk than her. I'm Will Pott's daughter. Genetically anyway. Even though Uncle Mark and Mum have now got Harry and Isaac, they still seem to worry about Alysha and me. Not that Alysha will ever believe this. She's been jealous of her dad's attention towards the boys ever since they came along. And she and Mum haven't got on since Mum got together with Uncle Mark. When she stopped being her auntie and became her stepmother. Mum doesn't take Alysha's attitude towards her personally; she knows she'd have been a cow with anyone trying to fill Auntie Lauren's shoes.

We've got the weirdest family set up ever, it has to be said. Because Mum's married to my uncle, he's become my stepdad too. Which makes Alysha my stepsister, as well as my cousin. Harry's my full brother, but he's Alysha's cousin, and now stepbrother. Isaac's easy enough – he's half brother to both me and Alysha. Me and Isaac have the same mum and different dads, and with Alysha it's the other way around. But we've all got the same surname, Potts, so, we probably look like a normal-ish family to the outside world. Those that don't know our background. Anyone who thinks we're normal couldn't be further from the truth. I've always wanted to change my name and hopefully one day, I'll get married, so I can. Uncle Mark and Mum discussed us all changing our surname years ago, but decided it was a common enough name not to drag us down even further than we were at the time. As the years have gone by, much of the mud which was initially slung at us has dried up and crumbled away.

"Heidi." Mum's breathless as she thuds up the stairs to the lounge door and bursts in. "Did Uncle Mark call you? Have you heard what's bloody happened?"

"I saw it on the news." Now that Mum's here, I'm slightly more panicked than when I first heard. The terror on her face is unmistakeable. The same as twelve years ago. She's never got over any of what happened, and she's had even more counselling than me. This will be like all her worst nightmares rolled into one. Though if I know her correctly, she'll be more scared for me than for herself.

"It's alright Mum. He's absolutely miles away. I've Googled it. It would take him hours to get up here from where the crash was."

"One thing I've learned love..." She grabs my gym bag from the top of the pile of stuff on the armchair, and thrusts it at me, "is never, ever underestimate Will Potts. Come on. Get some things together."

"What about Alysha?" I say. "Shouldn't we wait for her to come back?"

"Mark will find Alysha. My priority is you right at this moment."

I want to remind her that I'm nearly twenty, but I can understand her being protective. She always has been. "What about uni tomorrow? I'm supposed to be doing a presentation."

"If he's been caught by then, you can go in," she says, like I'm ten years old. "But until he is..."

I empty the contents of my gym bag onto the sofa, and race into the bedroom. My room is spotless compared to Alysha's, so I quickly find my night things and a couple of changes of clothes. Not that we'll be there that long. Surely even a man like Will Potts can't get very far. I'd imagine that every police force in England will be looking for him.

"I'll pack some things for Alysha," Mum calls from the next room. "She won't want me to, but tough. Uncle Mark's just texted. Alysha's not answering but he's left her a message to go straight to our house. Do you know where she is Heidi?"

"She doesn't tell me anything Mum. Not anymore. In fact, she accuses me of getting on her case every time I speak to her."

"Typical Alysha. Bloody hell. Look at the state of this bedroom." Mum opens and closes drawers and doors whilst I grab what I need from the bathroom. "I'm so glad she doesn't live with us anymore."

She's telling the truth. And it's more than just about the mess. But I still don't know how I feel about Alysha being foisted on me instead.

"Do you really think he'd make his way up here?" I ask Mum as we arrive back at the lounge at the same time.

"If he has the chance, then very possibly. He'll want to get to you more than anything. That's why we need to make sure you're safe."

"And Harry," I add. "Now that he knows about him."

Mum's face falls. We've still no idea how he found out about Harry. "That bloody letter he sent..." She zips Alysha's holdall and I notice the flecks of grey in her hair as she bends forward. She's still got a figure to die for though. It's far better than mine and I'm twenty years younger than her. She's got nicer clothes than me too. I spend most of my life dressed in black. That way I don't stand out as much. That bastard has left his mark on me in more ways than I can count. "Anyway, his last letter went to Alderton, didn't it? Hopefully he has no idea that we moved to Filey. He'll go there first, if anywhere."

"We should make sure Auntie Claire knows what's happened," Mum says. "Although I'm sure either Uncle Mark or the police will have let her know by now."

"Imagine the people living in our old house opening the door to him." An image of the semi-detached we used to live in emerges in my mind.

Mum shakes her head. "I've never known a house get so much interest after I put it on the market. Anyway, come on."

"I can't believe anyone wanted to buy it though. Not after he had lived in it."

"I know." Mum gives me a gentle push towards the door. "Get a move on. Let's get out of here. Safety in numbers and all that."

I lock the door behind us, shivering in the late October wind as we make our way towards Mum's car. The waves are leaping to the top of the promenade railings. I enjoy watching the sea normally, as long as I'm at a distance. It's as though it's alive. Especially tonight. I can taste the salt as I lick my lips. "He won't survive for long in the open Mum," I say. "I reckon he'll hand himself in. Who could spend a night outdoors in these temperatures?"

"That's what I'm trying to tell myself." She closes the car door against the roar of the waves. "His face is all over the news."

"But that's an old picture of him." It gave me the creeps when I saw it. It was exactly as I remembered him from when I was a child. Before I knew who he really was. Who he really is. A person like that doesn't change. He's evil to his core. I cross the seatbelt over myself and hope by now that Uncle Mark has got hold of Alysha. We all need to stay together until he's caught. Mum might not be overly concerned about her, but I am. Whether she likes it or not.

"Have you spoken to Alysha yet?" I'm asking the question before we've even shut the door behind ourselves. We always use the side door here, straight into the kitchen. The front door is the 'posh' entrance. As I step inside, the blast of warm air is welcoming. Even though I moved out nearly a year ago, it still smells like home. A mixture of washing powder and fresh coffee.

"I've left her a voicemail and sent her a text." Uncle Mark rakes his fingers through his fringe. He's going grey too. He and Mum must have that effect on each other. "Maybe she'll come straight here without replying first. I'm trying not to stress too much. There's always the chance she's not answering because she's driving." He sips at the brandy I rightly suspected he'd have poured for himself.

"You won't find any answers in the bottom of a brandy glass." Mum hangs her coat on the back of the kitchen chair. "I think we should keep the boys off school tomorrow Mark. Unless they get him, that is." I've never quite got used to hearing Mum and Uncle Mark refer to 'the boys.' It was always 'the girls,' Alysha and me. Despite this, I adore my brothers, whilst Alysha only seems to resent them. They can be irritating at times, but they drive her mental. She has a much shorter fuse than me.

"Of course we'll get him." Uncle Mark always says *we,* as though he's part of absolutely everything that goes on in the police force, no matter where in the country he's referring to. I suppose he's quite senior now though.

"Have you found anything out on the official side yet?" Mum fills the kettle. She's always the same in a crisis. Let's have a nice cup of tea. Like that solves anything. "Can you find out if there have been any leads?"

"I'm still trying to find out who's heading up the case," he replies. "It's likely to be one of the teams in Suffolk, since that's where he's escaped. Though they'll be liaising with Alderton in case he's on his way up here."

My gaze falls on the photograph of Uncle Mark receiving his latest police promotion, hanging above the computer desk. There's a special name for what he does now. I can't remember it, but I know that he has a gun at work. Isaac is always excited to tell people about it, even though he's not supposed to. It's a shame we can't have a gun in the house right now, in case a certain someone turns up here.

"I've left a message for Alan Jones." He glances at the clock. "But I bet he's not back at the station in Alderton until the morning. I wonder if he's heard yet."

"He'll be in there now if he's heard who's escaped." Mum plucks the milk from the fridge door. "He'll be having kittens, given the background to all this. Do you want a drink Heidi?"

"Can you try Alysha, Heidi?" Uncle Mark says. "She might answer if it's you."

"True. I haven't tried her yet." My phone's already in my hand so I put it on loudspeaker and press on her name. "Get your arse home," I say, as I get voicemail. She's probably drunk somewhere. "Your dad's house, not the flat. And hurry up." I turn to Uncle Mark as I end the call. "Have you told her what's going on in the messages you've left? Otherwise, she might just keep ignoring you."

He shakes his head. "I don't want her to panic. Not if she's driving. Flick the news on love." He gestures to Mum. "I can't believe no one's been in touch with us yet to be honest. Officially, I mean. He's been at large for four hours now."

I smile. The phrase 'at large' always amuses me. Like I've anything to be amused about right at this moment.

Then Uncle Mark's phone rings.

2

HEIDI

"WHY THE DELAY?" Uncle Mark drains what's left of his brandy. "He could be anywhere by now. Including on his way here."

Mum, sitting beside him at the kitchen table, grips his arm and I see the fear in her face. I'll never forget the night we were on our own in the house when he was trying to get in. She was so terrified that she called the police. I felt sorry for him at the time. But I don't anymore. I had no idea of who he was and *what* he was back then.

At least Mum's got Uncle Mark to look after her now. It shocked everyone when they first got together, though I'd suspected there was something going on for a while. Harry was born not long after the sentencing and Uncle Mark was around all the time. He's always taken care of Harry as though he's his real dad, whilst he and Mum just got closer and closer. Out of anyone Mum could have ended up with, I'm glad it was Uncle Mark. I would never have trusted anyone else. Though Alysha has never been happy about them being together. Not one bit.

"OK, so when will they be here?" Uncle Mark says. I strain to hear the words at the other end of the phone. When will *who* be here?

"I take it all ports and airports are on alert? Though he's not likely to have any funds, is he?"

Uncle Mark looks pale as he ends the call. "They're putting a response unit at the end of our road," he says. "And they've told me that according to the person escort record, which was recovered from the van, it looks like he's got a change of clothes and his wallet with him. They're missing from the property bags that were being transferred with him. The record also shows his wallet had a fair whack of cash in it."

"Why was he being transferred?" I look from him to Mum. "He got life, didn't he? And wasn't he in a secure hospital?"

"Yes, he's been there since his sentence. But according to the call I took earlier," Uncle Mark says, still looking at his phone. "They've assessed him as being fit to be discharged. He's well medicated and has complied with all their interventions."

"What does that mean?" He might as well be talking in a foreign language. "I don't understand."

"It means," Mum replies, "that they think he's well enough and safe enough now to mix with others back in prison. As if!"

"Alan told me on the phone just now that he might even have been considered for a move to a Cat B in five years if he'd continued as he was." Uncle Mark curls his fingers around the brandy bottle in the middle of the table. "Though he'll have blown any chance of that for the foreseeable, that's for sure."

"If they don't catch him," Mum continues, "I'm certain he'll kill again. The streets aren't safe with him on them."

"Well, he is on them, isn't he? Anyway, what does Cat B mean?" I should know all this. I've been around this sort of talk my whole life. With a Detective Chief Inspector Uncle and a maniac murdering biological father.

"Cat B means less security and more privileges - mixing with different sorts of criminals. Unlikely, but possible. But as I said, they might have looked at it in five years or so from now."

"How the hell could he ever be moved anywhere after what

19

he's done?" A sickness spreads throughout me. "He killed thirteen women, for God's sake. He's wrong in the head and should stay in that hospital."

"We got a call this afternoon about the transfer," Mum says, "but we wanted to wait and tell you face to face, not over the phone."

"They must have known they were going to transfer him before today."

"They will have done," says Uncle Mark. "But they don't tell anyone until the day itself. It risks security."

"That's a laugh." Mum bangs her cup down. "*Security!* After what's happened."

"We all know he was ill," Uncle Mark continues. "I'd be the last person to defend him, but everything he's done is down to the psychosis. From what they said on the phone, Will thoroughly regrets everything he's done."

"Talking the talk, like you said," Mum says.

"If he'd robbed a bank." I stand and walk to the window. "If he'd burgled a house. Those things you can regret. But to kill thirteen women." I don't think I'll ever get over being the daughter of a serial killer, but I have to. He's damaged my life enough already. I can either get on with my future, or I can let him and what he's done rule it forever. Anyway, Uncle Mark's my dad now. Even though I still call him Uncle Mark. I once tried calling him Dad, but it felt really strange, so I stopped. Alysha felt threatened by it as well.

Mum snorts. "Will just knows exactly what to say and who to say it to for the best results. I'd be surprised if he's changed at all. Cat B. My arse."

"I can't believe he's escaped." Uncle Mark shakes his head. "It's literally a one in a million chance. I want to know what the hell happened."

"I'm sure we'll find out soon enough." Mum reaches for his

hand as he brings the phone to his ear for what seems like the tenth time since I arrived.

"Where the hell is Alysha?" He slams it down on the table.

"Do the boys know anything yet?" I realise it's a stupid question as soon as I ask it. Isaac's only five, too young to fully understand anything, and Harry's totally unaware of the past of his biological father. He's been told that he left before he was born. I don't think he even knows his name, but I expect they'll have to sit him down in a few years time and tell him the truth. Or maybe they'll decide not to. I guess he's got a right to know though.

He calls Uncle Mark, Dad. He's the only dad he's ever known, so it's different for him than it is for me. This is something that irks Alysha enormously. Though I suppose with having lost her mum when she was only five, she's bound to be insanely possessive over her dad. I wouldn't have minded sharing Mum with her, though. That's if Alysha had wanted to share her.

Mum shakes her head. "We've not said anything yet. And I want it to stay that way if possible."

"I'm sure he'll be caught before they even wake up." Uncle Mark swallows a mouthful of brandy. "Even if he has got over five hundred quid in his wallet."

"Really?" I gasp. "That much! How come?"

"It was in his wallet when he was arrested before..." Mum begins.

"You mean...?" My voice trails off. If I close my eyes, I can almost see the glint of moonlight on the river's surface. I can nearly hear Alan Jones's voice. *I want him found,* he had yelled. *Shoot him again if you have to.*

I'll never forget when Will Potts took me on the run. How petrified I was when he left me on my own at night. All I could think about was how I might never see Mum again. I know how lucky I am to have survived. He's pure evil. And now he's free. I feel with every bone in my body that he's on his way for me. To finish what he started. If he couldn't have me in his life, he didn't want anyone else to have me either. Perhaps he'll kill me this time. I'm not going anywhere. I'm safe here. Not knowing what he looks like anymore, I wouldn't even be able to watch out for him.

"Heidi!" The bedroom door bursts open, and I wheeze with the force of Isaac landing on my stomach. Much as I love him, he weighs a ton.

"Why are you sleeping at our house?" Harry asks from the doorway. "Are you moving back in?"

"Yes, yes, she is," yells Isaac. "Aren't you Heidi?"

"Gerroff." I push my wriggling brother to the floor. "Thanks a bunch for letting me have a sleep in, you two."

For a split second I ask myself the same question Harry just asked. *Why am I sleeping here?* Then it all comes rushing back, slapping me as hard as the waves against the sea wall last night. Will Potts escaped from a prison van yesterday. Though surely they'll have him by now. I reach for my phone. The battery has died, so I'll have to go downstairs to find out if there have been any developments. Gosh, I'm turning into Uncle Mark. *Any developments.* Maybe I should have joined the police force too, instead of going to Art College.

"Is Alysha back?" I ask neither of them in particular. "Is she still asleep?"

Harry looks puzzled as he turns towards Alysha's old room. It's been made into an office since she moved out, but there's still a sofa bed in there for if she wants to stay over, though she never has, apart from last Christmas. I've slept in my old room, although they've redecorated it as a guest room, which makes me sad. Part of me wishes they hadn't changed a thing, so I'd always have somewhere safe to run back to. I hate feeling like this - I'm a grown woman and I've lived in the shadow of who my real father is for long enough.

Isaac trots behind Harry, glances into the other room, then hurtles back towards me, a cheeky grin on his face. I'm now perched on the edge of my bed as he launches himself into my lap.

"Not now Isaac." I slide him from my knee. "Look, I'll be downstairs in a minute. Let me get dressed."

"But where's Alysha? She'll play with me if you won't."

I want to tell Isaac that he has more chance of nailing jelly to the ceiling than Alysha playing with him. It's a shame she's so jealous of him being Uncle's Mark's son. Not *pretend son* as she sometimes refers to Harry when she's bitching about things. Who could be jealous of a five-year-old anyway? I think he's the cutest thing on two legs.

The hallway is still in semi-darkness as I reach the bottom of the stairs. The heavy curtain is drawn across the front door, and the low drone of the TV echoes from the lounge. Despite what's going on, I like being back at home again.

"Any news?" I open the door and try to read Mum's face. It doesn't look promising. It's only really since she and Uncle Mark married, and she had Isaac, that she's relaxed. What happened tortured her for years.

"Uncle Mark's gone to check your flat. For the third time. To see if Alysha's turned up yet. I can't believe how selfish she is at times."

"You mean she hasn't been back? All night? Hasn't she even rung?" I ignore the selfish comment. Things are strained at the best of times between Mum and Alysha without me chipping in. Much as I'm often tempted.

"Nope. We've rung her and rung her. Uncle Mark's starting to really worry."

"She'll be crashed out on someone's sofa. Or with some lad."

"Don't tell Uncle Mark that. I'm sure he still thinks the sun shines out of her backside." Mum laughs, though the sound is hollow. "I just hope he can manage to barge his way through all those reporters and can get back in here again. Have you seen them out there? Vultures, the lot of them."

I pull back the curtain and gasp. There must be over ten of them. One's even got a stepladder. A camera flashes and I let the curtain drop back down. Who knows why they'd want a photo of me?

"It's exactly like it was last time. I thought all that was behind us." Mum points the remote at the TV. "I'm waiting for the news to come on. Though I'm sure someone would have phoned from the station if they'd caught him."

"What do you mean? Last time?"

"When you were missing for four days. With *him*." Mum refers to Will Potts as *him* usually too, rather than by name. Thankfully, he's not mentioned as much anymore. "They were camped out on Uncle Mark's doorstep for ages."

Now Mum's brought it up. I remember it well. After I'd got back home, that is. For what felt like forever, we were like prisoners in the house. We had my beloved dog, Biscuit, and couldn't even take him for a walk. We had to wait until it was dark, and they'd given up for the day.

"So, I take it he's still out there Mum? They haven't even seen him yet?"

She shakes her head and sighs. "Uncle Mark's been up most of the night. Well, so have I, really. His priority right now is finding Alysha, then I expect he'll get into work to help with the search. That's if they'll even let him." She tilts her phone towards her face. "Are you sure you've no idea where

Alysha might have gone Heidi? You're not covering for her, are you?"

"Don't be daft. We've got totally different friends." I plug my phone in next to the TV. "And we go to completely different places. But if you give me five minutes to get some toast and charge my phone, I'll get onto social media and start asking around."

Though what Alysha's glamorous salon and college friends will make of her far-less-cool and slightly overweight cousin getting in touch remains to be seen. I usually make myself scarce when she brings anyone to the flat.

"Just hang fire until Uncle Mark gets back. See what he has to say first. We can't do anything that might jeopardise things."

"I don't see how we can. It's already out in the news."

"Which he might have access to as well. If he gets wind that Alysha hasn't come back, who knows?"

"What are you going to do about Harry and Isaac?"

"They're on the games thingy at the moment." She raises her eyes to the ceiling. "In Harry's room. I haven't even told them they're not going to school yet. I'm going to have to tell them something of what's going on shortly, much as I don't want to." She tightens her dressing gown as she tucks her legs under herself. "Gosh, it's so cold in here. The fire's gone out."

"I can't imagine they'll put up too much of a fight about a day off school."

"Ssshhh." Mum raises her hand. "It's on."

I sit beside her.

"The search is intensifying this morning for an escaped prisoner, William Potts, aged fifty-one, and formerly of Alderton in Yorkshire. He absconded yesterday evening from a prison van which was involved in a traffic accident whilst travelling North East along the A14. The van is thought to have skidded off the road before rolling down an embankment near the junction at Thurstan in Suffolk.

Potts was being transferred to HMP Suffolk when the accident happened at around seven pm yesterday. The alarm was only raised just before nine pm when the van failed to arrive at the receiving prison. Potts is thought to have acquired a change of clothing and a substantial amount of cash from his belongings, which were in transit with him.

The public can be assured that all resources are being allocated to find this man, and are advised not to approach Potts, but to call 999 immediately if they see him."

"I bet that looks nothing like him now." I nudge Mum as I stare at the photograph of the man who was once my father. Why are they not showing something more recent? God knows how Mum is feeling. She was actually married to him. I had him forced into my life, whereas she actually chose him once upon a time.

"Ssshhh," she says again. "Sorry love. I need to listen to this."

"*Potts is five feet, eleven inches tall, of average build, with medium brown, receding hair and blue eyes. He is usually clean shaven. The change of clothes he has means he may be wearing dark-coloured trousers, a white shirt and brown brogue-style shoes like the ones now pictured.*"

"How could he have been out all night if he's only wearing a shirt?" I stare at the garments being shown on the screen.

"Heidi! Let's just listen!" Mum's voice is a shriek. I definitely feel eight years old again.

"*It is believed Potts is heading North towards Yorkshire, where his family live. Ports, airports and all train and bus companies have been alerted nationally. The public are once again urged to remain vigilant at all times until he is found, and not to approach him, but to let the police know straight away if they have any information or believe they have seen him.*"

A video of the crashed van being hoisted up the embankment is shown as the reporter finishes speaking.

"*The two security officers responsible for transferring Potts, who are yet to be named, were pronounced dead at the scene of the crash. It's not known yet if Potts played any part in the crash or the deaths of the security officers. We will bring you more information as we have it."*

"Poor buggers," Mum says. "As usual, Will Potts's name is up front and central, whilst the two dead men are only mentioned as an afterthought."

3

HEIDI

MUM and I sit in silence for a few moments. His being on the run again must bring things back for her as much as it has for me. I spent three nights like that. Though I knew things were far from OK, I never realised how much danger I was in. After all, I thought 'my dad' would always protect me. How could I have ever known he was a psychopath? Who would know what a psychopath is when they're eight years old, anyway? For two of the three nights we slept in a car he'd borrowed, and only for one of those nights did we sleep in a proper bed. At scary Granny's old house. All I can really remember from that time is being locked on my own in the car a lot, and feeling cold and dirty because I couldn't change my clothes. I was also worried in case scary Granny came back. Neither I nor Alysha liked her very much when we were little. And with good reason, as we later found out.

His final killing happened whilst he was 'looking after' me. Sara. She'd been friends with Auntie Lauren and became Uncle Mark's 'sort of' girlfriend. Alysha was only five or six at the time and couldn't bring herself to speak to Sara. However, a couple of years ago when Alysha and Mum were in the thick of an argument over something, Alysha had screamed something at her along the lines of, *Dad should have married Sara, not you. She was miles better*. Mum was heartbroken, hearing that.

When I heard Sara was dead, I couldn't take it in. I'd heard it on the news whilst I was in hospital. Drowned in the River Alder, the same as all the others. Nearly me too. I'm just so relieved I'm nothing like him. That I take after Mum. All the time I worry that anything of him, or Scary Granny, might be in me. I'm prone to dark moods, say when I've got PMT, but I try to counteract that by being nice to everyone all the time. I've certainly never heard weird voices inside my head, so I should be OK.

Harry's shovelling cereal into his mouth at the kitchen table. I'm sad to say that he's a mini version of his real father, though he'll hopefully never know that. It's often been on the tip of my tongue to comment on this to Mum, but so far, it's remained unspoken. Not only does Harry look like him, but he's also got his temper. Like now.

"But I want to go to school Mum." He slams his spoon down. "It's Art and PE today. It's the best day." He glares at her from beneath his heavy eyebrows. "You're spoiling my life."

"Look. There's a bit of trouble with Dad's police work, that's all." Mum sits beside him and pats his hand. "And we've all got to keep safe at home. It's only for today. Just while it all gets sorted out."

"Me too?" Isaac asks, wide-eyed. "Can I stay at home as well?"

Harry pushes his bowl away. "Can't we go anywhere?"

"What are we going to do then?" Isaac asks.

"We can draw pictures if you like," I tell him.

"Boooring," he replies. "I'd rather play on the racing game with Harry."

"Fair enough."

"Just for today." Mum raises her cup to her lips. I expect she hasn't got the energy to amuse them in any other way. The lines are deeper around her eyes today. They always are when she hasn't had much sleep.

We all jump as the back door crashes into the cupboard.

"Careful Mark." Mum stands. "Boys, take your games console into the conservatory where we can keep an eye on you." She points towards the door. "And don't open the blinds, whatever you do."

The breeze from outside causes Isaac's paintings taped to the fridge to flutter. I shiver in the sudden chill, glad to be in here, but feeling an insatiable urge for freedom all at the same time.

"Why can't we?" says Harry. "It's too dark in there. And it's morning."

"Just put the light on," I say. I don't know why they're not allowed to open the blinds. The reporters are hanging around the front of the house, not the back. Though last time, one or two of them climbed over the back gate. We'd ended up going to stay with Uncle Mark and Alysha. Not that things had been any better there. But at least there'd been more of us with Brenda and Auntie Claire there too.

"But I haven't finished my breakfast," Isaac wails.

"Take it with you." Uncle Mark kicks the door shut with his foot. "*Now*, if you don't mind. I need to speak with your mother."

"What's going on Dad?" Harry stands and looks straight at him. "Who are all those people outside? And why can't we go to school?"

"It's grown-up work stuff, that's all," Uncle Mark replies. Even though Harry knows that Uncle Mark isn't his real dad, they're really close. I'm not sure if they'd have told him, if it hadn't been for Alysha letting it slip. She was in so much trouble after that. But what he doesn't know is that the man who's his natural father is also a convicted murderer, who's escaped from a prison van and is probably making his way up here to do God knows what as we speak. "It's nothing for you to worry about son."

Except it is.

"Any sign of Alysha at the flat?" Mum rises from the table. "I'll get you a coffee love."

"Nope." He sits facing me. "I don't think she's been anywhere near the flat all night, but it's difficult to say. There's stuff all over the place."

"That's her. Not me." I smile, despite the circumstances.

"Does she often stay out all night Heidi?"

There's something in Uncle Mark's voice that sounds as though he's blaming me for not keeping more of an eye on Alysha. But it's not my job to babysit her, and in any case she's not a kid anymore.

"Not really. Sometimes."

"She's not Heidi's responsibility love."

I smile at Mum who must have read my mind.

"We should never have let her move out," Uncle Mark says to no one in particular. "Not when she can't even be bothered to let people know where she is?" He takes a cup from Mum. "Thanks love."

"You couldn't have really stopped her to be fair," Mum says. "You can't, once they're sixteen. Look, she'll be alright. You know what she's like. Have you tried her phone again?"

"Of course I have." He's snappy, which isn't like him. "It's going straight to voice mail now. Her battery must have died."

"I'm sure she'd have rung back if she'd seen your messages. And Heidi's." Mum rests a hand on his shoulder. She's normally the one who stresses, and Uncle Mark's the calm one. They've reversed roles all of a sudden. "She might not know what's going on yet."

I'm surprised at Mum. She's usually the last person who'd stick up for Alysha.

"She must do. It's all over the news. Local and national. She's going to get a right telling off for not getting in touch."

"She really might not know Uncle Mark. Alysha's not exactly someone who takes much notice of the news." She's too wrapped up in her own little world. But I don't say this.

He ignores me and continues with his rant instead. "And I can't believe it was two hours after the accident before anyone thought to raise the alarm. Imagine how far he could have got in two hours."

"We're safe in here love." Mum sits beside him. "All together."

Except we're not all together. Where the hell is my stupid cousin?

It's hard to imagine Mum being married to anyone other than Uncle Mark now. And it's hard to imagine him being with anyone else either. I have vague memories of him living with Auntie Lauren, but that's such a long time ago. I loved Auntie Lauren. One of my nicest memories is her taking me and Alysha out to find our flower girl dresses, and then for afternoon tea. We were only five and seven and felt like princesses. She never made it to her wedding day though.

"No one's going to get past those reporters and the police guard, are they?" Mum adds, her words slicing into my thoughts.

"But that doesn't make Alysha safe, does it?" He glances at his watch. "She's due to start at the salon in half an hour. I'll try there. She might get in early."

"Alysha. Early." I snort. "You've got to be joking. It's a miracle she's still got that job, if you ask me."

"I'll get it." Mum rises from the table in response to the doorbell echoing through the house. She tightens the cord on her dressing gown.

"It's probably a bloody news reporter," mutters Uncle Mark. "I'm sick of them. As if we're going through all this again."

"I'll get it," I say. "You drink your brew Mum." The last thing I want is pictures of my mother in her dressing gown all over the news. Everyone's going to be gossiping about our family as it is. We've already been hounded out of Alderton. Other kids whispered about me at school, and we even had people shouting things at us in the street. And apparently, whilst I was missing, someone chucked a brick through Uncle Mark's window. You'd have thought it was one of us that had killed someone. Like we hadn't been punished enough. Like we hadn't been through enough.

People have left us alone since we moved to Filey. I've told close friends here about my past, but only those I can really trust. Mostly they've felt sorry for what I've been through, and the person my biological father is, rather than blaming me.

No one at university or at my restaurant job knows anything yet, as far as I know. And I really had hoped to keep it like that. Since I've moved out of home and into the flat, I've just wanted to get on with my own life. But now, with all this going on, everyone's going to know about our family. And Harry may well be in for the same rough ride at school that I got. Even Isaac could be in for it and really, it's got nothing to do with him. Will Potts is nothing to do with him.

What also worries me is that even if he still thinks we're in Alderton, somehow he'll be able to find where we moved to. One of the reporters is bound to give it away. They're taking photos of the house, after all. No matter how hard I try, I can't shake the thought that he might try to finish what he started when I was eight. He might even break in here through the night whilst everyone else is sleeping.

. . .

I peer around the door so that any reporters who are pointing lenses at it will only get a photograph of the top of my head. My attention is immediately drawn to them, rather than to the person who rang the doorbell. There are even more people than when I last looked out half an hour ago. The neighbours must be going mad with this. Finally, I turn my attention to the woman standing on the porch.

"Hi there. I'm your Family Liaison Officer. North Yorkshire Police. Adele Fisher." She flashes a card at me. I glance at it, then hold the door wider for her. I don't see what good she can do. Uncle Mark's in the police. What do we need a liaison officer for?

As I close it behind her, Mum and Uncle Mark appear in the hallway. "Adele." They nod at one another. He must already know her. "Back in there," he says to the boys who curl their heads around the lounge door. The lounge door bangs, followed by the slide of the conservatory door. They know when he uses that tone, he means business. They must be wondering what the hell is going on. Mum will have to tell them something soon.

"Come through." We all troop back to the kitchen and face one another around the table.

"So, what's the latest?"

Give her a chance to sit down, I feel like saying. No one has even offered her a drink, so I do.

"Yes please." She smiles at me. "DSI Jones is on his way across from Alderton," she begins. "To offer his support both to you and to the search. And I'm here now to liaise with everyone and keep you informed and supported."

"We don't need support," says Uncle Mark. "And I can liaise for myself. We just need him found. He's a category A prisoner, and he's been out all night."

Adele clasps her hands together on the table. "From what I've learned, there was talk of him being moved to a B if he continued to comply with his regime." She ignores Uncle Mark's comments about her not being needed.

Mum shakes her head. "He should rot after what he did. In fact, they should bring back the death penalty."

"I hear what you're saying," says Adele. "And after this, who knows what will happen? When we have him back in custody, he certainly won't be going anywhere anytime soon."

"He just needs to be caught," replies Mum. "I can't rest until he is."

"Have there been any further leads?" Uncle Mark yawns as he speaks. His hair is on end and his chin is stubbly. He looks as knackered as Mum. I hope the photographers outside don't get any pictures of him either. All I want is a normal life.

"I'm sorry not to be able to tell you much at this stage," Adele replies. "All I know is that the van transporting your brother was scheduled to arrive at HMP Suffolk at eight thirty five pm. He was being transferred at night to negate against the volume of traffic, and minimise public risk."

"Don't refer to him as *my brother*, if you don't mind." Uncle Mark is so snappy today. I guess he might calm down when Alysha turns up. He hates having Will Potts being referred to as his brother though. It's the same when anyone refers to scary grandma as his mother. He won't stand for it. Auntie Claire is the same. As far as they're concerned, they're the only two left from the family.

"How do they know the crash happened around seven o'clock?"

Uncle Mark gives me a look as though I've asked a daft question. I don't think it is.

"From the ice that had frozen over the tyre marks after the van had left the road. Also, from the mobile phone signals from the officer's phones. They became static just after seven."

"Right." From her answer, Adele doesn't think it was a daft question either.

"So... he's been on the run now for thirteen hours and there's still been no sightings?" Uncle Mark drags his fingers through his fringe. "None whatsoever. Is that what you're telling me?"

"Absolutely nothing." Adele looks almost guilty. As though it's her fault. "And clearly we don't know how injured he might be from the accident."

"But evidently able to get away from it." Mum scrapes her hair up into a ponytail as she speaks. "He can't be that injured."

"No. I've been told there are footprints leading away from the van, and there's evidence of him getting up the embankment. We're still looking at that. And very closely at the CCTV of the surrounding area."

"It was freezing last night," Mum glances towards the kitchen window, looking almost hopeful. She's probably wishing he's frozen to death, like the thirteen victims whose lives he so callously ended in the river, over two winters. I don't know what to think or feel. I feel bad wishing him dead, but after... Then an image flashes into my mind. It's the word *embankment*. I have a sudden image of being driven down an embankment from the motorway when he took me. The same night, he filled my pink princess coat pockets with stones. The night I nearly died. Uncle Mark saved my life. I look at him. If he were to look back at me, he'd probably see the gratitude in my eyes. He's my dad now. I might not call him it, but he's always been here for me. Alysha doesn't know how lucky she is to have him.

"I'll keep you updated every step of the way from now on," Adele nods around at us. "As soon as we get any news, you'll be the first to know."

"You're staying here with us, are you? Until he's caught?" Probably another daft question, but how am I supposed to know what exactly a Police Liaison Officer does.

"Well yes. Me and a colleague will keep swapping over."

"I'm sure that won't be necessary. We'll have him soon." Uncle Mark snatches his phone from the table. "But if they've sent you here, then so be it. Anyway, I'm going to try the salon. There should be someone there by now."

He looks up the number and then waits to be connected. I watch, willing Alysha to have turned up at work. I'll start to worry as well if she hasn't.

"Hi there, this is Mark Potts, Alysha's dad," he says, clearly talking to an answerphone. "Can Alysha ring me the minute she arrives please? It's urgent. I'll try again in ten minutes." He places his phone on the table.

Almost as soon as he's put it down, it bursts into life. He swipes at it as though his life depends on it.

"Ah, Alan," he says. "DSI Jones," he mouths at Mum. "Hang on, I'll just put you on speakerphone. I've got Eva, and my... erm, I've got Heidi with me and also Adele, the FLO."

Heat rises in my face. He never knows what to call me. Niece, daughter, step-daughter. I really wish I was his daughter, and not related in any way, shape, or form to Will Potts.

"Tell me what's going on? Bloody nightmare, isn't it?"

"Now we've got daylight, we've widened the search around the crash site." The gruff voice at the other end of the phone sounds reassuringly familiar. We saw a lot of DCI Jones, as he was then, when it was all going on, but I haven't seen him for ages now. "We're still in the process of obtaining CCTV," he continues, "and obviously he can't get anywhere on public transport. Every train, coach, bus and taxi company in the county has been sent an image of his face."

"Which county?"

"Well Norfolk and Suffolk, for starters."

"Just Norfolk and Suffolk?" Uncle Mark leans closer to the phone. "He can get a long way in what has it been..." He tilts his watch towards his face. "Fourteen hours now. Fourteen bloody hours. I mean, how the hell has he escaped from a secure prison van? I can't get my head around it Alan."

"I agree with you. Totally. And from the pictures I've been shown, it's a one in a million freak of whatever – I don't have the words. The transfer van has taken the impact on its side; a concrete post has not only pierced the window where he was travelling, it's also forced the door straight opposite. And it's gone down a hell of a steep embankment so it wasn't spotted from the road."

We're all quiet, just staring at the phone in the centre of the table. I look up and search Uncle Mark's face for signs of how he's feeling. This is still his brother, no matter how much he tries to forget that. His other brother died when he was a teenager, so he's lost both of them really. But all I can see in his face is anger.

I don't think any of it has sunk in with me yet, although it's feeling more real today. When I went to sleep last night, I honestly thought I'd be waking to news that he was back where he belonged.

"This is like history repeating itself Alan. Anyway, never mind nationally, I reckon word will get out internationally before long. Our police and prison services will be the laughing stock of the world. How the hell have we managed to *lose*," he draws air quotes with his fingers, "a prisoner convicted of thirteen murders? Heads are going to be on poles after this. The media will have a field day once the initial shock and sense of danger has passed."

There's silence at the other end. It's as though DSI Jones is letting him have his rant and is making sure it's definitely over. "I know." He sighs eventually. "But rest assured that everything that can be done is being done."

"Is there anything I can do? I feel useless just waiting..."

"I'll ask around and let you know Mark. Until he's caught, we need as many officers involved as possible. But for now, until you hear from me, just sit tight. Stay there with your family for now."

"OK, but only for the moment. I need to find my daughter first anyway."

"Alysha? Why? Where is she?"

"At work, I'm hoping. She's been out all night."

"Really? Do you know where she's been? Have you spoken to her at all?" There's concern in his voice.

"We've no idea where she is," Uncle Mark replies, looking at me like I secretly know, or something. "And she's not answering her phone either." The way his stare pierces me makes me feel guilty when I've nothing to feel guilty about. I guess it's a side effect of being the daughter of a murderer.

"Well that is quite worrying," DSI Jones says after a long pause. "Especially in the current circumstances."

"We're about to step up our efforts to look for her." Mum leans towards the phone on the table now, joining in the conversation for the first time.

"Right. Well, keep me informed the minute you find her. And if you haven't got her in an hour, two at the most, we'll escalate things further."

The phone beeps with an unknown incoming call. "Sir. I'll have to go," Uncle Mark says. "I've got another call coming through. It might be her." He presses the button. "Shit. Voicemail's already got it."

We sit watching him for a few moments. It's after nine. I'm supposed to be doing my art presentation at uni in an hour. I sigh. It's been twelve years, we've moved eighty miles away, and he's still affecting my life.

My attention's brought back by a loud beep. *Hi, this is Jess from Filey, Polish and Hair. Just returning your call. Alysha hasn't come in yet, but the minute she does, I'll get her to call you. Hopefully she's just late. From wherever she's been all night.*

4

WILL

I TAP my foot as I stand by the desk, willing the woman to look up and notice me. Hurry up. Hurry up. The longer I'm out in public, the more chance I have of being recognised. It's an old photo that's doing the rounds, but still.

The receptionist's on the phone. Whatever happened to *the customer comes first?*

"Yeah. It's not a million miles from here... I know. Someone said that at the time. That I could look like one of The Yorkshire Dipper's victims. Dark hair, green eyes, you know." She laughs. She's talking about me. "He was far enough away then though." She pauses. "Yeah. It's quiet at the moment. I should get finished early... No later than ten. I'll have a quick swim then maybe see you in the pub... I'll see how I feel... Yeah... I know it might sound creepy to you, but I like the pool when it's quiet. Besides, I know this place like the back of my hand. I've worked here since I was a Saturday girl."

I cough. I'm sick of waiting. She notices me at last.

"Sorry, I've gotta go." She drops her phone into her pocket. "Sorry about that, sir. I hope you haven't been waiting long." She steps towards the desk and smiles whilst tossing her hair behind one shoulder. There isn't a flicker of recognition on her face as she looks straight at me. "How can I help you?"

"I was wondering whether you have any vacancies for this evening?" I've been surrounded by southerners for twelve years, so can ensure not a shred of northern twang enters my voice. It's bound to have been reported where I originate from.

"Do you have a reservation with us?"

I almost laugh at the irony as I clear my throat. Like I'm going to have thought to have booked a hotel room in advance of my escape. "Erm no, but I'm only after a single room." Surely a place this size will be able to fit me in.

"We only have double rooms sir. With a single supplement, I'm afraid."

"That's fine." I refrain from adding, *unless you'd like to join me.* "I'll pay cash if that's OK?"

She eyes me with what could be curiosity. I keep my eyes firmly fixed on her face, trying with everything I've got not to allow them to venture south. It's been a while since I could feast my eyes on the outline of a bra beneath a sheer blouse.

Not that someone like her would look twice at me right now. She definitely would have done twelve years ago though. I've been in these dishevelled clothes since I got clear of the transfer van. It's been quite a day, and night. Mostly I've been travelling, apart from a few hours' shut eye in a freezing outhouse in the middle of nowhere. Still, at least it was dry. Luckily both men who picked me up and have helped me get further North have been foreign drivers. They didn't ask too many questions. My stars have certainly aligned over this last day or so. I only hope it continues. If my luck holds out, maybe I could get myself abroad. Perhaps with my kids. And eventually, I could make a killing selling my story. Though, I'd have to go somewhere I couldn't be extradited from.

"We usually ask for a card on account." The woman's voice

cuts into my wild thoughts. "Just to cover any other items you may wish to charge to your room."

"I'll just use cash if you don't mind." I laugh. "I guess no one pays cash these days. Only, as a tradesman, that's how most of my customers pay me. Lots of them are elderly." I laugh again. I'm not sure what I'm laughing at.

She smiles then. "OK. Is it just for the one night?"

"For now. I'll let you know if that changes."

"If you could just fill this out."

She pushes a card towards me, which I begin to complete with false details, trying to pay attention whilst she gives me restaurant times, swimming pool times, and tells me when I need to check out. I've never been any good at doing two things at once and she's expecting me to write whilst listening to her. In my current knackered and stressed state, it's irritating to say the least.

I slide six twenties across the counter. *A hundred and twenty quid.* Things have certainly gone up since they incarcerated me. She plucks a white card from a drawer and holds it against a machine. I wonder what on earth it is as she slides it towards me. I want to ask her what I do with it. After all, it's been a while since I inhabited normal life, but that might draw more attention than paying in cash already has. I'll work it out for myself. At least I'm in here - with no questions asked. But I need to get moving before someone else turns up behind me at the desk. It's a miracle someone hasn't already recognised me.

The TV in the corner of the reception area is switched off, thankfully. My face is probably being splashed all over the news. But other than the girl at reception, there's no one around to take any notice of me. There're a few people beyond the glass doors in the bar area, but to them, from a distance, I'm just another guest.

I'm keen to get to my room, order some food, wash my clothes out in the sink and take stock of the situation. One thing I won't be doing is shaving. Not that I've got a razor handy. With over a week's growth now, I look totally different from the picture I caught sight of earlier. My current unruly grey mop of hair looks nothing like the groomed short style in the photograph either. Front page news, no less. Back in the day, I would enjoy making the front pages. I can sure sell newspapers.

This latest newspaper was folded in half on the dash of the second wagon, and the driver who'd agreed to take me either hadn't looked at it or had just turned past it. I couldn't read the headline – I think it was French or Hungarian or something. As if they're flashing a picture of me around from twelve years ago. Idiots.

I take the stairs to my room. There's probably a camera in the lift. In fact, there are probably cameras everywhere in this place. I'm not going to look for them like the old me might have done. That could draw attention, and right now, one wrong move and it's curtains for me. Instead, I bow my head and focus on getting to the room as quickly as possible. Any fool could operate the card thing, but I take a few minutes once inside the room to work out that it needs inserting into a holder for the power to work. I flip the switch on the kettle, then devour both packets of biscuits, not realising how hungry I've been until I've finished them. The only thing I've eaten since leaving Aylesbury yesterday is a sandwich the first lorry driver donated. The same one that took pity on me as he dropped me off, and let me have an old fleece jacket, which he said didn't fit him anymore. Without it, I might have frozen to death in that outhouse.

I fling myself onto the bed, beyond grateful for this unexpected freedom. However long it may last, I don't regret taking the chance I was given. Only an idiot would have stayed at the crash scene, waiting to be taken on the rest of the journey to Suffolk Prison. I stretch my legs out, smiling at the proper bed beneath me, instead of a skinny bed on the hospital ward at Her Majesty's pleasure. It's amazing what's taken for granted until it's snatched away.

I order room service, then peel my clothes off and fill the sink with water to soak them in. Then I stand beneath the shower, wincing as the water pressure stings the cuts I've sustained to my limbs and head. This doesn't stop me luxuriating beneath the powerful jets of water though. It's the first time in twelve years where someone hasn't been staring at me.

After a few minutes, it feels as though I'm hallucinating. Perhaps I'm going to suddenly wake up and find myself back on the ward. I feel really peculiar. Disorientated, as though I'm not really here. Then a bit nauseous. I've not had my meds for thirty-six hours. That's bound to have an effect. Or maybe it's that bang to the head I had yesterday. After all, it was enough to knock me unconscious.

The knock at the door nearly sends me skyrocketing towards the ceiling in fright. "Room service."

I let a long breath out and poke my head through the bathroom doorway. "Just leave it out there please," I call into the lobby area of my room. "I'm just getting out of the shower." My voice sounds strange. Like it's not mine. Shit. I hope I'm going to be alright without my meds. I've been on them for years and don't know how I'll be. I've never been without them. Not since...

"I don't mind waiting sir."

He'll be wanting a tip. Wrong place. Wrong time. "No. Just. Go."

"Right you are," the male voice calls back quickly. I listen until I hear the squeak of a nearby door, hopefully meaning he's gone. I leave it a few minutes before I go anywhere near the food I ordered.

I practically inhale my pasta and vegetables. It's certainly a far cry from the processed crap I've endured for so long. At times I haven't even known exactly what I've been eating. I feel another wave of nausea as I try to drink the tea I've made. I haven't eaten such a good meal in a long, long time. My body probably doesn't know what's hit it. I lay back against the pillows, feeling as though I've died and gone to heaven. Why didn't I make sure I hung onto my freedom and my family? I wanted to change with every fibre of my being. Everything, and more to the point, *everyone*, conspired against me.

The room is shrouded in darkness as something jolts me awake. The net curtain flaps in the draft caused by the window's air vent. A faint light filters through it. I blink, expecting to hear the bustle and chaos of the hospital I'd been transferring from. All I can hear is the distant squawk of seagulls and a nearby door falling closed. Then I remember where I am. Norfolk. And I'm on the run.

I switch the lamp on, sit up and reach for the information folder on the bedside table. It's incredible that I'm here, holed up in a hotel. I'm not far from the coast. Not far at all. I'm probably best trying to hitch my way up the coastline, rather than the motorway, to get to Yorkshire. There'll be fewer police about on the A and B roads. I tighten the towel around my waist and shiver. These places should provide a bathrobe. I'm going to have to sort out some more clothes. All I've got is the court outfit. When I see Heidi again and meet my son for the first time, I want to look presentable, be someone they'll want to come away with. I can't wait to get to them. Once I've spoken to Heidi, I'll make her see how unwell I was back then. And how much I've sorted myself out. She'll have to forgive me. She was a decent kid when all's said and done. There's a bond between us that can never be broken.

Over the years I've gone from overwhelming fury to crushing misery, as my letters have gone unanswered. I've even sent visiting orders to Claire with Heidi named on them. Again, nothing. But once we see each other... And Harry will just be over the moon to finally meet his dad. His *proper* dad. I only found out about him recently. No one's ever confirmed it officially, but his birthday ties in with the last holiday we had before my ex-wife ruined everything. The holiday I broke my back to pay for. Harry's my son. They're my kids. My flesh and blood. Mine. I blame Eva completely for turning Heidi against me, and as for hiding information about Harry from me, I don't know how she lives with herself. She's played God with the wrong person here.

My jaw clenches as I think of Mark muscling in on my family like he has. The courtroom doors had barely swung behind me when he made his move on them. He's always been the same, wanting what I've got, and when I get the chance, I'm going to make him pay. Eva too. If I'd known she was pregnant back then, things could have been so different. I completely blame her for how I acted. She caused me to be labelled a Paranoid Schizophrenic. She pushed me there and was the cause of me becoming so unwell. Women have always triggered the downfalls in my life.

I don't want to put the TV on. I don't want to see the news. But I need to find out what time it is. See how long I've got left before I need to take my next course of action.

"Hello." It's the same girl who was at reception earlier. The same syrupy voice.

"Silly question, but can I ask what time it is?" I laugh. "I seem to have slept the evening away."

"Certainly. It's twenty past nine."

"What time did you say the pool closed?"

"Ten pm sir. I've just walked past. You'd have it all to yourself if you grabbed the last half hour in there."

"Cheers."

I stride into the en-suite and pluck my now-dry clothes from the towel rail and drag them back on. I want a swim more than anything. It's been years. The last time I enjoyed any kind of luxury was when Eva booked me in for a massage when we were in Florida. The masseuse said she'd never come across anyone as wired as I was. She said that the strain of trying to relax my taut muscles had left her feeling nauseated.

I could get picked up at any time at all, so I might as well make the most of what's on offer here. I can swim in my pants. There's no one else in there – that's what the woman just said. The last thing I need is to draw attention to myself.

I grab a towel and my key card before heading swiftly to the top of the stairs. There don't seem to be any cameras covering the stairwells, unless they're hidden within the wall. You never know these days. I follow the signs to the pool area and fold my clothes onto a chair beside the jacuzzi.

The pool is lit underwater. Never has anything looked more inviting. I dive in, my arms powering through the water as my anxiety drifts away from me. Who needs medication? This was all meant to be. Somehow, I'll get to my kids. I can feel it. And I have a way to get to them. The best go-between imaginable.

Maybe I should lie low here for another day or two. Allow this beard to take hold even more. Or maybe I should keep moving. Now I've had some food and a rest. As I continue to motor up and down the pool, my mind twists with indecision.

·   ·   ·

I glance at the clock. Three minutes to ten. I haven't been in the steam room or the jacuzzi. They're not chucking me out of here yet. I haul myself from the pool whilst doing a recce of what's around me.

The lights for the pool are next to the door. After turning them off, I dash towards the steps which lead up to the jacuzzi area. Then I throw my towel over the security camera. If I'm in the steam room, or ducked down in the jacuzzi, anyone who comes in to check the place is empty won't see me. And I need this. I deserve it.

The heat in the steam room makes my thoughts race and swirl as much as the steam. I can't breathe. I need to get out of here before I pass out. I have a cold shower before sliding into the jacuzzi. If anyone had told me yesterday that this is how I'd be spending this evening, I'd have laughed at them. As if.

I close my eyes as the jets pummel at my back and shoulders. I shift around a bit to ease the pressure against my bruises. At least the back of my hair is no longer matted with blood. The jacuzzi's motor roars in my ears. Then…

"Excuse me sir. We're actually closed in here now. I'm sorry."

It's the woman from reception. She stands before me in a green two-piece, her hair tied up in a band. Yes, I'd have laughed like a drain at anyone's forecast of me being here, like this, and now with her. She's exactly my type. However, I can't allow thoughts like this to take hold. It's been twelve years and I need to keep it that way. Getting to where my children are is all that matters. There. Sudden clarity. At least I've decided. Keep moving.

"Oh. I'm erm really sorry. I must have lost track of time." I remember her saying on the phone earlier that she was planning to come in here at ten.

"I'm going to have to ask you to vacate the area, I'm afraid." To her credit, she looks slightly apologetic.

"Just five more minutes." It's better than saying, *I'm going nowhere.*

"I'm afraid you'll have to leave now. You really shouldn't be in here after closing time."

"But you're using the area, aren't you?" I suddenly remember that I'm wearing my prison-issued pants. I'm not walking past her wearing these. No way. Nor is some poxy woman going to tell me what to do.

"True. But I'm a member of staff here. Having the pool to myself is one of the perks." She rubs her hands against her bare shoulders and looks thoughtful. "Look alright, you can have a few more minutes. Though I'll have to buzz through to the night porter. Just to let him know we're in here."

"There's no need to do that. I'll be out of here in a few minutes, won't I?" There really is no need to do that. If there's a porter feeling as though he's got to prowl around here, he might recognise me when I leave, or he might realise I've thrown a towel over the camera. This woman clearly doesn't have a clue who I am, nor has she noticed the towel.

"I have to. It's regulation." She turns away from me.

"You don't have to."

Something in my tone must stop her in her tracks. Shit. She turns back and stares straight at me, just like she did this afternoon. Then, she seemed like she could almost be checking me out. But this time, she's wearing a completely different expression. Instinctively I place a hand over the scar on my shoulder from where I was shot on the night they arrested me. It's quite a scar and she's probably wondering what it is. After a moment though, I realise that I'm seeing the same look in her eyes that I've come to know from so many women over the years. Her hand flies to her mouth, and she backs away. "You're... you're him."

"What the hell are you on about?" I spring to the side of the jacuzzi and hoist myself onto the ledge. "Come back here. I don't know what you mean." I wish I'd just got out when she asked me to. This situation can only have one conclusion. *Get rid of her.* It's not as if she can un-see me now that she's recognised me. *Get rid of her.*

She backs towards the steps. "I've seen you on the..." She clutches the rail at the top of the steps as she retreats, her mouth forming a blue circle in the light that keeps changing colour. "I'm calling the police."

Her seeing my pants is the least of my worries. Her eyes don't leave my face as I raise my legs from the water. *Get rid of her. Get rid of her.* The voices are back. They're as familiar as if I'd only heard them yesterday, instead of twelve years ago. My meds must have kept them away. And they're just as loud. I spring to my feet and dart towards her in an instant.

At least half of my previous victims would freeze in terror when they realised the danger they were in. The other half fought back or tried to get away from me. This woman is in the first group, and more than frozen – she's paralysed. Her hands grip the rail of the steps as though it's going to save her. The only thing that could save her is someone coming in and stopping me. I didn't plan this, but I've got to do what I've got to do. I'm not ready to give myself up. Not yet. *Get rid of her.* She turns as if to run, but I'm too quick. I push her to one side and stand in her way at the top of the steps, blocking any chance of her being able to go further.

I notice her gaze flit to the panic alarm and something shifts in her face. She clearly thinks she might have found a way out.

"I don't think so." My voice is a growl as I close the gap between us and take hold of her, squeezing the bones in the back of her neck and gripping her arm with my other hand. She throws her head back and looks as though she's going to scream, except no sound escapes her. *Get rid of her. Get rid of her.*

"Please. Please. I won't say anything, I promise," she

whimpers as I frogmarch her towards the water. "Please, just let me go."

Get rid of her. Get rid of her. GET RID OF HER! I didn't want to do this again, but what choice have I got? I've got to do as the voices say, and they're more insistent than ever before. My only chance of getting out of here is if I listen to them. They are here to protect me, just as they always have been.

In bare feet, we slip on the tiles as I drag her back to the edge of the jacuzzi from which I've just emerged. She tries to tug herself from my grasp, but she's got no chance. I'm not letting her go and she knows it. As we crash into the water, she seems to find her fight.

"Someone. Someone help me!" I'm in there right behind her, trying to maintain my hold on her neck as she flails her limbs in all directions. Her foot smacks into my chest. It's already bruised, so it hurts even more than it normally would.

"Fucking little bitch." I release her arm and grab for the front of her neck. She gurgles as I push her as far backwards as the space will allow.

"Help! Somebody." *Get rid of her.* She's all nails and slaps as she tries to fight back, but she's obviously no match for me. Although I nearly let go of her on one occasion when her nail scrapes the length of my bicep. But I grip her tighter.

Twelve years of pent-up rage is finally releasing. All those years of trying to work it out of myself in the hospital gym has only made me even stronger in order to deal with anyone who crosses my path. Twelve years of attempting to show remorse has gone. They can keep their group discussions and their one-to-ones. Will Potts is back.

"Help!" She manages to load power into her voice. "Somebody."

I'll be lucky if someone hasn't heard that. I need to end this. End her. Get out of here. Loosening my grip on her neck, I force my weight onto her shoulders. She's squirming like a fish and is as slippery as one too. I never imagined that the next time I'd have my hands all over a woman's body, it would be in these sorts of circumstances.

She manages to get up and take another breath. I press her head back down, forcing her to take a lungful of water instead of air. Then the fight begins to drain from her. She's on her way. Finally. By the time she becomes limp in my grasp, I'm shaking like a deprived drug user. Except I've now had my fix. I gasp for breath as I survey my handiwork.

Eventually, I push her head further underwater and hold it there. Just to make sure. I wait for a few moments until my breath slows and I can be certain that no one has heard anything. I'm ready for them if they have. There's plenty more where this came from. I glance up at the towel still draped over the camera. I can get out of this. For now, anyway.

I swoop down beside her under the water. I need this, at first glance, to look like an accident when she's found. No one should have any reason to come in here until the morning. I slide the cover from the drain by my feet and yank her hair downwards, feeding it into the hole. It's sucked in straight away until her head is firmly wedged where I want it. Whoever discovers her body will initially think that getting trapped by her hair was the cause of death, giving me more time to get away before she's properly examined.

My actions have silenced the voices. They've come and gone like old acquaintances. I hoist myself from the water and towards my clothes, still folded on the chair. I dry myself on the towel she's dropped, then dress, whilst staring at her outline beneath the bubbles, feeling a familiar surge of excitement. Will Potts is back alright. But this time, he's invincible.

I hit the stop button on the jacuzzi and turn off the remaining lights, before picking my way through the darkness down the steps and back to the poolside. In the faint light from the corridor alongside the pool, I spot her bag on the seat. A quick rummage inside offers up several notes inside her purse. I shove the bag behind a large plant pot and slide the money into my pocket. As I'm about to walk away, I notice a large key labelled pool, glinting in the faint light. I can hardly believe my luck. Chances for me are lining up like dominoes. Perhaps it's the only key. It could be even longer until she's found.

I check up and down the corridor before slipping onto it, locking the door behind me, and darting towards the foot of the stairs, hoping to get to the safety of my room with no one seeing me.

I thought I was going to have to run tonight. But now the pool's locked up, I should be safe staying here, at least until daybreak. Then I'll get the hell away. After what's just happened, I need to settle myself back down. I'd rather spend a few hours in a comfy bed than standing on a cold road, trying to hitch another lift. Soon, I'll be calling on the only person who should be willing to help me. And if they aren't, I can be very persuasive.

5

HEIDI

ALYSHA ROLLS HER EYES. "Alright, alright Dad."

"Don't you *alright* with me. You didn't even have the common courtesy to reply to my messages. As usual."

"Just stop going on at me, will you? My head's banging." Alysha drops her head into her hands. "I feel like shit as it is. You've made your bloody point."

"Don't speak to your dad like that." Mum turns from where she's standing at the sink. It's unusual for her to chip in. Normally she leaves them to it. "And I won't have language like that in front of the boys."

"*The boys.*" Alysha mocks as she stares back at her. "This conversation is between me and my dad. It has nothing to do with you."

"Alysha. Stop it." I glance up from my phone. Normally I wouldn't butt in either, but I won't listen to her talking down to Mum, even if Uncle Mark has gone on a bit. He paces up and down the kitchen like he always does when he's stressed.

Adele, the 'FLO,' as Uncle Mark calls her, has taken herself off into the lounge under the guise of making a phone call. She's been here all day – it must be such a boring job, just waiting, but it's the same for all of us. It's the worst thing, the waiting. Until something changes, we're all stuck here – Will Potts's hostages.

It's been a while since I've seen Uncle Mark so annoyed. "It's time you learned some respect as well as responsibility." Mum and I exchange glances as he continues, and she comes to sit at the table, probably to back him up if need be. "It's bad enough that you disappear off the face of the earth for the best part of twenty-four hours," he yells, "but not even to let your work know."

"I've said I'm sorry, haven't I? Look Dad. Please stop shouting at me." Alysha sounds as though she might cry, which might have worked for her once upon a time, but probably won't have much effect right now. "You ought to try having a hangover like I've got."

"You bloody well deserve it. Look, this isn't working out, is it?" His gaze swerves to Mum, then back to Alysha. "It might be for the best if you move back here until you can behave more like an adult."

Mum opens her mouth to say something, but Uncle Mark shoots her a look which must stop her. Perhaps he's just saying it to scare Alysha. I know for a fact that her moving back would be the last thing Mum would want. She's put up with her for enough years. Her words, not mine.

"No chance." Alysha stares straight back at him. "You can't make me."

"I think you'll find I can. Who pays the…"

"Don't you think…" Mum rises from her chair, "that the boys are upset enough as it is with everything that's going on, without having to listen to you two?"

"I'm sick of hearing about *the boys*." Alysha slaps the table.

Uncle Mark glances towards the door, then back at Alysha. He lowers his voice. "You know who's on the run, don't you?"

"Of course I know." Alysha's voice bears the sarcasm that's

getting worse as she gets older. Apparently Auntie Lauren could be quite sarcastic too. "I'd have had to have been on the moon not to have heard about it all."

"And still you didn't think to call us?" He rests his hands on the back of an empty chair as he surveys her over the top of his glasses. "Do you know how many times I tried to ring you?"

She looks sheepish for the first time since she sauntered in. "I was drunk Dad. Really drunk. I'm sorry."

"Where the hell were you anyway?" His voice is rising again, despite what Mum just said.

"Mark." Mum pulls a face.

Alysha slumps back in her chair and sighs. "It doesn't matter. I'm here now, aren't I?"

"It matters to me." He strides over to the sink and fills a glass with water.

I wonder for a moment if Uncle Mark would be this upset if it had been me who'd cleared off somewhere overnight. Probably not. Mum might be though. But I've always been the sensible one, in any case. *Boring*, according to Alysha. Maybe I should do something really 'out there' one of these days. I'd have to lose some weight first. And get out of my black clothes. I get sick of her calling me boring.

But Alysha's a danger to herself sometimes. They don't know the half of the scrapes she gets into. And most of the time, neither does she until she sobers up. I'll have a word with her later. When Mum and Uncle Mark have gone to bed. Find out where she was. She can't handle her drink and I just hope whoever she was with looked after her. Maybe Uncle Mark's right. Maybe she should move back here.

She can be totally off the rails and he'd only blame me if anything were to happen. If I'm honest, I was worrying about her as well. It's fair to say that she doesn't give a crap about anyone apart from herself. It's probably not even crossed her mind to ask me if *I'm* alright under the circumstances.

"What did they say at the salon?" She drags her fingers through her long, blonde hair, which looks like it could do with a good wash.

"I got you off the hook." Uncle Mark rinses his glass and places it face down on the draining board. "For now, anyway. I told them there'd been a family crisis, and you were probably reacting to that."

"I didn't even hear anything about Uncle Will until this afternoon," she says, with a hint of amusement on her face. She's a cow. And she knows exactly what she's doing with her emphasis on the word *Uncle*. I watch as she searches Uncle Mark's face for a reaction. He'd be better off ignoring her, but she always knows exactly which buttons to press.

"Uncle Will!" he repeats, throwing a tea towel onto the counter. "He's no uncle, father, brother or anything to anyone in this family, not after what he's done. Do you hear me?" He swings around to face her.

Alysha's face is bare of makeup for once. Her skin has a green tinge, and she looks rough. I almost feel sorry for her. Almost. Until I hear what she says next.

"Uncle Will would never hurt me." Her chin juts out as she switches her gaze from Uncle Mark to me. "I don't know what you're all panicking about. It sounds as though I've been well out of here over the last day."

"You've no idea what you're on about Alysha. I can't believe your naivety."

She twists in her chair to face Uncle Mark. "He's been locked up in a hospital, hasn't he? And he was getting moved from there. That's what I heard." She flashes what can only be a mock-smile at Mum who looks as though she's fit to burst. But she's learned over the years to keep a lid on it. Things blow over quicker that way.

"Which means he's better now," Alysha continues, avoiding

eye contact with me throughout her next sentence. "Besides, he was always good to me."

I can't stand my cousin sometimes. I can see why she gets under Mum's skin so badly. More and more as she's got older. But then I have to remind myself that she is two years younger than me. And definitely more spoiled and immature. "People like him don't change," I say. "Grow up Alysha."

"You can shut up too. If it..."

"Until he's caught," Mum cuts in as she fiddles with a corner of a place mat, "you're both staying where we can keep an eye on you." She looks at Uncle Mark as she speaks, as though seeking back up.

"You can treat Heidi like she's still six years old," Alysha whines. "But I'm not your problem. Besides, I've got to work tomorrow. I've got a full day of appointments. That's if they don't sack me first."

"Well, I'll be dropping you off and picking you up then," says Uncle Mark. "And you'll have to take some lunch with you, instead of going out for it. You must stay safe."

"That's not fair." It's my voice that sounds like a whine now. "Why is it one rule for me, and another for her? I wasn't even allowed to give my presentation at uni today." I wouldn't have gone anyway, but they don't need to know that. Alysha and I have often been treated differently, which has caused a ton of problems for all of us. And driven a wedge between me and Alysha at times.

"To be honest," says Mum. "I'd be very surprised if they still haven't got him by the morning. Then we'll all be able to get back to normal."

"That's what you said last night." It's true. And the longer it goes on, the more unsafe I feel.

"It could be minutes. It could be hours. It could even be days, though I bloody hope not." Uncle Mark sits heavily on a chair at the table. "I think that from tomorrow, whether or not they've caught him, we've got to keep going to wherever we need to be. Just work or school though. There'll be no gallivanting." He looks at Alysha, then back to Mum. "We'll have to let the boy's school know not to let them out of their sight."

"I don't know about that Mark." Mum looks at me and I know what she's thinking. I was safe at school, or so she thought. Look what nearly happened to me.

Adele curls her head around the kitchen door. "I'm going to leave you all in peace for the night," she says, half-smiling. She's obviously heard us from the other room. "Well as peaceful as you can be, given the situation."

"OK." Uncle Mark nods at her. "Thanks Adele."

"There's an armed police presence outside and obviously if anything changes overnight, you'll be informed straightaway. Either myself or Emily will be back first thing."

"Right you are," Mum says. "Thanks for all your support today. I'll see you out."

What support? She hasn't done a thing. We're no closer to knowing any more than we did last night when we first found out he'd escaped. Alysha might feel safe going to work, but I'm staying right where I am. I can't imagine Mum letting Harry and Isaac out of her sight either. But she's obviously got no say over Alysha. She's Uncle Mark's problem.

Amongst my circle of friends and people who are just being nosy, I've suddenly become the centre of attention. Not that I want to be. I've been getting messages left, right and centre all day. From people I've stayed in touch with from Alderton, to friends I've trusted with my secret here in Filey, and now unfortunately, it seems word has got around uni and the restaurant I work at. Everyone knows who my real father is now, and what he did. Who he was. And probably still is. No one will ever treat me the same around here ever again. They're bound to think I might be like him in some way. It's a nightmare.

Suddenly, I can barely keep my eyes open. I'm knackered from the racing brain I've put up with all day. "I'm off to bed," I announce. "Wake me up if there's any news." I can't sit around all night listening to everyone bicker. I can't be arsed.

Harry and Isaac are less energetic this morning and don't come jumping on me like yesterday. They've probably got used to having me around, and might have gone to jump on Alysha instead. Well, they'll be daring one another to jump on her. To say she's less tolerant of them than I am is an understatement.

Mum decided last night that she's going to keep them off school until after the weekend, depending on what happens. They're even less pleased than they were yesterday. I heard Harry shouting at Mum whilst I was dropping off to sleep last night. I didn't have the energy to get up and get involved. But there's only so much time indoors in front of a games console any five- and eleven-year-old wants.

Everyone is really subdued around the breakfast table. The only conversation that takes place between us over the first five minutes of sitting there is when I ask Uncle Mark to pass the milk. I just want things to be back to normal. I never wanted to have to think about that man again and here I am, cowering in my mother's house because of him.

"Get a move on Alysha, if you want me to drop you at work before nine." Uncle Mark reaches for the cafetiere. I love the smell of fresh coffee. We only ever have instant at the flat.

"Says you Dad. You're still in your dressing gown." Alysha looks better this morning. Her hair might be on end, but her face is pink again, instead of green. I'll speak to her later; I wouldn't have got much sense out of her last night. Normally, tonight, with it being a Friday, she'd be out doing it again. She's not going to be pleased at being confined when she gets home from work. I was supposed to be going out too, but I've already cancelled it. Even if he's caught today, I don't fancy being quizzed about things by my friends all night.

"I can be ready in five minutes." The mug looks small in Uncle Mark's huge hands. "Unlike you." The tone in his voice suggests last night's row is over with.

"I'll take Alysha in if that makes life easier," Mum says. "I need some bread and milk from the shop anyway."

"I'd rather go with my dad." Alysha pouts.

It's almost like a normal conversation.

Uncle Mark ignores Alysha. "It would make life easier. But come straight back love, won't you? Drop Alysha at the salon, go to the shop, then get straight back here."

Mum rolls her eyes. "Erm, grown adult here."

"Can we come Mum?" Isaac says between spoonfuls of cereal.

"You can both go and get dressed. Then we'll see."

Uncle Mark opens his mouth, probably to protest, but anything he's about to say is averted by the doorbell.

"I'll go," Mum says, putting her cup down. "Since I'm the only one here who's bothered to get dressed this morning."

Adele is speaking into her phone as she steps into the hallway, bringing a gust of cold air with her. "Can I take this into the other room?" she asks Mum who gestures towards the lounge door in response. It must be a personal call. She doesn't even say good morning. Not that it is. *Good.* Until he's caught, nothing can be.

"Are you going to tell me where you were the other night then?" I lean against the bathroom doorway where Alysha's putting her makeup on. She looks far better without it, not that she ever believes me when I tell her this.

"Just with some mates I was at school with." She tilts her head back to rub foundation onto her neck. "It turned into a something it wasn't meant to."

"What does that mean? What mates?"

"Heidi! You sound like my bloody dad." She turns to look at me with narrowed eyes. "Chill, yeah. Look I got wrecked. I couldn't get home, and I was too hungover to even speak yesterday, let alone ring Dad back."

"He was really worried about you, that's all. Even I was worried." I sit on the edge of the bath.

"I bet Auntie Eva wasn't though, was she?" Alysha twists the lid back onto her foundation.

"Of course she was. Look Alysha. We need to be careful. Honestly, we do. He really could be anywhere by now."

"You mean Uncle Will?" She drops a lipstick into her makeup bag.

"Don't call him that. He stopped being your uncle, and my dad, the moment he began murdering innocent women. He doesn't deserve a family. Look how many families he robbed of someone they love."

"He was ill Heidi. Everyone deserves a second chance."

"How can you say that?"

She zips up her makeup bag and turns to look at me. "I'm glad he's got out."

"You're being an absolute idiot. You really are." Where the hell is her head? What's got into her?

"I hope he gets away." She picks up her hairbrush and turns back to the mirror.

"Alysha! He tried to kill me, for God's sake! Don't you remember?"

"I'm sick of hearing about it all. I really am. Anyway. I've got to get to work," she mutters as she breezes past me. "God, what I'd give just to be part of a normal family."

I'm certainly with her on that one.

6

HEIDI

I SIGH as I sink onto a chair back at the kitchen table. It feels like I've been here longer than since Wednesday night, and I'm climbing the walls now. There's nothing worse than being cooped up, and I really don't know what to do with myself. There's plenty of university coursework for me to be getting on with, but I doubt I'd be able to concentrate. I might have to try later, just to keep myself busy and distract myself from my thoughts.

Uncle Mark has ordered the boys to muck their rooms out and Mum's taking Alysha to work, despite her moaning. I bet Alysha won't start with the Uncle Will stuff when it's just the two of them. She wouldn't dare. I wonder if Alysha and Mum get on any better when they're on their own, or whether they just ignore each other. Alysha plays up more in front of an audience.

Other than a bit of thumping around upstairs, the house is eerily quiet. The same can't be said for outside the house though. There's the same crowd of reporters as yesterday. They shout questions and try to get pictures of everyone who comes and goes. Who'd be interested in a picture of Mum, or Uncle Mark coming in or out of the house? It's hardly front page news. I open my phone. Let's see if they've even reported anything yet. Until he's caught, there's nothing to say. They're hanging around in the wrong place. They should be in Suffolk or wherever he is.

I've got another four messages.

> You OK Heidi? Can't imagine what you must be going through.

> Any news? Have they found him yet?

> Did your cousin turn up OK? I know you were worried about her.

> Will you be back in uni on Monday? Don't worry. We'll all look after you.

The last message brings tears to my eyes. I hope they mean it. Especially after the cruel things people were saying when we were back in Alderton. We might as well have been murderers ourselves. There were even kids at school who had their parents telling them not to play with me. We had no choice other than to move in the end.

Uncle Mark's raised voice in the lounge cuts into my thoughts. It sounds like he's in there with Adele, so why is he shouting? He seems to be struggling with what's going on the most out of all of us. Something must have happened for him to be raising his voice.

"What's going on?" I let the lounge door close behind me and look at them in turn.

"We know nothing for certain yet..." Adele begins, looking uneasy.

"What? Tell me." My voice is loud in the pause.

"It's him. It's got to be him." Uncle Mark sinks to the sofa, his anger seeming to deflate from him, possibly for my sake. He might have forgotten I was in the kitchen when he was shouting before.

"What's *got to be him?*"

"Let's just wait for more news." Adele places her phone on the coffee table beside her. "And for the forensics."

"More news about what?" They exchange glances as I sink to the sofa beside him. "I've got a right to be told what's going on, you know." I look from Adele to Uncle Mark. "Come on. I'm a big girl now."

"Can I?" Adele asks Uncle Mark.

"I'm nearly twenty years old, for God's sake."

Uncle Mark nods as he lifts his glasses and rubs at his eyes.

Adele takes a deep breath and sits forward in the armchair. I can tell by her face this is going to be something serious. The wait for her to speak is maddening. "It's looking like he could have killed someone," she says eventually. "The body of a woman has been found in a hotel – in the spa."

Her words take a few moments to sink in. I swallow. "Where? When?" I can't believe how calm I am considering what I've just been told. "And why do they think it's him?" This is my biological father, however, I feel far, far removed from him now. What's going on seems as though it's happening to someone else whilst I watch on from the outside. If only.

"The hotel they found her at is only a hundred and twenty miles from where he escaped."

"But that's quite a long way. He wouldn't have had any way of getting there, would he?" I don't know why I'm saying this. I shouldn't be surprised if it's him, but I really don't want it to be. I guess it's to do with what people will think of me. God, what a selfish cow I am, thinking that. I'm as bad as Scary Granny was.

"It's yet to be officially confirmed," Adele continues. "Her post mortem should tell us more. But we have seen a man who looks like him, on the CCTV, entering the hotel yesterday afternoon, and leaving this morning. They're pretty certain it's your father."

"He's not her father," Uncle Mark snaps. "He forfeited that right years ago."

Something inside me feels warm at his words, and the way he says them.

"What the hell is he doing in a hotel anyway?" I ask. "He's supposed to be locked up." I really can't get my head around it. How does a man who's done what he's done manage to escape?

"Never mind how he's got out. He just needs to be caught. Then they can look at the whats and the whys." Uncle Mark leans forward in his seat to the point where he looks as though he's hugging himself. "A woman is dead. Another sodding woman is dead at the hands of my brother." His voice rises and I realise that he's trying not to cry. I put my arm around his shoulders briefly and then let go. I don't really do proper hugs as a rule. Growing up, I've had to be so tough that it's made me less able to show affection easily.

"What actually happened?" I feel sick as the reality of what's going on washes over me. If it's really him, that's *fourteen* lives now that *he's* taken. Fourteen innocent lives. Mothers. Sisters. Daughters. Wives. Friends.

And it would have been fifteen if he'd had his way with me. I've got Uncle Mark to thank for saving my life. Mum admitted to how useless she was that night. When I was thrown into the water, she's told me how she just couldn't move, as though she became paralysed. I still have flashbacks, though not as often as I used to. That river. The cold was as sharp as knives through my body. When I couldn't breathe, it felt as though something was breaking inside my head. Then I had a strange floating feeling.

"Nothing official has been put out yet." Adele's voice

interrupts my thoughts as she tilts her phone screen towards her face. "But they'll have to release something soon." She looks at Uncle Mark. "The authorities are going to come under so much fire for this."

"Did the woman drown?" My voice sounds strangled. If she was drowned, then it's definitely him. It's his method. Perhaps I should go back to bed, pull the covers over my head, and stay there for the rest of the day. Work out what I'm going to do next. I'm going to have to move again. I can't bear everyone knowing who my father is. Mum's always said that what he's done doesn't reflect on me, but I don't agree. In my age group, we're all judged. Who I am makes me different. Far too different. No one will want to know me, or even if they do, it will just be out of curiosity, or because they feel sorry for me. Now that everyone here is finding out about who I really am, I'll have to get away and start again. See if I can transfer courses at uni. But this time I'll change my name and won't tell a soul anything. I'm old enough to make my own decisions now. If this lot want to wait here like sitting ducks, that's up to them. I'm out of here. As soon as possible. It will break Mum's heart, but enough is enough.

Adele nods. "I'm afraid so."

A gasp catches in my throat.

"One of the hotel cleaners found her this morning. At first, it looked like her hair had got caught in the suction and pulled her under. But..." Her voice trails off, and she looks at Uncle Mark as though she's seeking permission to continue.

"When they got her out of the water they noticed there was bruising all over her neck and arms," Uncle Mark continues. He thumps the arm of the sofa, startling me. "She's been there all night. He's an utter maniac." His voice cracks. "No more than that, he's pure evil. What the hell are we going to do now?" He drops his head into his hands. "I thought all this was behind us."

"What on earth's going on?" Mum appears in the doorway and, taking one look at us all, drops her bag and rushes to Uncle Mark's side. "What's happened?"

"He's murdered another woman." My voice is flat. I think I'm still in shock about the whole thing. And who knows how Mum will take it when I tell her I'm going to get out of here as soon as it's over? When he's back where he belongs. She'll try to talk me out of it, but I'm going.

"Oh my God! When? How?" She throws her arm around Uncle Mark's shoulder and pulls him toward her. That's one thing about him and Mum. They always support each other. There was never any of that when she was married to *him*. Only rows and bad atmospheres. I always knew when to keep out of the way.

"We're not sure of the time of death yet, or the exact cause." Adele pushes her glasses up her nose. "I've been told there's to be an urgent postmortem. And obviously, the search for him has intensified now. To a full-scale national manhunt."

"It should have been a *full-scale national manhunt* right from the start." Mark shakes Mum's arm off and gets to his feet. "They messed about again if you ask me, focusing on where the accident happened." He slides his feet into his shoes. "I'm going into work. See if I can make myself useful."

"No. Mark." Mum tugs at his arm. "Please. You need to keep back from this. Well back, in fact. You're too close to it all. You're better off staying with us."

Adele's phone beeps. "There's to be a briefing at the station," she says, looking at it, then at Uncle Mark.

"Why a briefing *here* if he's in Suffolk, or wherever he is?" Mum asks. She's pretty calm, considering. I guess she's trying to hold it together for Uncle Mark's sake. Maybe she'll fall apart when he's left.

"He was seen on the CCTV leaving the hotel just before seven this morning. That's nearly three hours ago. We know nothing for certain, but we believe now he could be heading for Yorkshire."

Mum's face turns from calm to panic. "Haven't there been any sightings? There must be... something."

"That's why I need to go in love." Mark looks down at Mum and squeezes her shoulder. "I need to hear what's going on first hand. To be honest, I'm surprised DSI Jones hasn't been in touch yet today."

Adele's phone beeps again. "And the Suffolk Police are holding a press conference in half an hour."

"On the TV?" My God. It might sound selfish, but I'm never going to be able to hold my head up ever again. It will be all everyone at uni will talk about today, and the next day, and the next. I loved being at university and just being me. I was loving my course. I didn't want to have to move from there. But how can I stay now? *I know his daughter,* they'll say. Even though I'm not his daughter anymore. I'm nothing like him. Tears are dripping from my chin onto my legs. I didn't even realise I was crying, so they come as a surprise.

"Come here love." Uncle Mark sits back down and pulls me towards him. I sob into his shoulder. "What if he's coming back for me next? And what if he gets Harry?"

"What if *who* gets me? What's going on?"

Shit. Harry and Isaac are standing in the doorway. I feel terrible now. But they're not daft. They'll have realised something big is happening.

"Go to your rooms you two. Now."

"But..." Harry looks at Uncle Mark with an expression that's somewhere between fury and bewilderment.

"Now!"

"I'll come and talk to you in a moment Harry," Mum calls after them.

"OK," Harry calls back, but I can hear tears in his voice.

We wait in silence until they're out of earshot. "I'm going to have to tell them something Mark. Especially with him overhearing what Heidi's just said."

"I'm really sorry Mum." I pull away from Uncle Mark and wipe my face with the back of my hand. Adele passes me the box of tissues from the mantelpiece.

"It's time Harry knew the truth anyway," Mum goes on. "He was going to have to find out one day. I'd just hoped he'd be older than eleven. It's a lot to take in."

"I can't... I don't want..." Uncle Mark's voice wobbles. It's been a long, long time since I've seen him this upset. The escape on its own is bad enough. But what's happened next is the stuff of horror films. *As if he's been able to kill someone.*

"OK, right. You go to the station," Mum says. "Find out exactly what's going on, and then let us know straight away. At the moment, we seem to be the last people to be finding anything out. Whilst you're gone, I'll speak to Harry."

"We really should tell him together," he says. "It's not exactly run of the mill to discover at eleven years old that you're the son of a serial killer."

"What about Isaac?" I ask. "Are you going to tell him as well?"

Uncle Mark shakes his head. "Tell Isaac as little as possible. In fact, tell Harry as little as possible too. Just the bare facts."

"Look. You go Mark. Leave this to me." There's an air of impatience to Mum's voice. I've heard it before when they're discussing me or Harry. It's like she's saying, *my kids. My way.*

"Will you both be alright here?" He looks from Mum to me. "Should I bring Alysha home before I go in? Given what we've found out."

"I'm here with them," Adele replies. "And like I've said before, no one will get past that lot outside anyway."

"When's the briefing?" Mum asks.

"Eleven o'clock." Adele checks her phone again. "They want to hear the news conference first. Is there any chance that Will could know where Alysha works?"

"None whatsoever," Mum replies. "None of us have had any contact with him since he was arrested twelve years ago."

"He probably still thinks we're living in Alderton," Uncle Mark adds. "I can't imagine anyone having told him about our move out here."

"Right." Adele clasps her hands together as though we have a plan. I wish we did. "We'll revisit whether to collect Alysha once the press conference and the briefing are done." She turns towards Mum. "That should give you a chance to speak to your boys. I know they're young, but I agree you should tell them something now." She nods in time to her own voice. "Especially with what's happening. You don't want them to hear it from someone else."

"Is it definitely him?" I ask. "Who killed the woman at the hotel? When will we know for certain?" I just can't believe it. The realisation it's going to impact on Harry's life as well brings fresh tears rushing behind my eyes.

"It's certainly looking that way," Adele replies. "There are some checks being carried out before they'll confirm anything though." She gets up from the chair. "Look. I'll make myself useful and put the kettle on whilst we wait for the press conference."

"I'll ring you from the station as soon as I know something." Uncle Mark kisses the top of Mum's head and ruffles my hair. "And then, I'll collect Alysha. I can't rest whilst she's at work. We all need to stick together."

"That includes you Mark," Mum says gently. "You need to be here with us more than you need to be at work. Don't be long."

. . .

Only Adele drinks the tea she's made. Mine goes cold beside me as I listen to Mum's low tones upstairs. My stomach's churning with nerves. I wonder what she's saying to my brothers and how they've taken it. I offered to sit with her, but she was having none of it.

Harry's asked me before about why Uncle Mark 'chose' and adopted him when he was a baby, but he's never asked me anything about who his 'real' dad could be. Mum's right though – he had to find out one day.

All goes quiet and the top step creaks as Mum steps on it. She must have finished telling the boys. She looks close to tears as she shuffles into the room, then sits on the sofa where Uncle Mark was. I wouldn't have envied her, her job this morning.

"What have you told them?" I reach for her arm. We're lucky to have each other, me and Mum. She used to do my head in, but now I've grown up and left home, we've become more like friends than mother and daughter.

"The truth," Mum says. "Both of them. Obviously in child speak. It's quite enough for now."

"How much of the truth?" I keep my eyes on the TV screen. It's been half an hour since we switched it onto the news channel, so there might be some more headlines on the way.

"I started by reminding them that Mark isn't yours or Harry's biological dad." She stares at her hands as she wrings them in her lap. "Although obviously that means nothing in the scheme of things. He loves you both as much as he loves Alysha and Isaac."

"I know Mum. He's the one that's always been there for us." I've got a lump in my throat the size of a tennis ball. "*Put shoes on our feet and clothes on our back. I know.*"

Mum laughs. Probably at the memories of my shrieking *you're not my dad* when I was a younger teenager. Usually in response to being bollocked for something. *The shoes on your feet* phrase was his stock answer.

73

"I wish he was." She looks at me with watery eyes, and her smile ebbs away. "Your dad, I mean. When I think what I subjected you to... Even before Will took you from school that day. There was always an atmosphere. He was a nightmare." She blinks rapidly, as though trying to shut out the memories.

"It's not your fault Mum. I've never blamed you. Not one bit. Only him."

"Perhaps it is my fault, some of it... indirectly..." Her voice trails off. "I should have left him long before I did. Anyway, then I told them how the man who is yours and Harry's real dad is a very bad man." Her voice is wobbling. She's clearly found it really difficult speaking to them. I should have sat with her whether or not she liked it.

"A very bad man," I echo. "That's putting it mildly." I'm fighting my own tears again, particularly seeing how upset Mum is. And poor Harry and Isaac. Especially Harry, who is old enough to understand now. One minute they're ordinary kids about to go to school, the next, they're in the middle of all this and like prisoners in their own home.

"I've had to tell them that Will is supposed to be in prison for killing people," Mum continues. "That he was safely locked away, but that he's managed to escape." She reaches for a tissue. "Gosh, it sounds like a novel or film plot, doesn't it? I'm not even sure the boys believed me when I told them. In fact, Isaac looked half excited." Mum nearly laughs. "But at least they know why I'm keeping them off school again."

"Are you going to say anything to the school about all this?"

"I'll have to. It's all over the news."

"Have you told Harry about what happened to me?"

She shakes her head. "Not just yet. I will at some point, but for now, I think the whole thing needs drip feeding to them."

"I agree." Adele reaches across from the armchair and pats Mum's hand. "I think you're doing great – both of you." She looks from Mum to me. "This is a terrible situation for you both to be living through again. Especially after..."

"It's brought it all back to be honest." Mum blows her nose.

"They'll catch him soon. You'll see. Then you'll be able to put all this behind you and get back to normal."

"I just never thought I'd be watching over my shoulder again." Mum pushes her hanky up her sleeve, but the tears keep coming. "I just want to keep us all safe from him. I'm certain he'll be on his way here. Where else would he want to go? And I can't believe he's killed again."

"We don't know anything for sure yet," Adele says, "But... oh look, it's starting."

We fall silent as we turn to the TV.

"Good morning. The purpose of today's press conference is to pass on information and to give you an update on the growing search for escaped prisoner, William Potts.

At approximately 2100 hours on Wednesday 27th October, we received the news of a major road traffic accident on the A14 junction with Thurstan in Suffolk, which had claimed the lives of two of our prison officers. We also became notified that fifty-one-year-old William Potts had escaped from the custody in which he was being held, whilst transferring from a secure hospital in Aylesbury to HMP Suffolk.

Potts, formerly of Alderton in Yorkshire, is serving a life sentence for the killing of thirteen women spanning three years.

As you may be aware, a full-scale hunt has ensued for him. As the hours pass, this search has been escalated, and in another development this morning, it has now become a nationwide manhunt.

At around 0800 hours this morning, the body of a female was discovered at a hotel in Aldeburgh. Formal identification has yet to take place, but it has been confirmed that she sustained significant bruising in the attack she suffered prior to her death. Early indications suggest the cause of her death to be drowning. CCTV footage shows a man who we believe to be William Potts leaving the same hotel just before 0700 hours this morning."

"That's him. I'm sure of it. I'd know him anywhere," Mum hisses as we watch the grainy footage flash up. This is followed by a still of the hotel, where a reporter is standing behind police tape. Just after we moved here, we found a roll of the tape in Uncle Mark's car and were playing cops and robbers games in the street with it.

A chill creeps over me as I observe the figure of the man who was once my father. A hood obscures his face, but I agree with Mum. It's him. I too, would recognise him anywhere. It's taken me seeing an up-to-date image to accept this.

"Early evidence suggests that the attack happened late last night."

"Sick bastard," Mum says. "He's just left her there and gone back to his room. How could he? If he didn't leave the hotel until early this morning..."

"Shush a minute Mum."

"Police are currently interviewing guests and staff at The New Hall Hotel in Aldeburgh, whilst police forces across the country continue the search for Potts. We have circulated his details to all ports, airports, public transport and private hire companies. Meanwhile, members of the public are urged to be vigilant and not to approach Potts, but to let the police know immediately by dialling 999 if they think they see him. We will now take questions."

The twelve-year-old photograph is flashed up again and I stare into the eyes of the man who was supposed to love and protect me. I shudder as they seem to bore into me. Then the camera moves to the audience in front of where the police officer has been speaking.

"Don Walker. Daily Mail. You must have some idea of how he's managed to get a hundred and twenty miles away from the crash site?"

The officer nods. "We're pursuing all lines of enquiry with that. Everything seems to point to suggestions of him hitching lifts. We're contacting haulage companies to find out about drivers in the area."

"But surely he was handcuffed?" the Mail reporter asks.

"The transport records show he was."

"But he couldn't have been."

"Rest assured. A thorough investigation is being carried out into that."

The reporter looks as though he's about to say something else, but a female voice shrieks out of nowhere.

"I hope there'll be a full scale inquiry into how the hell any of this has been allowed to happen. It's an absolute disgrace, especially after the failings found by the Police Complaints Commission twelve years ago."

"Too right," Mum says then we both turn to the rustle in the doorway where Harry and Isaac appear. "How long have you two been standing there?"

Adele points the remote at the TV to turn it off. For a moment I'm annoyed, but then I've probably heard all there is to hear for the moment. And now that Uncle Mark has gone into the station, he'll keep us posted with what's happening first-hand.

Harry shrugs and Isaac pushes past him. "Was that the bad man on the TV Mum? I want to see him. Can you turn it back on?"

"Yes. Yes it was." Mum draws Isaac onto her lap. "That's why we're staying safe here. Because he's run away from the prison van and the police are trying to find him."

"Is that where Dad's gone?" Harry looks from Mum to me with wide eyes as he sits in the chair facing us.

"Will Daddy shoot the bad man?" Isaac's eyes are equally wide.

"At least we could go outside again then." Harry sighs. "Has Dad really gone to find him?"

"Kind of," Mum replies, and I wonder if she's mentioned to Harry that Will Potts is actually Uncle Mark's brother.

7

WILL

I'M HERE. And it's nothing short of a miracle that I've made it so far. Everywhere I go, there are sirens. Unless it's my mind playing tricks. At times, I'm struggling to think straight, and I'm not sure whether things I hear are even real.

I stare at the house which holds memories of a time before everything went to shit. Hopefully, Tina still lives here. She did when I last carried out a licence check back when I was in the police. She'd changed her surname though. Got married, presumably. I recall how betrayed I'd felt as I stared at it, there in black and white on the screen. Although I'd moved on too, and was with Eva, I felt like Tina could only ever be mine.

Everything seems much the same as last time I was here, even after all these years. Except the conifer tree at the front dwarfs the house now, rather than the other way around. There are new windows and a different car outside but the garden's much the same. Tina would never have sold this place, but she could have easily let it out. It was left to her in trust by her grandmother and I recall believing her to be even more of a catch when I found out about it. Body, beauty and bounty.

Tina talked endlessly about Norfolk when we were together

as teenagers and would often say this was where she'd end up. She once brought me here, and we stayed all weekend. It was weird, at the age of seventeen, having this huge house that was just for us. Life then was the most normal it's ever been. I could never have imagined how everything would turn out. How everyone and everything would be taken from me.

We were happy, me and Tina. She was the only person, apart from Dean who I really thought something of. Then she fucked it all up by saying I was too much, too intense, and she was far too young to settle down. I found out not long after that she'd murdered my kid.

I look down at my feet and my fists ball in my pockets at the acknowledgement of the real reason I'm back. For the last thirty-five years, I've always sensed I'd get my chance to make her pay for what she did. And the day has finally come. I know only too well that I might never get this chance again. As I got away from that van the other night, I was initially only planning to make my way to my kids, but now I've done away with that bitch at the hotel... what's that saying, I might as well be hung for a sheep as for a lamb.

My face will be everywhere by now. I've stayed out of public places like shops and cafes, but I imagine I'm on every front page and the first item on every national news bulletin. The thought excites me – it always has. My notoriety will live on long after I've gone. People will never forget the name William Potts. And for now, women up and down the country will feel unsafe. As well they should. Some more than others.

According to the headlines I heard on the radio on the journey here, they've now come across the body of the receptionist in the jacuzzi. And they're calling the search for me a national manhunt. My beard wasn't mentioned when they described me though. They even referred to me as dark-haired, which might be greying. I grin to myself. I'm completely grey. They got the clothes spot on though. They had my property documented in the van, so they couldn't really go wrong there. As soon as I can, I'm going to have to get hold of some different clothes. Even if I have to pinch them off a washing line. I tug the fleece I was given yesterday around myself.

I don't know how the driver who I hitched up the coast with this morning didn't recognise me. Even when the news headlines were on. He was Polish, I think. He tried making conversation when he first picked me up - probably just testing out his broken English. Thankfully, he soon took the hint that I just wanted to kip. He was a decent bloke really. If he'd known who I was, a sandwich as he dropped me off would be the last thing he'd have given me.

He was continuing up the coastal road for another hundred miles. It was a real dilemma whether to stay with him and get closer to where I need to be. This, though, is probably the only chance I'll ever get to settle this particular score. So here I am. Outside what I hope is still Tina's house.

I dart up the drive and quickly wedge myself between the garage and the wall of next door's garage, hardly daring to breathe for a few minutes in case anyone has spotted me. Before long, I relax. No one can see me here. Now it's just a waiting game. And I've always been good at those.

As dusk falls, my hands are numb and I can't feel my face, but it'll all be worth it. I just have to bide my time until the opportunity presents itself. Which it always does.

There is finally movement. Simultaneously, a door at the front of the house bangs and a middle-aged woman strides towards a car. Is it her? It's hard to picture the slim brunette I knew as a girl in this woman. They all look the same when they get to a certain age. Wide-hipped, frumpily dressed and usually hiding their sagging chins behind scraggy shoulder-length hair, attempting to hang onto long lost youth. We men age far better.

I try to peer from my hiding place, but where she's standing is obscured by a bush. Bollocks. Bollocks. I can't tell if it's her or not. Surely she wouldn't have let herself go that much. Then as she's about to get into her car, another car pulls up beside her on the drive. A man and a sullen-looking teenage girl get out. She'd be the same age as Heidi is now.

Heidi. The mere thought of her name evokes both misery and fury within me. I can't believe she could reject her own father like she has. She's part of me whether she likes it or not. As I'll make her see.

"Are you setting off already love?" The man speaks in a broad Norfolk accent and the girl flounces away from them towards the house without a word.

"I've got to be there for half past four," the woman replies. "Just a few drinks and some dinner. Then I'll be back." It's her. It's Tina. She hasn't lost her Yorkshire accent over the years as much as I have whilst I've been inside, that's for sure. Although it's hardly a million miles away, the sound of the Yorkshire accent cheers me. A couple more hitches and I'll most likely be there.

"Don't you be rushing back love. Just enjoy your evening with the girls. I'll sort our mardy arse in there out."

"Teenagers, eh?" She opens the car door. "I'm sure they're more horrible than we were at that age." She laughs and my blood bubbles at the memory of what she did to me when we were teenagers. If it wasn't for her... she's definitely a huge part of who and what I became. When I went through all that shitty counselling at the hospital, her name came up time and time again. Anyway, it's feeling as though everything is about to fall into place.

"Where are you going anyway?"

"Just to *The Ship*."

"The one on the front? It's alright in there since they've

done it up." He kisses her forehead. "Let me know if you need a lift back."

Despite the many years that have passed, I feel a twinge of jealousy towards the man who's placed a kiss on her head. She should have been mine. That should have been my kid. Everything could have turned out so differently. And I want to know why she decided to keep that kid who's just gone into the house, and not mine.

"I'll be fine. But thanks anyway. It's Friday night. You have a beer or three. I'll either drive back or jump in a taxi."

I remain where I am for what seems like thirty minutes or so until darkness has completely fallen. It's much safer to wait. As I slide out of my hiding place, I notice a window being opened upstairs and steam billowing out into the garden. What I wouldn't give for a shower. I think of the home I once shared with Eva. When outwardly, my life was ordinary. Eva's another bitch who was part of my downfall. And coming to the top of my list.

I'm as stiff as a stick as I do my most nonchalant walk away from the house. I used to watch people, really watch people, so as I follow the slope of the street, I ensure I carry myself in a way I have previously observed - one that will make me appear as insignificant as possible. Rounded shoulders, a downward gaze, and hands thrust firmly in my pockets. The guise of the unconfident. Not unlike how I used to carry myself after Dean was run over and Mum kicked me out of the house. When I was a nobody. Now I am a somebody. Will Potts will go down in history.

Despite my hatred towards Mum, the grief that engulfed me when I found out about the stroke which had killed her five years ago came as a shock. I even cried – and I never cry. It wasn't for her, more for the mother she never was. Not to me, anyway. And if there is such a thing as an afterlife, I hope Dean told her to piss off after how she treated me for as long as I can remember.

Though if anyone had ever asked me whether I would want to go to her funeral, I'd have laughed in their face previously, but after I heard the news, I found myself wanting to be there. I wasn't sure if this was to get a temporary licence and be out for the day, or whether I genuinely needed to lay the ghosts to rest. Perhaps I was simply looking for confirmation that she was really dead. As it happened, I wasn't even allowed to apply to go. Instead, the hospital chaplain offered to hold a short service with me. But rather than bring any sort of closure or comfort, it made me angrier than I'd been for a while. We didn't even finish the 'service.' I felt like I'd totally lost the plot for a few days.

They upped my meds after that for some time and kept waking me through the night to 'check' on me. Like anyone really cares whether I'm alive or dead. Then I was forced to talk about her. It was crap.

I've talked about her in therapy before and look where that got me? I'd wanted to change and to be a normal family man but ended up spilling my guts to some charlatan with an axe to grind. Another target on my list. Him and his sidekick. Suzannah Peterson escaped me once. It won't happen again.

I buy chips and a hot drink from a girl serving out of a kiosk on the seafront and head to where I can watch the entrance to *The Ship Inn* from the beach. The tide's right up but I find a patch of sand by the sea wall, spot on for keeping watch on the doorway.

I wrap my numb fingers around the polystyrene cup. The food and drink warm me, but not for long. The rhythm of the waves has a sedative effect on me and I lean against the wall, fighting an overwhelming fatigue. I crunch the cup in my palm and clench my jaw. I don't want calm. Chaos and anger are what I need to deal with what is going to happen next. The face of the receptionist emerges in my mind, and I clench the cup tighter within my fist.

As I drop into a crouch against the gap in the sea wall, thoughts of both Tina and Eva leap over one another. I see their faces, twisted with hatred towards me. Two bitches that equally robbed me of my chance to have a son. As I keep my eyes fixed on the door of *The Ship Inn,* the voices resound inside my mind again. They're back like old adversaries, chanting the same words as last night. *Get rid of her.* Over and over again.

"Shut the fuck up. Leave me alone," I shout back at them as I get to my feet and try to focus my attention on the plough formation in the night sky above me. The inky-black tide looks to be slowly going out. I glance up and down the promenade. Hopefully nobody heard me shouting. There's not a soul to be seen.

I tuck my hands up opposite sleeves, grateful for the temporary warmth this provides. I need to get inside somewhere – I'll freeze to death out here. When I've taken care of business, I need to find somewhere to sleep tonight.

It's possibly not a good move, but I'm getting too cold to reason with myself. I edge towards the doorway of the pub and peer through the windows from the shadows. To say it's a Friday night, it's dead in there. I bend to the ground, as if adjusting my shoes, and try to take a closer look. There's a group of four women in the corner, but I can't make out if Tina is one of them. To make sure, I need to hear her again. The last thing I need is to make a mistake here. Not when I've come this far.

A young lad is serving; I can't imagine he'd take much notice of me if I walked in and ordered a drink. He's glued to his phone anyway. And he doesn't look the type to be a news watcher. The only time I ever watched any news at his age was after Dean had been killed in the hit and run by a pissed-up Pat Ingham. Another bitch who's thankfully snuffed it. I felt nothing but joy at the news of her heart attack. She was no age in the scheme of things, but after what she did to Dean, she didn't deserve to rebuild her life after being released. *What goes around comes around.* One of Mum's favourite sayings. I wish I could stop thinking about her. She's the last person I want to think about. She can rot for all I care.

For a few minutes, I deliberate over my next course of action. Go inside, or freeze out here? With me having a beard and grey hair now and having closely cropped dark hair back then, there isn't an immediate and obvious likeness between me and the photograph that's being peddled all over the media. The lad behind the bar is unlikely to look twice at me. He'll just think I'm some old fogie.

As I'm checking around for CCTV, I spot a hat that someone must have dropped. Excellent. It's been dumped on top of the railings surrounding the outdoor seating area. I slide it onto my head, shivering as the wool chills my ears.

When I was leaving the hotel this morning, the only exit seemed to be the main exit. The only other way out was through an emergency exit, which looked to be alarmed. That would really have drawn attention to me, so there was no way out other than through the revolving doors at the front.

If they've got me on camera as I was leaving, I had my hood up. So any images they put out in the media will be of a man in a hood rather than a woolly hat.

Nobody seems to notice as I push the door into The Ship Inn open. The four women seem engrossed in each other's company. I can't recall the last time I had a decent conversation. Perhaps I never have. No one seems to be on the same wavelength as me.

I stride up to the bar and order a pint of orange juice. I

guess most men my height and build would order a pint of beer. No way will I ever drink alcohol again. Not after what happened to my brother. Though I guess that if anything's going to make me stand out whilst I'm on the run, ordering orange juice in a pub might.

But, as I suspected, the bartender barely looks up from his phone as I give him my order, and he can hardly see through his fringe when I pay him. I grab a newspaper from a rack beside the bar, take my drink, and sit at a table with my back to the women. I'm close enough to listen to their conversation. The other tables are empty. The deserted promenade suggests they'll stay that way.

I let a long and grateful breath out. At least I'm indoors for a while even if the conversation I'm listening to is sleep-inducing. Who is doing what on bonfire night? What universities their kids are applying to. What someone's mother-in-law has said... and on... and on. Tina used to have an edge to her when we were young. Evidently, she's become as tedious as the woman I went on to get married to. However, she must also find the conversation boring, as she eventually announces her departure. At least I'll know which one of them she is when she stands up.

"Aww, stay for a bit longer Tine. It's Friday. It's not like we have work tomorrow."

She most certainly doesn't. She doesn't have anything tomorrow.

"No, I'm going to get off. I haven't been sleeping well for the last couple of nights. And I've got an early start tomorrow. I'm taking Jennifer up to Newcastle for an open day."

"Is Dave picking you up?"

"He offered, but I'm just going to jump in a cab. I told him to have a beer." She's slurring her words. I suppose she's been in here for well over three hours. And she never could handle her drink.

"Where's your car?"

"I'm going to leave it outside work. Dave'll bring me for it tomorrow."

"Shall I walk with you?" A different voice asks.

No. No. No, you shan't.

"No, you stop here where it's warm. Honestly. The taxi rank's only round the corner."

"I don't know Tina. You shouldn't be walking around on your own."

"Give over. If anyone comes near me, I'll kick them in the balls."

"Has that bloke been caught yet?" A different voice asks. "That *Yorkshire Dipper* or whatever he was called?"

"Oh God yes, I've heard about him. It's enough to give you the creeps. You make sure you get a taxi."

"He's my ex-boyfriend."

"Who is?"

"The Yorkshire Dipper."

"What?? Noooo. You're kidding, right?"

For only four women, their laughter is raucous. I curl my now-warm hands into fists. I've never been able to abide drunk women at the best of times, but amongst them is one drunk woman in particular. One who decided that it was acceptable to murder my unborn child without my knowledge. And now they're all laughing at my expense. Maybe I should come back for the other three.

The laughter subsides. "Shit! Are you really being serious Tina?"

"I'm afraid so. It's not often I think about it these days."

"When? How old were you?"

"I was a teenager. And an idiot. I liked them mean and moody back then. I guess, for a time, I thought I could change him somehow."

"Wow! Well, he's certainly mean. Gosh, I can't believe you used to go out with him."

"Me neither. I had a very lucky escape, didn't I? When I think of what my life might have been... I could have been that poor woman he married."

Poor woman. Eva ruined *my* life, not the other way around. Wait until I get my hands on her. And I wonder if Tina's going to tell them about the baby she aborted. Whore.

"I felt sorry for his wife when it happened." Another voice jumps into the conversation. "Really sorry. They all got hounded out from where they lived, didn't they? He had a daughter as well. Poor thing. Do you remember what he did to her?"

"He tried to kill her, if I remember correctly?"

Is this what I've been reduced to? Idle gossip amongst pissed women in a pub. And how dare they mention Heidi? They don't know the circumstances. She was my kid to do what I wanted with. She still is. And so is Harry.

"He's a maniac. I hope they throw away the key when they catch him."

I bury my head deeper in my newspaper. What would they say if I jumped up now and said, *Will Potts. Pleased to meet you?* I almost laugh at the idea.

"Have they got him yet?"

"I haven't watched any news since lunchtime, but I'm sure they will have done by now. Someone like him won't get far." It's her voice again, Tina's. The adrenaline, anger and chaos are certainly swirling now. And I'm soon going to get the chance I've been waiting for.

"Does Dave know you used to go out with him?"

"Yeah." She laughs. "Of course he does. He often jokes about how my taste in men has drastically improved. It's not really funny though. Is it? What he did to all those poor women, well..."

What he did. It's no worse than what *you* did. I want to ram her up against a wall. Shout in her face. See fear in her eyes. *You're just as much a murderer as I am.* But what I did was a service to society. I cleansed the streets of pathetic drunken women whilst she butchered a defenceless unborn baby. My baby. Perhaps my son. I think then of the son I *have* got, the son that's out there, growing older without me, and my gut twists with the anticipation of finally getting to meet him. I wonder if he looks like me. Then the familiar anger rises with the memory of who's playing dad to him now. Mark's taken anyone and everyone who belonged to me. It should have been *him* killed in that hit and run, not Dean.

"Drop me a text when you're home safely." One of the women calls after Tina.

"Of course I will," she calls back over her shoulder. "I'm just nipping to the loo before I go."

I've seen this time and time again. Women who are either too comfortable sat on their fat arses at a pub table, or too tanked up to ensure someone in their group is safe. I hate the bloody lot of them. As a traffic cop, I was always pleased on the occasions when it was a woman I pulled over for a traffic offence, especially drink driving. Being part of their criminal record and driving ban held a lot of job satisfaction.

As the remaining women return to their boring conversation, I take the opportunity to slip back out the way I came in. Again, no one seems to notice.

The dimly lit promenade is shiny with the fine mist of rain. There's something about the seaside in winter which really depresses me. I hurry to retake my place behind the gap in the seawall before Tina follows me out of the pub. The tide has gone much further out whilst I've been in there, which is exactly what I need.

. . .

A few minutes pass before I spot her, framed in the pub doorway. She pauses, pulling on her gloves and a hat. She won't need them where she's going.

I hold my breath as she looks left and right. Finally, she ventures beyond the tables and directly towards where I'm lying in wait. After the winters I spent in Alderton, I know exactly how an animal feels whilst stalking its prey. The head rush of anticipation, the surge of power.

Eventually, she passes me. I rise from my crouch and emerge from my place behind the wall. As she passes through the shuttered-up amusements, I catch her up and fall into step with her.

"Hello stranger." I catch her arm as she swings around. She searches my face for a moment before seemingly recognising me, horror replacing curiosity.

Like so many women before her, she appears to freeze. Her eyes bulge. She's even worse close up. Blimey, she's really let herself go. Even more than Eva did. Eventually she stammers, "what do you want Will? What the hell are you doing here?" Her voice wobbles with fear. As well it should.

"I want to talk to you." I tighten my grip on her arm. "We'll head this way, shall we?" Taking hold of her shoulders, I attempt to steer her towards the gap in the wall where I was hiding.

"No. No. Get off me. HELP!" She tries to break free of my grasp. I cover her mouth with my other hand.

"Shut it, do you hear me?" Now fully behind her, I'm able to frogmarch her towards the beach. Her legs are carrying her whether or not she wants them to. Her squealing is somewhat irritating though. She squirms to escape my grasp, but she's hardly a rival to me. Especially with the volcano of unspent anger I've carried for so many years.

As we get onto the sand, she stumbles and nearly takes me over with her. I quickly recover myself and tighten my fingers into her flesh. Again she tries to scream out, but I'm ready for her this time. I squeeze at her jaw, aware that I could crack it in two here and now. That will really give her something to squeal about. However, what I've got in store for her is much more fun.

It takes an age to drag her to the edge of the water. She's so busy trying to tug herself backward and downward, she drops her handbag on the sand a few metres from the sea. I'll go back for that. Hopefully, there'll be something of use like there was in the woman's from the hotel. Fate has done nothing but shine favourably on me for the last couple of days. Starting with the opportunity to escape.

"Please," she gasps as I relax my hold. "Please. Let me go." There still isn't a soul around, and even if there was, any sound she makes is likely to be carried out to sea from here. "Will."

"Don't you even say my name." My voice is a growl in my throat. *Get rid of her.*

"But you cared about me once. Please don't hurt me. Think about what we had."

"What we had." I keep my grip on her chin whilst allowing her mouth to be free enough to speak. Only for a moment. "You're right. I cared about you once."

"Look Will. I know you. Really know you. Remember?"

I grab her even tighter. "No, you don't. Not anymore."

"Look why don't we go for a drink or something? Come on Will. You don't want to do this."

"I told you to shut up. You had your chance with me."

"Remember when we came here Will? Just me and you?"

"Shut your noise. I know what you're trying to do."

"Come on Will. I know there's a decent person still lurking in there somewhere."

"I trusted you. And look how you repaid me."

She wriggles again. How can she possibly imagine that she's going to be able to get away from me?

"Carrying your kid inside me made my skin crawl." Her tone's changed now. "Getting rid of it is the best thing I ever did."

"And you're about to find out that leaving that pub alone is the stupidest thing you've ever done." We're so close she'll be able to feel the warmth of my breath against her cheek. "More stupid than murdering my kid."

Who could have foreseen this situation all those years ago? I loved her once, at least I thought I did. It was probably lust rather than love. She was worth lusting after back then. Now I've no choice other than to end her.

She lets out another scream, so I grab at her mouth again. *Get rid of her. Get rid of her.* With my free hand, I get hold of the back of her neck. I can feel each bone and every bit of gristle as I wrestle her to the ground.

"No! No!" Her final sound is a gurgle as she starts taking in the water.

She's stronger than she appears and writhes beneath me as I hold her face down. It takes everything I have to keep her there. Eventually, her thrashing subsides until it becomes a few twitches, and then stops altogether.

As I rise to my full height, I'm shaking from the exertion and I'm panting like a dog. I stare as a wave washes over her. I can't believe we were arguing a few moments ago... before I squeezed every breath out of her. And what she said about my kid making her skin crawl. I'll never forget that. Or the disgust in her eyes as she said it. Anyway, she's gone now.

The power of what I do unnerves me sometimes. It's as easy as stamping on a spider. One minute they're alive, the next they're a blot on the floor. She's had this coming for thirty-five years. I always knew I'd punish her one day.

I turn her onto her back with several stabs of my foot,

checking I've definitely finished her. This is no time for mistakes. I bend forwards and roll her over again. And again. And again, until I'm up to my thighs. Further, deeper into the froth of the waves. Deep enough in to be carried by the still outgoing tide. Giving me plenty of time to get away from here before she's washed up somewhere. Like she wasn't washed up enough as she was.

8

HEIDI

"I CAN'T BELIEVE you're not letting me go to work." Alysha sits cross-legged in the wicker chair. The sullen expression she's displaying reminds me of when we were kids. With her face bare of make-up for a change, and her blonde hair piled on top of her head, she looks more like the seventeen-year-old she is, rather than the twenty-one-year-old she pretends to be. She squints in the sunshine filtering through the conservatory blinds as she stares at Uncle Mark.

"It's only for today love. All being well. I'm just trying to keep us all together, so I know everyone's safe." Even Uncle Mark's tone reminds me of how he'd have spoken to us when we were kids. His chin is all bristly, which is unlike him. He's totally not himself. I can vaguely remember when Auntie Lauren died. Everyone used to have to tell him to shave, to eat, to wash. Alysha slept at our house more than at her own. Uncle Mark was a total mess. I'm glad he's happy with Mum now. They've both been through the same thing, so they're good together.

"I've told you a million times, Uncle Will would never hurt me." Alysha lets her gaze roam over us all. She's definitely waiting for a reaction. When she doesn't get one this time, she turns her attention back towards whatever message she was composing. She'll be feeling dejected if I know her correctly. Normally, at the very least, she can get a rise out of Mum, even if it is just a look.

In response to its beeping, Mum reaches into her bag for her phone. "It's yet another message of complaint." Her voice is matter-of-fact as she waves her phone in the air. "Next door but one this time. I can't blame them. It's getting worse out there. This is normally a peaceful place to live."

"Surely they must realise there's absolutely nothing we can do about it?" Uncle Mark reaches for her shoulder and squeezes it. The wicker chair creaks beneath his movement. "It's not as if they're trespassing or making an excessive amount of noise."

"I know, but people are struggling to get their cars in and out of their drives. And who wants that lot on their doorstep?" Mum tugs at her hairband, and lets her hair fall loose around her shoulders. "Gosh, that was giving me a headache."

The conservatory at the back of the house is as far away from the sea of reporters as possible. But the main reason we're in here is that the boys have taken over the lounge with their train set. This is our third day stuck in this house. We might as well be in prison too. Because of *him*.

"Once Will Potts is safely back where he should be," I say, "they'll all bugger off." I glance out across the garden, watching a bird in the birdbath. Normality. Looking at the stillness at the back of the house, it's hard to imagine the chaos at the front. Mum's right - this is a street where nothing ever happens. It was one reason they bought a house here.

"Why do you call him that?" Alysha raises her eyes towards me. "*Will Potts.* It's like me calling him *Mark Potts* when I talk about him." She nods towards Uncle Mark.

"Uncle Mark is your dad. A proper dad. Will Potts is

nothing to me," I say. She knows this. Why does she have to make a thing of it again now?

"You know you've always got me Heidi." Uncle Mark leans across to where I'm sitting on the footstool at the side of Mum and ruffles my hair. "Don't you ever forget that." I'm warmed by his words. Mum must be too, because she smiles. She spent many years being tormented by guilt at what I'd seen and gone through when I was younger. I've never blamed her though. Despite that, I don't think she'll ever truly forgive herself.

Alysha gives first her dad, then Mum the dead eye before scowling at me. She hates not being the centre of attention, and she hates it even more when her dad is nice to me. Alysha and I were best friends when we were small, before everything happened. When Mum and Uncle Mark got together, she started seeing me as a rival. She returns her attention to her phone and continues texting.

"Linda from next door but one the other way has messaged again now." Mum sighs. "She has a point Mark. The reporters are causing a nuisance out there." Mum drops her phone into her lap. "There must be something we can do. Imagine how we'd feel if it was one of the neighbours bringing this sort of drama to the street."

"If only," Uncle Mark replies.

We all stare at each other as the doorbell echoes from the hallway. Nobody moves.

"We're not expecting anyone are we?" Uncle Mark asks.

"Friend or foe?" Mum adds, half laughing. "Who knows anymore?"

"I'll go." I stand. "But what if it's a reporter? Do I just tell them to..."

"Just close the door on them, if it is." Mum raises her voice to drown out what I was about to come out with. "Though it's probably Adele. Hopefully she'll have something to report for a change. I'm sick of just sitting here. It's like waiting to be hung, drawn and quartered."

"I'm sick of it too," says Alysha without looking up. For once, she and Mum agree on something.

It *is* Adele.   And DSI Jones. I remember him from everything that happened before. Plus, he's been here a few times for dinner over the years. He and Uncle Mark are friends. Though now I've moved out, I don't really know what goes on here anymore.

"Heidi." He stretches his hand out, which I think means he wants to shake mine. "Nice to see you again. If only it was in different circumstances."   I nod as I look out towards the cul-de-sac. Flash bulbs go off everywhere, making my eyes ache. Me answering the door to Adele and DSI Jones is hardly front page news. Catching Will Potts is.

"Come in." I step back from the door. "Quickly. Before they take any more pictures of me looking like this." I've borrowed a pair of joggers and a hoodie from Mum and my hair is in plaits. I've certainly looked better.

Both of them look serious as they step into the hallway. Shit. What are they going to tell us? We just need some good news. Like he's back where he belongs.

"Uncle Mark and Mum are in the conservatory," I tell them, pointing towards the lounge. "Do you want to go through? I'll just grab another chair from the kitchen."

I should probably offer them a drink, but I don't want to miss whatever they've come to say. For DSI Jones to be here too, I reckon it's going to be something worth hearing.

"Sorry," I call after them, as I follow. "You'll have to step over my brothers and the train set to get in there."

"Alright Alan. Adele." Uncle Mark stands and shakes DSI Jones's hand as though they're about to do some sort of business deal. Shaking hands must be the done thing in the police. "Have a seat both of you." He gestures behind him to the two-seater and moves beside Mum onto the other sofa. Alysha, being Alysha, doesn't move a muscle. Hopefully she won't always be like this, but I do wonder if she'd even give up her seat on a bus to someone elderly. She's that selfish most of the time.

"You two carry on with your trains." I tuck my head into the lounge where it's all gone quiet. Harry looks at me inquisitively. "I'm going to close this door, but I'll find out what's happening and let you know."

He nods, wide-eyed. Poor love. I remember what it's like to wish I was older and could be told exactly what was going on. Although sometimes it's better not to know.

I slide the door between the lounge and conservatory closed, then drop onto the dining chair I've just grabbed from the kitchen.

"I take it we haven't got him?" Uncle Mark clasps his hands in his lap. "I'm sure someone would have let us know if he'd been taken in."

DSI Jones shakes his head and clears his throat. "To be honest with you Mark, I wanted to get round here before the next news goes out." He looks at Adele then back at Uncle Mark.

"What's happened?" Mum's really pale. I hope she's OK. She's not sleeping at all, and we've had three nights of this now. She won't confide in me properly, as she'll think I can't cope with her fear as well as my own. But I can. Me and Mum have been in this together the whole way through. She ought to know she can talk to me.

I can't believe they haven't caught him yet. How hard can it be? Dozens of police forces against one man. And with cameras all over the place as there are nowadays?

"I'm really sorry to have to tell you..." DSI Jones takes a deep breath. He also looks as though he hasn't been sleeping either as he rubs at the bridge of his nose.

The pause is maddening. "Tell us what?" Mum sits forwards.

"Everything is pointing towards him having struck again."

Silence descends over us all for a moment. Even Alysha's face drops.

"You're joking, aren't you?" Uncle Mark sits up straighter. Like this is really something they would joke about.

"You mean he's killed someone else?" My voice is too loud. I hope Harry and Isaac haven't heard me through the glass doors. I doubt it. "But when? How?"

Mum drops her head into her hands. At least she can't blame herself this time. One reason the press hounded her before is that she'd told the police that Will Potts was at home, sleeping on the nights when women were drowning in the River Alder. Something else she's never forgiven herself for. How could she have known, though? When you turn in and go to sleep in the same bed as your husband and he's still there the following morning, you don't expect him to have nipped out in the night and murdered someone.

"A dog walker discovered a body on a beach in Norfolk this morning." DSI Jones fiddles with his cuff as he speaks.

"A dead body?" My face burns as everyone turns to me. What a stupid question. Of course, a body is a dead body. The poor dog walker, I think. Imagine finding a dead body. They'd never forget the sight of it. And it's always dog walkers or early morning joggers that discover dead bodies. I'm never taking up jogging, but I'd give my right arm for another dog. The soppy face of my beloved lab, Biscuit, pops into my mind. God do I wish he was still here, even if he was originally bought by *him.* Biscuit had to be put to sleep the year before last, and I thought my heart was going to break. I didn't stop crying for days. And that's because of a pet dog. I can't get my head around what all the families of the dead women have gone through and will continue to go through. All at the hands of the man who is technically my father. And now, by the sounds of it, he's done it again.

"The body that's been found matches the description of a woman reported missing in the early hours of this morning." All eyes are on DSI Jones. "Not long after midnight."

"What makes you think it's him?" Mum rubs at her temples. She's probably getting one of her migraines. These days, normally, there's only really Alysha when she's being a cowbag that gives Mum a migraine.

"The woman's body was found washed up by the tide in Hemsby," he replies. "Only fifty miles from where the hotel receptionist was murdered the night before."

"Drowned?" My chest feels as though it's being squeezed from the inside. "Again?"

"That doesn't mean it was definitely him." Alysha uncrosses her legs. As if she's still sticking up for him. What will it take?

"The woman's husband identified his wife at the scene," Adele speaks for the first time since saying hello. "She's going to be named in the next news bulletin. Tina Atkinson. She was fifty-one. And according to the husband, she was Will's ex-girlfriend."

"Oh my God." Mum's hand flies to her mouth.

"Bloody hell. I remember Tina," Uncle Mark says softly, his chin dropping, so it almost touches his chest. "They went from being inseparable to detesting one another."

"He's never let..." Mum's voice trails off as she glances from me to Alysha.

"He's never let what?" I ask.

Suddenly, everyone in the room is looking at her.

"It doesn't matter." Mum rubs at her neck as she moves her head from side to side. A flush is creeping up her throat as it always does when she's uncomfortable. It surprises me sometimes how well I know my mother. And I never forget how lucky I am – in fact, it's often why I cut Alysha some slack.

MARIA FRANKLAND

The poor thing was so young when she lost her mother. She'd have probably been completely different if Auntie Lauren had lived.

"Yes, it does matter actually." Alysha glares at Mum. "You're keeping us all here like prisoners, so if there's anything to know about this woman they've found, we want to know too."

It's the first time Alysha has shown any sort of togetherness towards me since all this started. I jump on it.

"Yeah Mum. Alysha's right. We have got a right to know. We're not kids anymore."

"As it's just been said, Tina was Will's girlfriend when they were teenagers." I watch as Mum reaches into her bag and pulls out her migraine tablets. I was right. "What I was going to say before is that he's never let it go. And I mean never. He couldn't forgive..."

"Are you OK Mum?" I point at the box in her hand.

"I will be. Once this tablet kicks in." She presses one out and reaches for the bottle of water beside her. I wait for her to swallow, wondering what the hell is coming next. "Anyway, Tina was pregnant, so Will told me. But she ended the pregnancy, apparently without his knowledge."

"She had an abortion!" Alysha's voice is a shriek. "Without him even knowing? That's awful."

"In her defence, she was very young," Mum replies. "Seventeen, I think. Plus, she obviously saw something in him I was blind to."

"He's murdered her. Will has killed Tina." Uncle Mark's voice is flat as he raises his eyes to meet DSI Jones's. "What actually happened? She was a nice lass, as I remember. She wouldn't have hurt a fly."

"Tina left the pub she was in with some friends on her own. It looks as though he's waited for her, then dragged her onto the beach." The room is silent. "He held her face down in the sea until she drowned." DSI Jones closes his eyes for a moment. "We're keeping an open mind, but there's really no reason to suspect anyone else."

I notice Uncle Mark's shoulders are shaking. As if he's crying. He *never* cries.

Mum rests her hand on his back as she looks at DSI Jones. "He's been out there for three nights Alan. Why the hell hasn't he been caught yet? I don't understand."

"We've got officers crawling all over the place, don't you worry. House to house. And every shred of CCTV is being scrutinised. Plus, we've got roadblocks on all the routes out of there."

"She was definitely killed last night?" Uncle Mark raises his head to look at DSI Jones again.

"It looks that way. But the post-mortem hasn't been done yet, so I can't confirm for certain."

"Her body wasn't found until this morning though, was it?"

DSI Jones shakes his head. He's much older than I remember him. Old enough to be someone's grandad, that's for sure. I wish I had a grandad. Or even a grandma. Both mine are dead and weren't up to much when they were alive. I had Scary Granny, who I was terrified of, and my other grandma had dementia and had no idea who I was.

"The roadblocks and house to house. We've only implemented them this morning, right?" I can tell where Uncle Mark's going with this. I'm thinking the same, but he's always better at putting things into words.

"Yes." DSI Jones lifts his glasses and rubs one of his eyes as he squints in the sunshine filtering through the conservatory blinds. "We were more focused on Aldeburgh and the surrounding area until this latest killing. He got further than we thought."

"He could have got a lot further still in the last twelve hours." Uncle Mark's voice is matter of fact.

"From what I've been told," DSI Jones continues, "he'll be

suffering withdrawals from his medication quite badly by now."

"Meaning?"

"The best we can hope for is that symptoms such as nausea and the tremors slow him down."

"And the worst?" Uncle Mark looks at him.

"That those so-called voices he claims to hear are back, and he's going to strike again at their instruction."

The chill I've had for the past few days snakes further up my spine. He's killed two more women, and if he's managed to travel further away from where the prison van crashed, he could be getting close to Yorkshire by now.

But how the hell is he travelling? He wouldn't be able to hire a car like he did when he was on the run with me. I didn't think I was going to get out of that car alive. He was driving it away from the police up the motorway as fast as an aeroplane. I really thought we were going to crash. I was screaming and screaming and then he yelled something awful at me. Then I just closed my eyes. I didn't really believe in God back then, but I seem to remember that I prayed.

"Nobody leaves this house until he's caught." Uncle Mark sweeps his gaze over us all. "I mean it."

I glance over my shoulder at the boys on the other side of the glass sliding doors. They're playing so innocently with their trains, but I recognise the look of worry on Harry's face. This isn't fair. Why should they have to deal with the enormity of what's happening at their ages? Alysha and I went through enough when we were kids without it now affecting Harry and Isaac too. I reach for my phone. DSI Jones was right. Hemsby is fifty miles closer to where we are than Aldeburgh. He's on his way up the country. He's on his way for me.

. . .

"You need to let your sister know," Mum says to Uncle Mark after DSI Jones has gone. "You haven't spoken to her since last night, have you?"

"I wish she'd come and stay here, like I suggested. She's saying that no one's going to drive her out of her own home. But if he makes it as far as Yorkshire, our Claire's will be one of the first places he'll go."

"Try to persuade her again," Mum says. "She's so stubborn."

"I know. I'll ring her now." He glances around for his phone. "She's probably already heard about this latest one on the news. I'm not sure what they have and haven't reported."

"It's going out in the next bulletin," Adele says.

"Have a word with Claire too, Eva." Uncle Mark nods at Mum. "She's not coping very well with it all, from what I can gather. It's bringing it all back."

"What makes you say that?" Alysha's ears prick up. "Auntie Claire's got nothing to worry about."

"I don't know if you can remember, but Auntie Claire was lucky to survive an awful attack too," Uncle Mark begins.

"It was the same man who killed your mum. Then he went after Auntie Claire," Mum adds.

I close my eyes. Why couldn't I just have had a nice, normal childhood? "DCI Jonathan Ingham," I say. I might have been young, but his name has always stuck in my head.

"I can't believe you remember his name."

Alysha was only five, but her face still darkens at the mention of it all. She always used to say she was going to be a writer, like her mum, when she grew up. She was going to help catch bad men. Instead, she dropped out of sixth form and ended up training to be a hairdresser. Still, she seems good at it.

"I've an idea of how Claire's feeling." Mum nods towards Uncle Mark. "Pass her over to me when you've spoken to her."

The doorbell goes again. "I'll get it." Alysha stands this time.

"Blimey – it's not like you to do something useful." I grin at her. "You'll be offering to make a brew next."

"Yeah right."

"It's like Piccadilly Circus around here," says Mum. I smile. What's going on is nightmarish, but some things never change. Like Mum's predictable sayings.

I listen to Uncle Mark as he's connected to Auntie Claire. I haven't seen her for months. When I first moved into the flat, I loved having her around. Her being there a few days each week made the wrench of leaving home easier. But she's got a boyfriend now and spends most of her free time with him. Years ago, we were all quite a close family. But what happened blew us apart. I've spoken to Mum about it and she just said that there's only so much pain any family can take before it splits. What have we got in ours? A drink drive death. A murder victim, two attempted murder survivors, one of them me. We've got a serial killer. Then, of course, there was Scary Granny, who was a liar and covered up the killings. Then everyone in our family has been bereaved on some level.

"Grandma," Alysha shrieks from the hallway. "What are you doing here?" She sounds the happiest I've heard her in a long time. The boys race from the lounge to the front door. Brenda's no direct relation to them, but she's always made a fuss of them. She was the same with me – the nearest thing to a Grandma I've ever had. When we went to Mum's mum's funeral last year, it was like going to the funeral of a stranger. I'd travelled in the family car behind the coffin, feeling like a fraud for being there.

"Brenda's here." Mum jumps up, her face brightening too. Brenda's always had that effect. She's just what we all need right now.

Adele looks quizzically at me as Mark puts a finger in one ear and walks towards the conservatory door whilst he's on the phone, looking irritated. Mum always jokes that he can only do one thing at a time.

"Brenda's Mark's mother-in-law to be, well she used to be," I explain to Adele. "He was engaged to my Auntie Lauren, who was killed by DCI Ingham, before Auntie Claire was attacked." I point my finger around as I speak, as though putting everyone in their relevant positions.

Adele probably knows this history already. She nods, like I'm telling her run-of-the-mill stuff. Nope. This is our lives.

"Brenda's Lauren's Mum. So she's Alysha's grandma," I explain. And there's no doubt that Brenda is Alysha's grandma when she follows her into the conservatory. Holding her arms out to me, it's like looking at an older version of Auntie Lauren, and an even older version of Alysha. They all look so much like each other.

It must be strange for Mum when Alysha and Brenda get together. At times, I consider the fact that Mum's and Uncle Mark's marriage has only come about after so much misery. Without the evil, the loss and the grief, they'd have never got together. They'd still just be brother and sister-in-law. What a tangled mess our family is.

9

WILL

"Cheers mate. Safe drive now." I rub my eyes as I jump down from the truck's cab. The driver revs a couple of times before leaving me behind in a cloud of dust and engine fumes. Now I'm exposed again. There's a line of trees at the side of the road which I dart towards. I've come this far and I'm not going to get myself locked back up now. But I desperately need a change of clothes. Also, I'm starting to look like a tramp and I'm going to really draw attention to myself if I don't do something about it.

It would have been good to have made it closer to Alderton, but the driver's only going as far as Hunstanton before turning to go back to the ferry at Portsmouth. Thank God for foreign drivers, that's what I say. He didn't look at me twice as we drove here. He's probably got no idea what's headline news here in the UK.

I managed to get picked up at around six this morning after getting some kip on a sun lounger. I'd broken into a hut after walking for a few miles up the beach. It reminded me of the beach hut we had at Bridlington when I was still a constable. Heidi was a baby and east coast holidays were all I could afford. Those years were the closest I had to a normal life as an adult.

The voices were leaving me alone and I only had to suffer seeing my mother two or three times a year.

The beach hut even smelt the same. Sea salt, damp towels and vinegar. Vinegar was the only thing left in the cupboard. Though I was glad to be able to make a black coffee and then I'd found a packet of biscuits. Sugar and caffeine, combined with seeing Tina on her merry way conspired to keeping me awake for most of the night. The waves sounded alien, especially after twelve years of listening to banging doors, jangling keys and wailing voices, and not just at night.

I knew I'd have to get away from Hemsby before first light came. I've never dumped a body in the sea before and it seems that I didn't do a very good job, considering Tina's body washed straight back up first thing. Rivers are much better for the job. It usually takes at least a day and sometimes two, for them to surface.

I'm feeling braver this morning. The longer I'm out, the more invincible I become. I tug my hat over my ears and venture into a charity shop without hesitating this time. The two women are busy wittering at one another and don't appear remotely interested in me. One of them nods an acknowledgment in my direction before returning to the conversation, which sounds like typical women's crap. At least they're not talking about me. The lift I've just hitched has hopefully got me far enough away from where I might be the first topic of conversation.

I quickly pick out jeans, jumper, trainers and a thick coat. No messing. It doesn't matter what they look like so long as they fit me, and I can feel warmer. Dumping it all on the counter, I briefly raise my eyes, spotting something else as I do. One woman mutters something about having some pricing up to do in the back, whilst the other woman taps at buttons on the cash register.

"I'll just have a quick look over here," I say, wandering across to the 'new items' section."

"Right you are."

I catch sight of myself in the mirror as I go. The beard is coming along nicely, although I look haggard from twelve years in that hospital, three nights on the run, and two more dispatches of women. I've certainly altered considerably since the photograph that's being circulated. I grab socks, undies, another hat, a scarf and some gloves. At least I'll be able to hide behind the scarf now. I toy with the idea of asking to use the changing room but changing head to foot in there will probably only draw attention to myself.

As it happens, the woman serving me keeps her attention on a phone call she's taken whilst she rings my items through. The old me would have made a comment about her rudeness, but the current me is grateful for her lack of attention.

Next, a man's got to eat. Particularly one who's spent as much physical and mental energy as me over the last few days. Clutching my bag from the charity shop, I hover around a greasy spoon for a while. I need to get inside. It's hanging around out here like this that'll get me caught. But first I need to check that it's going to be safe for me to go in. I don't want it to be my final stop. After a few minutes, I know for certain that the café's empty apart from a bored-looking lad. He leans over the counter, scrolling through his phone. That's all anyone seems to do nowadays. Too busy with what's in their hand, rather than what's going on around them. But I can't grumble, that's just another thing in my favour.

"A bacon sandwich and a coffee please," I say as I walk in, making sure I disguise all traces of my accent. He looks irritated at my interruption, but thankfully, his face shows no trace of recognition. So far, so good. I know the risks I'm taking, but without food and a change of clothes, I won't get much further.

"It'll be ten minutes," he replies. "We close in twenty though." He glances up at the clock. "Is that OK?"

"Sure thing. Where's your toilet?"

I place a ten pound note on the counter then head in the direction he points me in. At least I can have a wash and change from the clothes that haven't been cleaned since I was at the hotel. I'll eat, then I'll head for the road and see about hitching another lift. Really, I want to bin all these old clothes, but I'll have to find a safer place for that.

I could have done with longer than twenty minutes in the café's warmth, but it serves its purpose. The key clunking behind me in the lock of the café door reminds me of the hospital I recently left. I'm pig sick of being locked up. Twelve years is long enough for anyone. Maybe I won't have to be... I seem to have the midas touch right now – everything is falling into place. There is no reason why this cannot continue to be the case.

As I've done before, I'll stand somewhere I can see the licence plate before I try to flag anything down. I don't try to stop anything with a UK number plate, and I only wave to wagons. It's asking for trouble to hitch a lift from anything else. Even if I have to wait for two hours, it's worth it. Maybe I'll be able to get all the way to Alderton today.

I consider whether I should leave it until darkness has fallen before watching for my next lift. At least I'm far enough away from where I chucked Tina in now. And from the newspaper I had a flick through in the café, that's where they seem to be concentrating their efforts. Total idiots.

Luckily for me, it's quiet out here. I woke to sunshine and seagulls in that beach hut this morning, but now it's turned into one of those dull November days which doesn't seem to maintain full daylight. Another thing in my favour.

Then, as I stride through leaves, scanning for signs to the main road out of here, I spot an interesting sign in a window.

Long & short-term holiday lets. 1 bed apartment. £60 nightly. £400 weekly.

I walk on, not wanting to be seen hanging around. But I could do with getting my head down. Just for one night. A whole night's kip. I could have a shower. Work out what to do next. And decide how I'm going to use my one and only alliance out here... I reckon it's time.

"Yes. Hello. I'm ringing about your holiday let on Swithen Street. Is it available?" I'm amazed to have found a phone box. They were a rare thing even before I got sent down, so I thought they'd have all disappeared in the years I've been locked up.

"We rarely have much call for it out of season, but yes, I suppose it is available. How long would you be thinking of and when?" The woman sounds quite old. Hopefully, this will mean she'll be more trusting of me and less likely to ask too many questions. In my experience, old dears never see what's right under their nose.

"Just for tonight, I think." This call box is making me claustrophobic. I haven't been in one of these things for years. It stinks of mouldy chewing gum. Some things never change.

"Tonight!" Her voice rises and then falls again. "That's incredibly short notice. And to be honest, I wouldn't usually let it go for just one night. And I'm due to be setting off somewhere shortly."

Her use of the word *usually* offers some leverage. "What if I paid you for two nights?" I do a mental calculation of what funds I have left. Still, I'll be able to get my hands on some more soon. "That way, we're doing each other a favour."

"I have a policy of a three-night minimum stay," she says. "You know, because of the need to get cleaners in afterwards."

"We'd keep it very clean and tidy." I attempt to load the edge into my voice that always used to win the girls over when I was young. "You won't even know we've been there." I realise she might be more inclined to help if she thinks I've got a woman with me. "You'd be doing us a massive favour to be honest. We've just had to leave our car at the garage to be fixed, so we're a bit stuck."

"How many of you are there?"

"Just me and my wife."

"And your car won't be ready today?"

"It won't be ready until tomorrow at the earliest. They've had to order a part in."

The woman goes quiet for a moment. "Right. OK. I'll let it to you both for one night. I won't see you stuck, but I'll have to take a hundred pound deposit from you. Just in case."

"That's fine."

"Can you meet me there? I was on my way out, like I said, so it'll have to be soon. What name is it?"

"Allan Hardisty," I say, giving the first name that pops into my mind. "And we can be there as soon as you'd like us to be. We're fairly close by." It dawns on me that I'll have to think of a reason 'my wife' isn't with me when I go to meet this woman. A good one. I don't want her changing her mind about leaving the keys with me. Still, I can be very persuasive. It's one of my best attributes.

"I'll be there in twenty minutes." She sounds hurried. Hopefully she'll take the cash, give me the keys, and then be on her way. I'm desperate for a shower and just to rest up.

Somewhere I can lie low. If only for just one night. Then I'll be more than ready for what's going to come next.

I linger in the phone box for a while, keeping the phone against my ear as though I'm still speaking. I used to do this as a kid. Shelter in phone boxes when it was raining. It had to be really tipping it down for Mum to let me back inside. She reckoned to be able to feel my presence in the house and didn't like me to be around. And even when she did let me in, I had to stay in my room. It's really no wonder I turned out like I did. An outcast.

It's not exactly a good idea for me to be seen on the street. All it takes is one person to recognise me or even to half think they do. The police would be here quicker than I could say nine, nine, nine. And hanging around outside a house will only draw attention to me.

The time takes forever to pass. I can't believe the memories are back of when my mother used to lock me out. I thought I'd well and truly buried those. I was allowed indoors at noon for lunch and at five o'clock for dinner. Until I got to ten years old, I wasn't even allowed off the street. I'll never forget that daily sense of homelessness, trying to find ways to kill the time. I feel like that again.

Eventually, with five minutes to go before the meeting time with the woman, I slam the phone onto its holder and walk the two streets back to the house, keeping my gaze downwards at all times. I'm so pissed off with myself. No matter where I am, the darkness always finds me. But at least the voices have quietened since last night. I hope they stay that way. I don't want to kill again. All I want is to get to my kids. But if dealing with these obstacles is the only way, then so be it.

There's a Ford Fiesta waiting outside the holiday let as I

turn the corner. My heart hammers in my chest. I'm ready to run if she recognises me.

As a woman steps from her car, keys jangling, my heart feels as though it's going to stop. She's the absolute image of my mother. It's the grey flecked, scraped back hair, a stripe of grey along the roots. She has the same high cheekbones as my mother, and God, she even has green eyes. I stare at her, wondering if she somehow is her. It's the same wide-hipped build. Same sort of tailored clothes. Same walk. But my mother is dead. Dead. Dead. *Get rid of her.*

"Mr Hardisty?"

"Erm yes." I avert my eyes towards the holiday cottage, flat, or whatever it is. I need to get a grip. "Thanks for agreeing to this. And for coming around so quickly."

"Where's Mrs Hardisty?" Her voice is hesitant.

"She's just called to the shop for some basics. Now we know we're staying tonight." I sound so convincing I'm even fooling myself.

"Will she be long?" The woman looks unsure. She should be very unsure.

"She tends to dawdle in shops. Perhaps we should get on with it."

"I don't know…"

"My wife will be fine with leaving this to me. Besides, you said you needed to be away somewhere?"

"Well yes. You're lucky you caught me to be honest. I'm driving down to Great Yarmouth for a couple of days." She looks beyond me, down the street as if having another look for my *wife*.

"We can just sort the payment out here if you'd prefer?" Anything to get her to leave me alone.

"I don't do business on the street," she replies.

My hackles rise. *Business.* Who does she think she is? She holds her car key aloft as she locks her car. Damn. She is planning on coming inside. So much for me paying her and then her leaving me alone. I only hope she doesn't insist on waiting for 'Mrs Hardisty.'

"Right. OK." I don't really want to get into a conversation. I just want her to give me the keys and then do one.

"Of all the places for your car to break down," she puts the key in the door. "It was probably best for you it was here in Hunstanton. I take it John Tate's fixing it?"

"Who? What?" A musty smell emits from the open door as I stand behind her.

"John Tate. Tate's Garage." She even sounds like my mother. I never saw her body. I never went to her funeral. What if..? *Get rid of her.*

"Oh. Yes. That's the one." This woman needs to go. I don't want anything to happen this time. I just want some sleep and a few hours of being ordinary. But things are stirring within me.

She bends to gather letters from the doormat. "Sorry. Come inside. I just need to get some details from you if that's alright."

It really isn't, but I walk in behind her like an obedient animal. I don't really have a lot of choice. She's still talking as she closes the door, wittering on about having looked after her grandchildren for the last two days, and now she's on her way to a spa. Like I'm remotely interested. She's different from my mother in that she barely had two words to say to me at every stage of my life. I used to think she'd be different once I grew up, but she was worse, if anything.

Being ignored used to really piss me off. And then I married someone like that. This woman might look and sound like my mother but there the similarity ends. It isn't her. Still, I can't take my eyes off her.

"Are you OK?"

She stops talking and looks at me. A little too closely.

"Yes. Fine. You remind me of someone, that's all."

I hold her gaze, loading a confidence into it, and into my

voice that I'm no longer feeling. Maybe this was a bad idea. I don't like the new expression on her face.

"What did you say your name was again?"

For a split second, I can't remember the name I gave on the phone. Then just as I sense more reluctance from her, it drops into my mind. "Allan Hardisty." I look her straight in the eye and try to smile. Though it probably looks more like a grimace. "I wonder where my wife's got to. Women and shops, eh?"

She laughs, but the nerves within her laugh are unmistakable. "You look like..." She laughs again and feels around in her pocket. "Oh, it doesn't matter."

Get rid of her. "Like who?" Shit. She can't have recognised me. Surely she wouldn't have entered the house in the first place with me if she had.

"Shall I pay you then? Then you can get on your way."

She steps back towards the door. She won't need me to tell her it's a bit too late to regret letting a stranger in off the street. Too trusting for her own good. In this sleepy seaside town, she won't have ever encountered anyone like me.

"I'm, um, really sorry, but silly me. I should probably get references for you first. Have you got any identification, Mr... erm..."

The change in her has made me forget what I said my name was completely this time. I've gone completely blank. "I'm only staying here for one night. Whilst my car's fixed. You said it was OK."

"You've got a look of that man who killed all those women."

I laugh now. What a stupid thing for her to come out with. Correct. But utterly stupid. "I suppose I have a bit. But I'm not him. Don't worry yourself."

"I'll just need to check with John Tate. That he's seen you, I mean. Can't be too careful nowadays, can you?"

"My wife went into the garage actually."

"Why don't I have a look out? See if she's on her way."

I slam my shoulder against the door as she steps towards it. She gasps as I hold my hand out.

"Give me the keys. Now." *Get rid of her. Get rid of her.*

"I've changed my mind about you staying. I'm sorry. Now let me get past you, if you don't mind."

I wrench the keys from her hand and throw them to the floor. "Move away from the door." Then I raise my voice. "Now! Do as I say."

Her eyes plead with me. She knows as well as I do that she's going nowhere. The course of her life has changed on a sixpence. She's worked out who I am and if I let her go, I'm done for. It's her, or me. This is going to be another despatch that I haven't planned. It probably serves me right for getting brave. First the charity shop, then the café. Then I thought I could get away with this. *She's your mother. She's your mother. She's your mother. She's your mother.*

"Don't hurt me. Please. I'm begging you. My grandchildren would be heartbroken."

"Stop! Shut up!" I clasp my hands over my ears as the woman lurches towards her keys.

"Oh no, you don't!"

I wrestle her down and she lands heavily with a grunt. *She's your mother. She's your mother.* And now she's going to pay for everything she's ever done to me. Before I know it, I'm sitting astride her chest, gripping her between my knees as she writhes beneath me. Finally, I'm the one with the power.

"Let me go." Her voice is a wheeze. "Get off me." She slams her knee into my back and gouges my chin with her fingernail. She's decided to fight, has she?

I allow her to tire herself for a minute, then catch her chin between my fingers. As she screams, I ram the back of her head against the floor. Though her eyes roll slightly, the bang isn't nearly impactful enough. She's still thrashing around.

She's your mother. Get rid of her. The woman's mouth is

moving, but I don't hear her words. All I hear are the voices. They're louder than they've ever been. *Get rid of her. Get rid of her. She's your mother. She's your mother.* Shall I keep slamming her head against the floor? Or end her another, quicker way?

A strange calm envelops me as I squeeze her squirming torso between my knees with everything I've got, and tighten my fingers around her scrawny neck until they whiten. Her mouth twists in her face, turning from crimson to purple. Her eyes bulge from their sockets to the point that I wonder if they'll pop out of her head. Her tongue droops to the side of her mouth. Then I realise that she's limp beneath me. I've got her.

After a few minutes, the voices quieten, then leave. I release my grip on her neck. It's the first time I've ever ended a woman where water hasn't been involved.

I'd planned for rest, a shower and to head further north tomorrow. As I reach along the floor for the bunch of keys, I know I'll have to get moving from here soon. Keeping going is definitely for the best. Her car's outside, which could draw attention to the house, and clearly she's expected by this spa place she was on about.

I stand and look around for somewhere I can drag her to. If I hide her body, perhaps I can delay it being found for long enough to be well away from here. The spa place might just leave it. Especially if they already have her money. I pull a door open beneath the stairs. Bent double, she'll easily fit in there. Then I can shower before I get out of here. And at least I've got transport now.

10

HEIDI

ADELE SMILES at me from the armchair. I'm stretched out on the sofa, feeling bone idle after barely moving since I arrived here. Normally I'd have been to the gym today. And I was supposed to be out with my uni friends tonight. They'll still go without me, and my ears will burn all evening with them talking about who I really am. It's horrendous, this is. What if they don't catch him? What if I have to hide away like this forever? I can tell Alysha won't be able to put up with much more, that's for sure.

I hear her and Brenda's voices echoing from the kitchen and wonder what they're talking about. And why I couldn't have been sitting in there with them? I was much closer to Brenda when I was younger, but Alysha doesn't let me have a look in if she can help it these days. She's become far more jealous over the last few years. Of everything and everyone. Me, Harry, Isaac, and even more than she already was of Uncle Mark's relationship with my mum. I don't know why she's so threatened, but I'd love to give her a good shake at times.

She really annoyed me earlier when she said, *I'm off to sit in the kitchen to spend some time with my grandma.* It was the way she said *my grandma,* as well as the look that accompanied her words. She might as well have added, *and you're not welcome.* I've always gone to great lengths to make sure she's felt included with me and Mum over the years - shopping trips and that sort of thing. I can't believe how left out she's making me feel.

Mum's having a soak in the bath and Uncle Mark has cleared off to work. It was obvious that he was itching to go, but he's still left his instructions that none of us are allowed to leave the house. I feel about five years old at the moment. "So why are you able to leave the house then?" I'd asked him.

"So I can join in with the hunt," he'd replied as he put his coat on. "Even if I'm not allowed to get involved directly, I can go over CCTV or ring around potential witnesses. I can't just sit here, not when I can do something to help make sure he's brought in. For all our sakes."

"But the rest of us have to," I'd said. "Just sit here."

I wouldn't last five minutes doing Adele's job. Once upon a time, I might have thought it sounded interesting, being a family liaison officer, never knowing what's coming from one day to the next. But what could be duller than sitting around all day, doing absolutely nothing? Waiting for information that doesn't arrive, and developments that never happen. She'll probably be going home soon. I bet she can't wait. It's nearly eight o'clock, and it looks as though we're going to have a fourth night of it. It seems like this is going to go on forever.

"How are you doing Heidi?" Adele must sense me watching her. She crosses one trousered leg over another. "I can't imagine how hard all this must be for you."

"I'm just fed up, to be honest."

"That's hardly surprising." She pushes her glasses up so they rest on the top of her head.

"And a bit scared," I continue. "I can't shake the feeling that he's going to turn up here." I shiver, despite the heat from the fire. "Try to finish what he started twelve years ago."

"He won't get this far Heidi." Adele shakes her head as though she's trying to convince herself too. Her dark curls wobble with the movement. "No chance. And even if he were to get anywhere close, there's an armed response unit out there, as well as enough news reporters to sink a ship. He can't get anywhere near you."

She stares at the TV screen as she speaks. I've muted it, as I'm sick of hearing the same news reports go around and around, with never any fresh news. I stare absently at the headlines which repeatedly scroll across the bottom of the screen, willing them to change to *Escaped prisoner William Potts has been found, and is in police custody.* But no, they just say the same thing repeatedly, *Police are appealing to the public for help in finding William Potts, aged fifty-one,* whilst they repeatedly force me to look into the eyes of a man who I once thought was my dad. I know I was only eight, but surely something should have made me realise he was a serial killer. *Is* a serial killer.

"We're really bored." Harry and Isaac flop into the lounge and flank me either side on the sofa. "When can we go somewhere? Can we go out tomorrow?"

"Not just yet," I reply. "Anyway, you'll be going to bed soon."

Harry sighs. I think he's gone beyond being angry, and I know exactly how he feels. The most exciting part of the day is going to bed and escaping the monotony of it all. He looks at me. "What about school on Monday?"

"I just don't know Harry." I squeeze his arm. "None of us do." I should do something with them. It might lift me a bit too. Play a game, watch a film - anything. But I've got no energy. Nor do I feel motivated to do anything that resembles getting on with life. Not whilst Will Potts is still out there.

"Have they put that naughty man back in prison yet Heidi?" Isaac curls into my side. Alysha would probably disagree, but I think he's the nicest little brother anyone could have. It's just a shame we've got such a huge age gap between us. I hope we're still close when we're older. Several times, I've been mistaken for his mum when we're out. This makes both of us laugh. I'd have had him before I was fifteen to be his mum.

"No Isaac. The naughty man is still not back in prison." Harry's reading the words scrolling at the bottom of the screen. He then turns to me. "Do you remember him much Heidi?" His tone suggests a slight envy. I guess that on some level, it could be just a bit interesting for him, all this. Hopefully, he won't have to put up with a fraction of the finger pointing and the behind-the-hand muttering I've had to over the years.

I nod, looking across at Adele. I guess I'm seeking her guidance on whether to continue answering Harry's questions, or to put a stop to this conversation. But I don't even think she's listening – instead she's typing into her phone. I wonder whether what she's doing relates to the search, or whether she's texting with her husband about what they're going to have for dinner.

"Yes. I was eight when he went to prison. So, I remember him well enough. Unfortunately."

"What was he like?"

Adele is still typing into her phone, so I guess I must be OK to continue. Whether or not she's listening. "I suppose I thought he was alright at the time," I reply. "I didn't know what was happening, did I? He brought Biscuit home for us to look after."

"I miss Biscuit." Isaac looks sad. "I wish we could get another dog."

"Did he give you anything else?"

"Not that I can remember. But he took me and Alysha on holiday. To Disney World."

Harry's eyes widen. Maybe that was the wrong thing to tell him.

"I want to go there," Isaac says. "To go on all the rides."

"Me too," says Harry. "What made him turn bad? He doesn't

sound that bad. Not if he got you a dog and took you to Disney World."

"People aren't bad the whole time," I say. Really Mum should probably be having this conversation with him – not me. "But he wasn't kind to Mum," I tell him. "And we didn't know what he was really doing when he was supposed to be at work at night."

"He was a policeman, wasn't he?" Harry sits forwards on the sofa. I don't know how much Mum's told him, but she seems to have covered the bones of it.

I nod. A policeman of the worst kind. I remember at school when we were told to always find a policeman or a shopkeeper if lost or in trouble. He'd be the last policeman anybody would want 'help' from.

"My daddy's a policeman," says Isaac. "And he has a gun too."

I ruffle his hair and laugh. "We know your daddy's a policeman."

"My daddy can shoot the bad man with his gun." Isaac forms a gun with his fingers and makes shooting noises. Mum will go mad if she hears him.

"He killed people, didn't he? Ladies?" Harry's not letting this go. "He threw them into the river."

Oh God. Harry's going to be the next one needing counselling. Even though Uncle Mark's the one who's always looked after him, there will be that voice that will always natter away. *Your dad's evil. What if you take after him? What if his evil can be passed on?* And that voice might convince Harry that he's different. Even if that doesn't happen, others will probably judge him anyway. As they so often do. It could even be worse for Harry because he's a boy. If I don't reply, maybe he'll change the subject. I wrack my brains for something else to talk about.

"Why did the bad man throw ladies in a river Heidi?"

Adele puts her phone on the arm of the chair. "Why don't you all play a game or something?"

"You're lucky you can go home soon," I tell her. "I can't stand much more of being stuck in here." I long for the peace of my flat. When Alysha's not in, that is. My own things. Normality. It's been well over a year since I moved out of here. And now I'm back, it's as though I've never been away. When these two have gone to bed, I might try calling Auntie Claire. If she came over, it might be more bearable here.

I glance from the window to the side of the front door as Adele leaves. There don't seem to be as many reporters now, but the flashing cameras tell me that there're still a few out there. Adele marches through them, without replying to any of the questions they're shouting at her.

Mum's out of the bath and sitting in the lounge with Alysha and Brenda now. Alysha can hardly shut Mum out of a room in her own house. Harry's in the shower in Mum's en-suite, and Isaac's reluctantly gone to bed. It's been the longest day ever. If they don't get him soon, then I'm going to die of boredom. I sink to the bottom step and close my eyes, wondering where he is right at this minute. Behind the closed lids, my eyes burn with tiredness and my head aches with overthinking.

I can no longer visualise the man, and when I try, I only see the photograph that keeps being shown on the TV. My strongest memory of him is from the night when he was thumping at our back door, begging me to let him in, telling me he had nowhere else to go and was going to have to sleep outside in the dark. Guilt gnawed at me that night. Guilt I still carry. Even my years of counselling haven't been able to completely shift it.

Another vivid memory I have is of being freezing, standing in the darkness, and wanting to get to my mum who was only metres away from me at the side of the river. He was telling everyone that was gathered there that if he didn't have me; he had nothing, whilst he filled my pockets with stones to weigh me down when he threw me in. I honestly never thought he'd throw me in, until he did.

Uncle Mark bursts in through the back door and appears in the hallway, making me jump.

"Where is everyone?"

I jerk my head towards the lounge and jump up to race after him, swapping the chill of the hallway for a blast of hot air from the fire. His face says he knows something.

"He's been seen. He's been bloody seen." Uncle Mark punches the air and there's a new energy in his eyes. "At last."

Is that it? I want to ask. Being seen doesn't mean caught. And nothing's going to change for us. Stuck in these four walls until he's actually caught.

"Thank God for that," Brenda says, massaging her neck.

"Where?" Mum points the remote at the TV, muting the sound.

"Mablethorpe. He's set about a woman as she left a pub."

"You're joking, aren't you? Another one?"

"She's one of the lucky ones and has managed to get free of him and raise the alarm. By the sounds of it, she had a close call. She's covered in bruises apparently. He had her around the neck at one point."

"Poor woman. But thank God she got away."

"Mablethorpe. But that's..." I do mental calculations. I remember a school trip when I was eleven. It only took a couple of hours on the coach from Alderton. That means... "If they've seen him, why haven't they actually caught him?"

"We will. He's been caught several times on CCTV. Driving a Fiesta."

"How's he got hold of a bloody car?" Brenda's voice is almost a screech. "First, he's swanning around a hotel, then he's driving a car. The man's supposed to be serving a life sentence."

"We've no idea. Not yet. But we will have soon. We're trying to track down the owner of the car at the moment."

"What about the woman he tried to attack?" Brenda asks. Her eyes are watery and I know she's probably remembering what happened to Lauren. "What's she said?"

"We got a good description of what he was wearing from the woman, and hopefully there'll be some clear CCTV shots that we can put out into the media."

Uncle Mark sounds almost excited. I really can't understand it. Until Will Potts is safely behind bars again, there's no cause for any excitement or celebration. He could still literally be on his way here. He could arrive at any minute. Perhaps, he'll break in through the night and kill me as I sleep. Maybe no one will hear him. They'll just find me dead in bed in the morning. It will be me he goes for out of all of us – I'm sure of it.

"Why hasn't he been caught yet?" Mum's voice is nearly a wail. Reading her expression, I can tell she feels the same as me. "I can't understand it. How many women have to be put in danger before you get him? It's exactly like when he went on the run before."

"At least I'm not with him this time." I try to smile, and Alysha gives me a funny look.

"This new intelligence has only just got to us," Uncle Mark replies, getting back to his feet. "But we're on it. I just wanted to get round here and make sure you all knew what's happening. It's going to be on the next news, but I wanted you to hear this from me. It's only a matter of time now. I can feel it."

"You're not going back, are you? To work I mean?" Mum reaches for his hand. "Can't you stay with us now?"

"I'm sorry love. I've got to see him caught. DSI Jones wouldn't let me hot foot it down to Mablethorpe to be front line on it, but at least I'm here, ready to act, if he gets this far. Since I'm firearms, there might come a point where I have to be at the front."

"But you're not here, are you? Not with us. And we need you right now. There are enough officers out there to take care of this. Surely they can spare you?"

"He won't get all the way here, will he, Uncle Mark? He'll definitely be stopped?"

"I don't know why you're making such a big deal about it." Alysha tucks her legs under herself. After how she's been these last few days, I'm not sure I want to go on sharing the flat with her. She really doesn't get what's going on here.

"I'm not scared of him," she continues. "I never have been. And I never will be. Like I said before, he was always good to me."

Then I notice Harry in the doorway.

"He won't come and get *me*, will he?" His bottom lip is trembling as he stares at Uncle Mark. "Does he know about me?"

"Come here son." Uncle Mark holds his arms open and drops into a crouch.

"Except he's not, is he?" Alysha uncurls her legs from under her and struts into the conservatory. "He's not your son. Not really. He's *his*."

Harry runs at Uncle Mark and Mum shakes her head after Alysha, as she slams the conservatory door. Mum looks seriously pissed off. Brenda reaches for the remote and unmutes the TV. She never gets involved when we're all falling out. If Auntie Claire had been here, she'd have torn strips off Alysha for her nastiness.

"Ah, here we go," Uncle Mark says, turning Harry around so he can see the TV. "Like I said son, we'll be able to catch him soon."

"These are the evening headlines at nine o'clock. We have a

confirmed sighting of escaped prisoner, William Potts, who is into his fourth day on the run after escaping the scene of an accident on Wednesday that involved the prison van transporting Potts from the Millwood secure Hospital in Aylesbury to Suffolk Prison."

Alysha must notice us all staring agog at the TV through the glass of the conservatory door, as she shoots back into the room and drops to the carpet in front of where Brenda is sitting. She might be in a grump, but she's never one to risk missing anything. She leans back against Brenda's legs.

"Since then, a manhunt has ensued, which has intensified. This follows the killings of two women, thirty-four-year-old Lydia Hancock, who was found murdered at the New Hall Hotel in Aldeburgh yesterday morning, and fifty-one-year-old Tina Atkinson, an administrator and mother-of-two from Hemsby, whose body was discovered on Hemsby beach this morning. Post-mortems are taking place to establish the exact times and causes of death."

They flash pictures of the women up, side by side, on the TV screen. To think that a couple of days ago, they were happily living their lives. If they'd had any idea what was going to happen to them... I stare into their faces. *The man who is my father did this to you.* Tears blind me for a moment. These are people's mums or daughters, and he's killed them. How am I ever going to be able to go back to normal after this?

"Why did this have to happen?" Brenda echoes my thoughts. "He should have been safely locked up. Look at them. Look at what he's done!"

"Sssh." Mum raises the flat of her palm. "Let's just hear what they've got to say."

"Don't you tell my grandma to sssh." Alysha pouts. I wait for Uncle Mark to bollock her for getting lippy with Mum, but he doesn't. Alysha always gets away with murder.

"In a further development, Potts has pursued and attacked a third woman as she took a shortcut home through a public park in Mablethorpe. However, she managed to alert a passer-by, who could

then raise the alarm. Potts ran off in the direction of a car park adjacent to the promenade."

The camera flashes up a scene of a cordoned public path, then moves to a car park. Then a different picture fills the screen.

"That's the e-fit the woman has done," Uncle Mark explains.

"Potts is described as wearing a thick black coat with a hood, blue jeans and black trainers. He's wearing a black beanie-style hat, with a dark-coloured scarf, which in some of the CCTV, is obscuring the bottom half of his face. The victim described him as having a dark beard."

Great, I think to myself. If he's somehow watching this, the first thing he'll do is to shave his beard off.

"Her rescuer saw him making his escape in a dark blue Ford Fiesta, registered SL02 9JR. The car is registered to a Ms Yvette Hargreaves of Hunstanton. Attempts to contact her have so far been unsuccessful but are ongoing. It is believed she may have gone to stay with family or friends in another part of Norfolk, and she is urged to come forward as soon as possible.

The public are asked to remain vigilant and to report any further sightings of William Potts immediately. They should also be assured that road blocks and surveillance is being used to its optimum in order to capture him, and return him to custody as soon as possible. It is thought that he may still try to head North to Yorkshire, where he lived before being sentenced to life twelve years ago. We'll bring you more on this story as it unfolds."

"You should see what all the headlines and commentators are saying about it all." Uncle Mark peels Harry from his knee and rises to his feet.

"I can imagine." Brenda sniffs.

"I can see another Police Complaints Commission in the offing," Mum adds.

"I don't think Alan Jones gives two hoots about that right

now. So long as he's caught like yesterday, we'll answer to any inquiry when we're put in front of it."

"Uncle Mark. Can't you stay with us? I'm scared. Even the news reports are saying he could head this way." I ignore Alysha's look of contempt towards me. I am scared. There's a good reason to be. It's alright for her.

PART II

ALYSHA

11

ALYSHA

HEIDI'S GETTING on my nerves with her weeping and moaning. She acts like she's eight again. Just so she can continue to lap up the sympathy. OK, so everything was awful at the time with what Uncle Will did, but I reckon what happened to my mum was far, far worse. She was about to get married to Dad and had her whole life ahead of her. At least Heidi is still alive. No one even talks about Mum anymore. Not since the tenth anniversary when we took some flowers over to Alderton. Auntie Eva didn't want to return to the stream where Mum was killed. Neither did Auntie Claire, with it being the same place she was attacked too. So it was just me and Dad, which I was glad about. We lit a candle and sent a balloon into the sky. Dad looked like he was trying not to cry, which I'd have really liked Auntie Eva to see. She needs reminding sometimes of whose shoes she's tried to step into.

I reach for my bag, which I've pushed beneath the bed. My phone has died in the night, so I plug it into the charger, then pull out my journal. I wouldn't want anybody reading this – I write everything I'm thinking and feeling, so I'd be mortified if anyone got hold of it. I slide a photograph out, which is resting between the back page and cover. It was taken in Florida. Me, then Heidi, Minnie Mouse, then Uncle Will. The edge is torn off. Auntie Eva was there, but I ripped her from the picture one day when she was doing my head in.

Heidi acts like she's all diversity and inclusiveness, but she forgets that Uncle Will was suffering from a mental illness back then. Surely allowances should be made for that. It's why he's been locked up in a hospital rather than in a prison. He was really poorly by the sounds of it. He had voices telling him what to do and everything.

I know he regrets it all. I can't help but feel sorry for him, especially as I know a different side to him. Though it's niggling me about what might have happened with these two poor women over the last couple of days. I'd forgiven Uncle Will until I heard about them. He told me in a phone call a year ago that he was cured now. That he was on tablets and still having counselling. He said he'd never hurt anyone ever again and would never have done what he'd done if it wasn't for the voices. But he said they'd gone away now. As long as he stays on the tablets, he'll be fine. That's what he said anyway.

I haven't seen him since I was six, but I've been writing to him since I turned sixteen. I pull the letter out of my journal that's tucked behind the photograph.

You're the person I miss the most whilst I'm in here, he's written. Do you remember when you were young? You were more like my daughter than my daughter.

I should show this to Heidi. It would certainly put her in her place. For many years, I've wanted to be able to write to him, but Dad would never let me, and couldn't understand why I'd want to. But I didn't need his permission once I got to sixteen. Though he'd go spare if he knew, so I've got to keep it a secret. So would Auntie Eva. I used to like her when I was young – when she was my auntie instead of my stepmother. Before she muscled in with my dad and dragged us all from Alderton to live here in Borings-ville. All there is to do here is get wasted with the local lads. Especially in the winter when everything is closed up. If it wasn't for my job and the college place, I'd probably go back to Alderton. There's always a spare room with Auntie Claire and she's not even there at weekends so I'd have the place to myself.

Sometimes I think it would be great to get away from the lot of them. For years, I've had to put up with one, then two annoying younger brothers. Only Harry isn't even my brother – we just have to pretend he is.

When Dad told me that my mum was pregnant when she died, I was heartbroken. I only found out about this a few years ago and can imagine I'd have been closer to my real brother or sister than I am to Harry. Once whilst I was grounded and was feeling pissed off, I told Harry the truth. It took Dad and Auntie Eva a long time to forgive me for that one, but things are better out in the open.

I've also told Uncle Will all about Harry. That's probably the reason he's escaped. To meet his son. Harry should have been taken to meet him well before now. It's not right what Dad and Auntie Eva have decided – to keep them apart forever. Harry should be allowed to decide for himself. Like I have. They're taking away his rights and his freedom of choice.

Of course, I haven't let them know that I've been writing to Uncle Will and hope they never find out. I'd get into about as much trouble as I've ever been in. The phone calls have been a bit weird though. He clearly remembers me as his six-year-old niece with pigtails, instead of how I am now.

The first time I spoke to him, all he seemed to want to know about was Heidi and Harry. Particularly Harry. I felt a bit put out by that, after all, it's been me, rather than them, who got back in touch with him. Only me that's made any kind of effort. Without me, he'd never have found out about Harry. Dad and Eva have never made it public that Harry is really Uncle Will's son, so hardly anyone knows. Perhaps even Uncle Mark's name is on the birth certificate.

I can't believe he'd never been told about Harry before. Even when Scary Granny died, someone in the prison let him know about it. I thought it was really unfair that he wasn't allowed to go to his own mother's funeral. None of us went either. Dad said she could rot in hell as far as he was concerned.

When I tell people at work that I'm taking a call from my uncle in prison, they're always interested, to the point of being impressed. Especially when they find out who he is. *The Yorkshire Dipper.* Because he's not actually my dad, I'm never going to get judged for it. Not like Heidi and Harry always will. Besides, if people are going to judge me on someone else's behaviour, then that's their problem, not mine.

Uncle Will has never been able to talk for long. He says it costs a lot to ring mobile phones from the secure unit he's in. When he called on Friday, whilst I was at the salon, we could talk for longer. That felt really weird. Hearing his voice, knowing he was no longer locked up. I got a few funny looks when I rushed outside to answer my phone. I left a woman halfway through her shampoo, but there was no way I was risking missing that call. And this time, I could hardly let the others know who I was talking to. Especially since there's an all forces police manhunt going on for him. It's exciting, being the only person who knows anything about where he is.

I'd been relieved to hear from him as I'd been worrying. Imagining him, possibly injured from the crash, trying to make his way up here, to the only family he's ever known. I worried about whether he's got access to food or warm clothes and felt guilty about being able to sleep in a warm house with a full belly. Heidi's talked about that sort of guilt from when she was young. After Auntie Eva first threw him out and he told her he had nowhere to go.

"I'll get to see you all soon," he had said.

"Are you really going to be able to get here?" Anticipation had fluttered in my belly. I don't care what anyone else says. I've only got good memories of Uncle Will. He was always kind to me.

"Hopefully. You and Heidi are still in the flat you gave me the address for, aren't you? I've memorised it to be honest. I always knew that one day I'd get my chance." He didn't sound like someone on the run from the police. Although I could tell he was outside, as I could hear the wind, he sounded just like normal.

"Er, yes. But we're not there at the moment Uncle Will. Dad and Eva are making us stay with them. Until you're caught."

"I won't get caught."

I believed him. But that was before I knew about what had happened with the woman in the hotel and the one on the beach. However, it probably isn't even him who's done it. His history doesn't make him automatically guilty. But he might not get up here as easily now. The finding of the two women means there are more news bulletins, more police looking for him, and more people who are feeling scared. I have to keep believing that it might not be him who's responsible for the latest deaths. No matter what, he's my uncle and I can't help the way I feel about him. And it's me he makes the effort with, rather than Heidi. Me, he's trusting now. After spending most of my life in her shadow, I'm enjoying the current attention from Uncle Will.

Heidi's always been better behaved and got better grades

than me. But it was me who lost my mum when I was so young. I don't know why the sympathy always went to her. She muscled in on my dad and even my grandma. I never used to mind, but lately I do. She and her mum can stick together. We were all better off as things were.

My phone lights up at the side of me. Three missed calls. I try ringing the number back, but there's no answer. I type the code into Google – it comes up as Alderton. It must be Uncle Will. I hope he's alright. I'll have to keep my phone charged and on me now. He was there for me when I was a kid after Mum died, and now I'm here for him.

If it *was* Uncle Will who hurt those women after escaping on Wednesday, it was only because they'd have reported him if he hadn't. They might have threatened to turn him in. He's done what he's got to do to survive. Either that or he's hearing the voices again.

I overheard Dad and Auntie Eva talking yesterday about how he would be much more dangerous without being able to take his medication, and how he could have gone for several days without his tablets by now. And so I blame that for whatever he could have done, rather than *him.* I've Googled *psychosis*, which is the word I heard Dad use. And I firmly think it's not Uncle Will's fault that he's like he is. It's an illness. I really can't hate him like the others do, as I remember the other side of him.

He's been locked up for twelve years now. Twelve years. It's a long time. I think he should be let out and given his medication, and be offered another chance to live a normal life. He's been punished enough for the past. Life sentences often only mean fifteen years according to Dad, so he might have been out in a few years anyway. Who knows what will happen now?

· · ·

Usually on a Sunday morning, I'd be rolling around in bed, nursing a hangover, but today, as I wake on the sofa bed in my old bedroom, my head is clearer than it's been for a long time. It needs to be. I don't know what might be asked of me today. Uncle Will told me on Friday to be on standby, whatever that means.

I can hear voices downstairs. Pots clanking, Harry and Isaac arguing as usual. They're only quiet when they're asleep. I wonder if the pointless Adele has arrived yet. That's what I've been calling her in my head. *Pointless*. I wouldn't say it to her face though.

Dad and Auntie Eva are always up early. They've got really boring since Harry and Isaac were born. I expect all this is the most excitement they've had for a very long time.

I type *BBC news*. The headlines haven't changed. They're still looking for him. I really think this will be the day I get to see him after twelve years. Maybe Heidi will change her mind about things once she actually has the chance to meet him again too. But for now, it's my secret.

As Grandma often says, *blood is thicker than water*. I'm off to see if she's awake. She slept in Isaac's bed last night and he bunked in with Harry.

"Grandma." I curl my head around the door. With the blackout blind down, it's impossible to see a thing.

"Yes. Good morning. I take it, it's morning? I haven't slept too well." She fumbles around, probably for her glasses. She's got the perception of an ostrich without them. "That's why I haven't got up yet. Despite the commotion downstairs."

"Why? You're not worrying, are you Grandma?" I raise the blind a little so I can find my way across the room. It smells of Grandma in here. A combination of talc and face cream. She sits up, so I perch on the bed beside her. Grandma's hair is grey now, probably because of all that stress, but she still wears it in plaits. She tells me that's how my mum had hers. I guess that's why I sometimes plait my hair too.

"Of course I'm worrying. Two more women have been killed, and well, it brings it back what happened to your mum."

I don't know what to say to that. Although I've been back to the stream, it really didn't bring anything back for me. I was too young when she died.

"To think you were the same age as Isaac is when you lost her." Grandma slides her glasses on. "It breaks my heart."

It makes me feel sad to hear that from her. Isaac is an utter pain in the neck, but the thought of him without Auntie Eva around to take care of him isn't a nice one. No kid deserves that. Even though at times I've wished that Auntie Eva would disappear off the face of the earth. Especially when she thinks she has the right to tell me what to do. I've reminded her many times that she's not my mum and she needs to stop acting as though she has any say over me.

"I take it nothing has changed? The news?" Grandma reaches for the glass of water on the bedside table. She looks funny, sitting there in her nightie, surrounded by a duvet and pillowcase covered in dinosaurs. She's even got a stuffed dinosaur tucked in beside her. Isaac must have already been in and done that.

I shake my head. "But I don't want them to catch him Grandma. He's been in prison forever. He should get another chance."

"Eh? I don't know where your mind is sometimes Alysha. How can you say that?" Her face hardens as she gives me one of her expressions. "Look at what he's done. Not just in the past but in the last few days."

"There's no proof it's him yet Grandma. I know everyone hates his guts, but seriously, I only remember good things about him. He never did me any harm."

"It's because of him that so many people, including you, have lost mums, daughters, sisters…"

"It wasn't Uncle Will who killed my mum."

She sniffs. "He might as well have done. He had as much blood on his hands as that DCI Jonathan Ingham in my opinion. Look, I'm really sorry Alysha. I don't usually talk to you about this, but if you're going to come out with rubbish like, *you don't want them to catch him,* then you need to hear it."

"Hear what?"

"The man's evil. Go and re-read the news stories. All the lives he's taken and even more lives that he's ruined of those left behind. In years gone by, he'd have been sent to the gallows."

"I thought you didn't believe in that sort of thing."

"It would be too good – for him. They should let all the families at him."

"But Grandma, you've always taught me that everyone deserves a second chance…" She would never normally talk like this about anyone.

"Grandma." Isaac slopes into the room, grinning. "Did you like sleeping in my bed? With Steve?"

It drives me insane that Harry and Isaac call my grandma *their* grandma. They haven't got one, the same as Heidi.

"Who on earth's Steve?" Grandma laughs. I'm well annoyed. She never laughs with me anymore.

"Steve the Stegosaurus."

Grandma pats the duvet at the side of her, next to me. "I'd like it better with a hug from my handsome grandson before I get out of it."

"He's not even your grandson." I glare at him as he skips over to the bed.

"We were talking." I push him back, but he just runs round to the other side. "Oh, what the hell. I'm off to get dressed."

12

WILL

It takes a moment to compute my whereabouts when I wake up. I stare at the cream interior of the car and shiver, despite the blanket I was fortunate enough to find in the boot, along with some chocolate and a torch. The woman was evidently the sort who listened to advice for making long car journeys. There was nothing much of use in her travel bag though. I'd already helped myself to the cash in her purse before I left the holiday let, which wasn't much either. Still, it's all in a good cause and she's safely tucked up in her cupboard under the stairs.

If she'd just got on her way yesterday, I could have had a bed for the night instead of having to hunker down like this. I had no plan to do away with her until she recognised me. Even if she was a reincarnation of my mother.

Once out again, I drove up the coastal road to Mablethorpe and, in behaviour quite out of character for me, found myself in a pub again. No good ever comes of it. I watched a drunk couple having an argument and when the woman stormed staggering from the pub crying and not paying attention to anything around her; she was easy pickings. Well, she nearly was.

. . .

I hoist myself to sitting and wipe the condensation from the back window with my sleeve. It's rained overnight and I've felt the wind on the car several times. But I've slept strangely well to say I'm a six-foot man curling up on the back seat of a Fiesta.

It feels bloody good to be nearly back on home turf. I'm at a disused airfield on the edge of Alderton. Its only purpose, as I remember, is for unofficial driving lessons. Dad brought me and Dean here a couple of years before he died. It's the first time I've been back since. I was nearly old enough to apply for my licence and Dad said I was a natural. I never thought then that I'd have ended up as a traffic cop – perhaps it would have been one of the few things that might have made him proud of me.

Things could have been so different if they'd both stuck around. Mum got much more hostile towards me after Dad died, and after Dean had been killed, well, she couldn't stand to be anywhere near me. They have frequently forced me to talk about her in therapy throughout my time at the hospital. At first I tried to get away with saying as little as possible, but I had to show I could talk the talk, taking part in the pointless group discussions. They were a requirement of eventually getting moved from that hospital and even being eligible for parole one day. It made me realise that maybe, from the talking I have done, she's got a lot to answer for. But she's taken all her explanations to the grave. The so-called anger management work they've done with me has done nothing to dispel any of the hatred I have towards her.

I'm returning to Alderton as I've got a visit to take care of – a rather large score to settle. Then it's off to Filey to finally see my kids – meet my son for the first time. I don't have the finer details yet of how I'll make this happen, but I've got an ally in Alysha. And I know she'll make it happen – I never could do any wrong in her eyes. *My son.* When I think of how I used to crave this, well, I could weep, which is most un-Will-like behaviour.

How dare that bitch of an ex-wife have kept his existence from me for all these years? It's nearly as bad as what Tina did to me. Killing my kid. But I had the last laugh with her. I will with Eva too. She's going to regret how she's treated me.

She even had the nerve to divorce me for unreasonable behaviour. I refused to sign anything, but she got her divorce anyway. It felt like shit getting the decree absolute in prison and gave them another excuse to put me on suicide watch and increase the therapy crap. Role play. Pretending I had Eva in front of me. What I'd have done to her if she had been.

I get out of the car and stretch my arms above my head, blinking in the morning's brightness. All around me is deserted. If anyone's planning a driving lesson here today, they've yet to arrive.

The overnight rain has washed away some of the mud that was obscuring the number plates yesterday. I'll have to do something about that. I know from my time as a traffic cop that dirty number plates are the bane of the job. The ANPR cameras can't read them. This car was filthy when I took it. It didn't need much more revving in a muddy puddle to ensure the plates were definitely unreadable. To be fair, it's hard to even say with any certainty what colour the car is right now.

I took a chance driving all the way here from Mablethorpe with dirty plates as they're a pullable offence. But I'd rather have risked that than the car being recognised as hers and tracked down. That's if anyone has reported her or her car missing yet – I'll check the news out in a minute.

I take a leak and brush my teeth with the woman's toothbrush from her bag. My stomach growls with hunger. I can't believe how little I've eaten in the last few days. I seem to be running on adrenaline.

A check on the car's dash, the clock tells me it's nearly nine, and I've still got half a tank. Good stuff. I'll get some food, then I'll be on my way. I flick the radio on and blow onto my hands to warm them as I rev the engine. Three beeps and the Radio Two music grabs my attention. In twelve years, it hasn't changed. Here we go.

"A police search is still underway for William Potts, aged fifty-one, formerly of Alderton. He is now entering his fifth day on the run from prison after absconding from the scene of an accident in which two officers died."

Has it really been five days? I must be pissing them off. I remember Mark when the hunt was on for Ingham, after he killed Lauren and attacked Claire. He was losing his shit with frustration at Ingham continually evading them. But I'm cleverer than Ingham. As I keep proving.

"Potts is believed to be either in the Lincolnshire or Yorkshire region, and we urge the public to continue to be vigilant as he remains at large.

He was sentenced to life imprisonment twelve years ago for the murders of thirteen women. An indeterminate minimum sentence was recommended to be initially served in a secure hospital. It is believed that the number of victims at his hands has now increased to fifteen, with two more women being named since his escape from the scene of the accident on Wednesday."

I smile. They clearly have no idea about the woman in Hunstanton yet. I can relax in her car.

Their numbers are skewed as well. They tried pinning two of the killings from twelve years ago on me from the time I was in Florida. I could prove those two weren't me. It's the one and only time Eva could give me a secure alibi. However, the man who'd been hired to carry out the killings in my absence told the police it was me who'd hired him to throw the police investigation off course. This was all a complete fabrication and more unfinished business as far as I'm concerned. It's been one of my missions whilst I've been inside to find out exactly who hired him and what they were hoping to achieve. Now it's time to get the business finished.

"A third woman narrowly escaped with facial injuries after being attacked by Potts as she left The Star public house in Mablethorpe yesterday evening. A passer-by who heard her screams for help rescued her."

If it wasn't for that bloke walking past...

"We're now going to hear from DSI Jones, one of the officers leading the Inquiry."

Get him. Detective Superintendent. That should have been me. They accuse me of taking the lives of people, but in reality, my life's been taken again and again by so many people. My fists curl in my lap as I listen to what he's got to say.

"My name is DSI Alan Jones and I'm the leading officer in this inquiry. William Potts is still on the run, and we urgently need the public to be both alert, and careful. The victim in yesterday's attack has given us a detailed description of Potts. He is described as wearing a thick black coat with a hood, blue jeans and black trainers.

Potts is also wearing a black beanie-style hat, with a dark-coloured scarf, which in some of the CCTV, is obscuring the bottom half of his face. The victim describes him as having a dark beard. As previously reported, he is six feet tall, with blue eyes and a slim build. I reiterate he should not be approached under any circumstances."

A detailed description! Hardly.

"We are circulating an e-fit image of Potts and would once again urge the public to be on the lookout for him at all times, and to call 999 immediately with any suspicions. It is also imperative that until he is caught, women take extra precautions to keep themselves safe. This would apply particularly in the Yorkshire and East Coast areas of England, but those further afield should also heed this advice, as we now believe Potts to have access to transport."

Shit. They know about the car.

"We are looking for a Ford Fiesta, blue in colour, registered to a Mrs Yvette Hargreaves of Hunstanton. We believe that Potts may have stolen this vehicle, registered SLO2 9JR, from outside her home whilst her house was unoccupied. Efforts so far have failed to locate her, so we would appeal to her, or anyone who knows where she is, to come forward as we are concerned for her wellbeing."

But they don't know about her yet.

"I would like to reassure the public that we are acting on a significant number of leads and sifting through hours of CCTV as this search continues. We will continue with our round-the-clock investigation until we find William Potts.

Any information, no matter how insignificant you feel it might be, should be reported to the incident room at Suffolk Police by dialling 0300 123 999, quoting reference 1091, or by calling three nines. Thank you."

Trying to get through to my kids without being caught is getting trickier. But I'll figure something out whilst I'm eating. A man can't deal with situations of this magnitude on an empty stomach.

I park in the furthest corner of the car park to the fast-food restaurant, chewing a hash brown. It tastes like caviar after the food I've become accustomed to. Getting served was so easy, it was laughable. Place order at one window. Feed money into a pay machine. Collect food from the window where the girl doesn't even look at you. Excellent. And I've never been so grateful for a decent coffee. I'm certainly in need of fuel for what I've got planned next.

. . .

Once upon a time, I had my sights firmly set on Suzannah Peterson. She was the whole package. From the way she moved to the way she looked. With brains to go with it too. But I misread the situation. The woman last night wasn't the first one to escape me. It turns out Suzannah had got away from me on the banks of the River Alder two years prior, and was set on making me pay. She did that alright. Along with her sidekick Daniel Hamer. Posing as my therapist, he'd recorded me speaking when the voices had got hold of me again. They both had the whole thing planned all along. To bring me down.

It's my turn now. My turn to ensure the same happens to them. At this moment, that's even more important than seeing my kids. I'd given up the whole Yorkshire Dipper thing back then, with a plan of leading an ordinary family life with Eva and Heidi. Then Hamer's and Suzannah's actions lured me back.

It's not doing me any favours being back in Alderton. It's full of ghosts. This darkness deep inside me, which I've spent most of my life trying to fight has descended over me with such intensity, I can hardly think straight. The voices are back, but they're too quiet to make much sense of just now.

I can't resist parking up outside the house I used to live in with Heidi and Eva, wondering if the current occupants know who used to live there. My anger rises in me again as I recall how hard I grafted to provide it. Look at the thanks I got.

The house is unrecognisable from when we lived there. I'm not sure how long Eva and Heidi stayed in it after I was sent down. I'm not even sure how long it took Mark to muscle in on her and my son.

Someone has plonked a dormer on the roof and a garage extension on the side. The front garden which I'd paid to have landscaped has been replaced by tarmac. It looks shit and part of me feels like marching up to the door and demanding my home back. I didn't get a penny out of it either. What I'd give for things to have been different. Still, I'm going to see my son and daughter soon and somehow, I'll get them on my side. No matter what it takes.

I've served my time and given a stellar performance in all the victim awareness crap. I've kept a convincing lid on my thoughts during the many reform programmes I've had forced upon me.

But no one can give me back the time I've missed seeing my kids growing up. Perhaps I can get hold of some passports and get us all out of here. One thing's for sure, I'm not going back inside. And when I get my kids back, I'm never letting them go again.

The curtains twitch in the lounge window of the next-door neighbours. I wonder if it's still the same nosy cow who was partly responsible for everything going so badly wrong for me. The one who gave two statements, making out like I was some sort of wife batterer. *Get her for this. Get her.* Maybe I should pay her a visit whilst I'm over this way. Nah. She'll keep. I have more pressing visits to make. I only hear the instruction once more. The voices know where I need to be and what I've got to do.

The short drive to *The Alder Centre* is like travelling through a village of shadows. Past the school Heidi went to, the church me and Eva got married in, the park, the row of shops. Different voices whisper at me as I turn each corner. *Get her for this* is the most prominent one. But now, it relates to someone else.

I pull up outside *The Alder Centre,* surprised it's still there. But my association with the place was probably good for business and I guess people will always need therapy. I can't imagine life is any easier than before I got sent down. None will have it as hard as I did though. A brother killed by a drunk driver, a father who was so distant, he barely left a dent when he died. And of course, a mother who hated every bone in my body, and Mark and Claire who barely acknowledged my existence.

Then there have been the shitty women I seemed to attract. Women like Eva, and Tina and Suzannah Peterson. No matter what had gone before, Suzannah wouldn't have been able to help herself from jumping into bed with me if we'd got the opportunity. Perhaps today we'll have our chance at last.

Blinds cover the windows at *The Alder Centre,* just as I would have suspected on a Sunday. I found out where Suzannah lived when I stalked her twelve years ago, so hopefully she's still there. If not, I'll come back here tomorrow and follow her home. At least I've got the car to sleep in now. Or perhaps I'll be able to do what I need to do in there if she's alone. I don't want to wait a moment longer than necessary. She's not the only person on my agenda, after all.

I make the short journey to the new housing estate, her last-known address. Except it's not new anymore. It's strange to consider how life's continued rolling, even whilst I haven't been a part of it.

She lives in a converted former mental health asylum - now luxury houses and apartments. Who would want to live here is anyone's guess? The irony isn't lost on me, given the place I've just been discharged from. If they catch me, they'll either send me back there, or at best, still go through with the plan to integrate me into a normal prison. I certainly won't have a chance of being moved to a Cat B now. They'll chuck me in with the real murderers. The ones who do it for kicks, rather than for good reason, like I did.

This isn't the first time I've driven to Suzannah's place. I recall it being at the end of a row opposite a kids' play area. I don't want to loiter for long. There's no one more likely to get noticed than a bloke parked up beside a play area. I pull up as close as I can get to the house without drawing attention to myself.

The motor outside looks like the sort of car she'd drive. I've always had a sixth sense as far as Suzannah Peterson's concerned, and somehow, I can feel that she's still living here. She's going to be the hardest of the lot to dispose of, given the connection I have with her. Despite everything that's happened, she's occupied my thinking many times whilst I've been locked up. She's entered my thoughts nearly every day. I've had no feelings towards any of the other women apart than revulsion.

As I edge further forward, I spot another car, a Range Rover, parked behind hers. She's bloody moved someone in. As far as I knew, she was single. Whore. I had fantasies of her living alone and us being together when the day came when I was free again. Like now.

I sit for a while wondering what to do. I don't know for sure if she's still even living here yet. Me getting myself all hot and bothered could be totally pointless. Eventually, my patience pays off. Like it always does. She leaves the house and saunters towards the car wearing tight clothes, and... Her belly is fucking enormous! Bitch. Bitch. Bitch. She's up the duff and with...

Daniel Hamer, yes Daniel fucking Hamer follows her out of the house. The bastard. I knew he had designs on her all along. No wonder he wanted me out of the way so badly. He could sense what was likely to happen between Suzannah and me, and wanted her for himself. He's won again. For the last time.

Suzannah reverses her car from the drive onto the road. Hamer follows her out. Then she rolls hers back onto the drive. He turns in the road before heading towards me. He looks mad. Distracted. Perhaps they've been arguing. I hope so. I let a long breath out and duck down as he passes me. He doesn't even look my way. I might have a beard now, but I'm certain that he'd recognise me straight away. After all those hours I sat facing him, trusting him with what was going on inside my head.

Personal things I've trusted no one with since. With the therapists at the hospital, I told them what they wanted to hear. It did the job though – I was on my way out of there. But if it wasn't for Suzannah and Hamer, and Eva, of course, I'd have never been locked up.

Things all keep just falling into place. So far, I've evaded capture and there's no reason this shouldn't continue. More proof that my actions are, and always have been, justified. I keep pinching myself on how fortunate I've been since Wednesday. When I was on the run with Heidi twelve years ago, I didn't even make it to four nights. And now another piece has fallen right where it should. I've been granted my big chance. Daniel's gone out, leaving Suzannah in on her own. At least I hope she's on her own. I'd better make sure before I make my presence felt.

I wait a few minutes and then step out of the car, striding towards where Daniel recently emerged.

13

ALYSHA

"I CAN'T STAND this for much longer," I tell Dad between spoonfuls of cereal. "It's alright for you."

"What's alright for me?" He rolls his eyes. He does that a lot lately. Every time he sees me, in fact.

"You get to go to work. Keep yourself busy. Carry on as normal. You can't keep us all chained up here forever." Another day looms ahead of me. I've never been one for staying in the house. When they used to ground me, I'd be out of my window, until they put a lock on it. In those days, Heidi used to cover for me. I don't know if she would now.

"Look here, young lady. I'm not *carrying on as normal* as you put it. Our force is one of the busiest in the country; we're doing all we can to find him."

"It's not as if Uncle Will is even that dangerous. Come on Dad, you grew up with him." Judging by the look on Dad's face, I should probably shut up. But I carry on anyway. "You should know him better than anyone? Didn't you share a bedroom?"

"Of course he's dangerous. Wake up Alysha." Dad slaps the table with the palm of his hand. "And he could easily be on his way up here. Which is why we have to be ready for him."

"I thought you weren't allowed to be involved. Being his brother and all that."

"DSI Jones would prefer me not to be on the front line. But I will be if it comes to it."

"What do you mean, the front line?" He always has to be so dramatic. He carries on like we're in the middle of a TV drama.

"If there were to be any kind of confrontation when we find him. Whoever's there would be considered to be on the front line."

"Like what sort of confrontation?"

"Like there was when he kidnapped Heidi."

It always comes back to Heidi. Always. "I like how you use the word *kidnapped*. He's her dad." I point my spoon at him. "You seem to forget that."

"Look I'm not getting into this Alysha. I need to be on my way shortly."

"But you've just said you're not on the front line?"

"I can help to go through the CCTV and the traffic cameras."

"So, do you reckon you'll find him?" *I know something you don't know.*

"Of course we will." Dad narrows his eyes. "It's just a matter of time. "

"What if you don't? When will you have to give up? What if he's too clever for you?" He has been so far.

"We'll never give up. How can we? A serial killer can hardly be left to roam free around the country."

I can never think of my uncle as a serial killer. To me, he's just my uncle who got ill. And with good reason. Who wouldn't be affected after walking along the street with his brother, then suddenly being run over by a drunk driver? Uncle Will watched them drive off, then he watched his brother die right in front of him. Dad's told me that his own mother didn't visit Uncle Will in hospital and told him that he should have been the one to die. No wonder he ended up with mental issues.

Scary Granny put on a front when other people were around – she made out like she was alright. But she wasn't very nice to me and Heidi if we were on our own with her. She'd just watch TV and ignore us, and we had to be really quiet all the time. Her favourite saying was that *children should be seen and not heard*. And we'd be lucky to get so much as a selection box at Christmas. She was the opposite of Grandma Brenda who's always been exactly like a grandma should be.

"Anyway," Dad sips his coffee. "This shouldn't go on for much longer. Then we can all get back to what we should be doing."

"But there's no need for me to stay here Dad. Can't I go back to the flat? I don't see what difference it makes, whether I'm here or there." My voice whines like it did when I was young, but I don't care. It used to work then with Dad. If I got on his nerves for long enough, he'd always give in. Perhaps it can work now.

"No chance. I can't keep you safe if you're at the flat."

"But you're not even keeping me safe here. You're going to work."

"I'm hardly leaving you on your own." Dad walks over to the sink and starts rinsing his cup.

"What if Grandma was to stay with me at the flat?" I brighten suddenly. That's the answer. "And Heidi."

"Give over. Brenda needs looking after too. And Heidi knows she's better off here until he's caught. She's said so herself."

"We're all grown-ups Dad. No one needs looking after. Besides, he wouldn't hurt any of us. Uncle Will isn't as bad as you're making out."

Dad gives me one of his most irritated looks. "Talk to your Auntie Eva if you want to be told again just how bad he is. Or look up the old news articles if you want something to do." A look of sadness crosses his face. Just saying the words, *news articles,* will have made him think of my mum. He straightens up as Auntie Eva's voice sounds from the top of the stairs. He hardly talks about Mum anymore. Especially in front of *her.*

"And besides all the horrendous crimes we locked him up for, your *Uncle Will,* as you so nicely call him, made your Auntie Eva's life a living hell. And Heidi's. Ask her as well if you want proof of how nasty he was. She had to watch it all. And that was before any of us knew the evil he was really capable of."

"So why did she give him an alibi then? I've seen the news articles. Saint Auntie Eva. She said time and time again that he was at home asleep whilst he was out doing what he was doing." I shudder to myself. Sometimes I think she's as much to blame as he is. She could have stopped him and got him some help.

"I'm not discussing this any further with you Alysha. You're out of line." Dad's face bears an expression I've grown used to. One that says he can't stand what I'm saying. He probably can't stand me either.

"I get sick of hearing about it anyway," I reply, aware that Eva's standing on the landing, listening. I can see her shadow on the wall of the stairs even if Dad thinks she's gone into one of the rooms. She needs to hear this anyway. It might put her in her place a bit more. "Year in-year out. There's never any sympathy for me losing my mum when I was so young. It's all aimed at poor badly done-to Heidi and Eva. Is that why you got married to her? Eh Dad? Because it was your brother who'd supposedly treated her badly? Were you feeling guilty?"

"I can't believe you're coming out with this rubbish Alysha." Dad slams his hand against the kitchen counter. "What is it? The ridiculous jealousy thing again? You need to grow up. There's no need for this, you know. We might not be a traditional family, but we're all making the best of it. Harry and Isaac..."

"Are spoilt little brats." I finish the sentence for him. "They do my head in. And you wonder why I want to go back to the flat."

"Does all this make you feel good Alysha? Cos it's doing the complete opposite for me."

"All this what?"

"Sitting there - bitching about everything and everyone. You'd feel better if you planted a smile on your gob and realised that we're all in this situation together. As a family, whether you like it or not."

"Yes." Auntie Eva strides in. "I heard most of what you said Alysha. Claptrap."

"I don't give a toss what you think of me." Although I know I'd better rein it in or I'm going to really get it.

"Do you not agree?" She rests her hand on her hip as she glares at me, "that we've got enough going on right now, without you regressing to the sort of behaviour that we'd expect from Harry and Isaac." I hate how she looks at me. As though she really dislikes me. No one looked happier than she did on the day I moved out.

"Well - they don't want me here either." I know I'm sulking, but I can't help it right now. If I do everyone's heads in enough, they might let me go back to the flat, where I can play some tunes and chill out. It's ridiculous that they're keeping me here like a prisoner. "All they care about is Heidi."

"That's because Heidi's nice to them," Dad replies. "She plays with them. She talks to them. You could take a leaf out of her book."

"Saint bloody Heidi." I drop my spoon into the bowl and glare at him. "You've always preferred her to me."

"Alysha. That's just not true. I love all of you."

"But I'm your daughter. She's just your niece." What I'm

saying here is right. Things would have been so different if Mum hadn't have gone and got herself murdered. Dad would still be with her, and I'd have a real family instead of this false one. A proper brother or sister. Tears stab at my eyes. As Grandma would say, *I've got out of the wrong side of the bed today.*

Auntie Eva slams a cupboard door. "Oh Alysha. Grow up, for goodness sake."

"I just don't want to be kept here like a caged animal. It's not fair." I stare into my bowl.

"None of it's fair," she snaps. "But I'll tell you what isn't fair most of all. Lives of innocent women being put at risk because that maniac is stalking the streets. And we're four days in now."

"We're doing our best to catch him love." Mark sighs. "I'll be on my way in a minute."

"Well, do better then." She glares at him now. It's good to see them having a cross word too. Why should it always be with me?

"What's up with everyone?" Heidi breezes into the kitchen, still in her pyjamas, with Harry and Isaac trotting in after her. "We could hear you all going on from upstairs."

"Nothing," replies Dad. "Alysha's got cabin fever, that's all. Hopefully not for much longer."

"What does cabin fever mean?" Harry slides two bowls from the cupboard and passes one to Isaac. "Can we catch it?"

Dad laughs. Yeah. He would laugh at something the precious boys say. "I think we've all got it. It means she wants to get back to normal." He reaches out and ruffles his already messed-up hair. "Like we all do."

"Hasn't the bad man been caught yet?" Isaac slides into the chair next to him.

"Not yet. Soon."

"So we still can't go out." Harry frowns. "How much longer Dad?"

"He's not even really your dad." I wave my finger from

Harry to Dad. "I don't know why you call him it. The bad man is your dad. And hers." I point at Heidi now, who turns from filling the kettle with her gob wide open.

"You rotten..."

"Get out of my sight Alysha." Dad steps towards me. "Go on. I've heard just about enough from you this morning. Sort yourself out."

"I'm going home then." I throw my chair back with a scrape and stomp towards the door. "Nobody wants me here anyway."

"You're going nowhere." Auntie Eva says. "Look I know you're upset Alysha. We all are. Just go to your room and cool off. Your dad will talk to you about it later." She shifts her glaring eyes from me to him.

"It's not my room anymore."

Auntie Eva does my head in. She hardly ever says what she really thinks to me and rarely gets mad. Which is why Dad never agrees with me when I tell him stuff she's said or done. OK, so I exaggerate sometimes, like the time I said she'd thrown me out of the car, leaving me to walk home in the dark. I made out like it was miles away, but it was actually just the next street. I caused a massive row between them after that.

"You heard her Alysha." Ooooh. He's shouting at me now. "Go upstairs. And don't come down until you've got a civil tongue in your head."

I stare from the upstairs window at the reporters. I could go down there and tell them I've spoken to Will Potts. That I know more or less where he is. I could sell them my story and make loads of money. Then I could really get out of here. Far away from the lot of them. I could tell Harry everything I know about the past. They've hardly told him anything, and Harry has got a right to know the full story. And Isaac should be told too. None of us here are real brothers or sisters – our whole family is just one massive make-believe game. It's not a proper family. It's a sham. Why should they get to have the nice childhood when that chance was snatched away from me?

I've thought about this lots lately and mostly blame that DCI Ingham and scary Granny. They made Uncle Will the way he is. And that wife of his too. I'm glad they're all dead. They deserve to be. Ingham's wife lied through her rotten teeth for years about everything. And she dragged my mum into it all. She'd still be alive if it wasn't for her. It should be me, Mum, Dad and proper brothers and sisters, living in Alderton, where we belong. Not a step-mother who's really my auntie, a half brother, where we've got the same dad and different mums, and a step brother and step sister who are really my cousins. It's all messed up. I'm so fed up with being different, of living half a life, of people either feeling sorry for me or thinking I'm weird. I'm –

"Alysha. Are you OK?"

Heidi pokes her head around the door. I jump back from the window and search her face for signs that she's going to have a go at me. She looks more worried than anything. That's the trouble with Heidi, she's too... nice. She totally does my head in.

"Can I come in?"

"I suppose so."

She always looks nice too, even for someone who's overweight and always seems to dress in black. I'll never be as good as Heidi. I never was.

"What's up with you? I mean, what's really up?" She steps further inside the room. "That was some carry-on downstairs. Mum's really upset."

"I don't care." I sit back on the windowsill.

"Well, she cares about you, despite what you think sometimes. How could she not?"

"I'm just fed up with it all." I drop my chin into my hands.

"We all are. But until they get him... Bloody hell, look at all those reporters. I wish they'd get lost."

"They might not." I look at her. "Catch him, I mean."

Judging by her expression, she must sense the hopefulness in my voice. She tightens the cord on her dressing gown and comes to sit next to me, taking up a bigger space on the windowsill than me. She's been trying to lose weight and has even joined a gym, but she's not doing very well at it.

"Look. You're a couple of years younger than me. It's understandable that you remember things a bit differently than how I do."

"I've got my own mind you know. I remember things my own way, that's all."

"Mum's right Alysha. I know you and her haven't got on brilliantly lately, but she's right about one thing. William Potts is a maniac. Look at all the women he's killed. I don't care what illness he's had or what voices are in his head, I'll never forgive him. And look what he tried to do to me."

"Grandma's always said that people deserve a second chance." I glance around the room, trying to visualise it as it was before I moved out. The posters, the clutter, my stuff. I bet it was Auntie Eva's idea to turn what was my space into something else the minute I was out of the door. Make sure I could never come back. No second chances for me.

"Some people deserve a second chance, but not him." She clasps her hands in her lap and turns to look at me.

"But he'd got better, hadn't he? Before he escaped? He'd been treated for whatever was wrong with him. The voices?"

"If he really was better, like they were saying – well enough to leave that hospital, then why is he accused of killing two more women in the last couple of days?" She gets up and sits on the sofa bed, so she's facing me square on, and tucks her hair behind an ear. "It might even be three."

"Why three? Who said?"

"It's not been on the news yet, but Uncle Mark's been telling us about that car that he's driving about..."

"Uncle Will?"

"Stop calling him that. He's not part of this family anymore. He's not your uncle."

"But he's your dad Heidi. Nothing you say or do can ever change that."

"Biologically maybe. But that's it. I never have to have anything to do with him ever again. Anyway, the woman, whose car it is, no one's seen her since yesterday."

"That means nothing. In any case, they haven't got proof that it was him with the other two, have they? It's probably just easier to blame him."

"I don't know about proof. Uncle Mark can't tell us everything. He's not allowed to."

"We've got a right to know whatever he knows, if you ask me. Just like Harry and Isaac have the right to know everything – not just some fairy tale about a bad man."

"Uncle Mark and Mum are just trying to act like they did with us when we were young. Shield the boys from the full details. They're too young to get their heads round it."

I stare at my cousin. We really are so different. She's boring. It's no wonder she doesn't have a boyfriend. Anyone that she's ever liked fancies me as soon as they see me anyway. I'm more interesting. More exciting. She might have her mum's glossy hair and big eyes, but who wants to be around someone who's so sensible? She likes art, for God's sake. And she's overweight.

14

WILL

I STAND IN THE GARDEN, watching Suzannah through the window of the cabin, or shed, or whatever it is in her garden. Eva would have called it a summer house. I'm reminded of the many occasions I used to watch Suzannah through the window at The Alder Centre as she moved around the reception area. I had the perfect view from a café over the road.

Fences and trees border the garden, so it looks as though I may have free and undisturbed rein here. Daniel, the snake, Hamer is hopefully out of the equation now. Wherever he's gone.

I notice a sign above the door as I creep towards it. *Dan's Posh Shed.* He must live here then. Domestic bliss, eh? Not for much longer. I'll be putting an end to that.

Suzannah's laid out on an exercise mat, staring at the ceiling, her ugly fat belly protruding into the air. I've never liked lycra on a woman, particularly a heavily pregnant one. I'm so disappointed. She's not nearly as attractive as she used to be. Pregnant women are the ugliest thing. I couldn't go near Eva when she was expecting Heidi, and I never saw her pregnant with my son. Bitch.

Suzannah's a far cry from the groomed, sexy woman that used to saunter around the office when I went for my counselling appointments. I wonder if she ever thinks about me. The recent news reports about my escape should have returned me to the forefront of her mind. It's time for me to make myself fully known to her again. *Right, go.* The door squeaks as I push it open.

Suzannah turns her head towards the sound, the shock in her eyes quickly turning to terror when she realises who I am. "How... What the hell are you doing here?" She hoists herself into a sitting position and begins to slide towards a mobile phone on the table. Does she think I'm stupid? Does she really think I'll just let her get to it?

"It's been a while Suzannah." I let the door fall closed behind me. "I thought I'd take advantage of my newfound freedom and pay you a visit."

She seems to know I'm watching her eyes on her phone. I reckon she'll make a sudden grab for it when she thinks I've lowered my guard. Except I won't be doing that.

"How... how did you know where I live?" Her eyes flit around the room. I reckon she's looking for something she might be able to use as a weapon against me. As if she could fight me off in the state she's in. As if she could fight me off at all.

"I've known lots of things about you for a long time Suzannah."

"What's that supposed to mean?" Her voice shakes. I'm glad. I hope she's petrified. Serves her right after everything she's done. And what she's become. She looks like the back end of a bus.

"Let's just say you were my favourite research project back in the day." I take a step closer to her. It stinks of perfume and flowers in here. "I thought I'd found out all I needed to know about you when I used to come for those appointments. Only, I didn't realise at the time just how far back our *connection* went." Grinning at her, I draw quotes with my fingers in the air as I say the word *connection*.

The scene emerges in my mind. Her ghostly face bathed in moonlight on the banks of the River Alder. It was almost romantic. As I'd predicted, Suzannah was one of the women who, seemingly resolute with her fate, or so I thought, didn't scream. Little did I know she was already planning how to get out of there. But I'd watched her. Seen her go under. And I'd waited. I've still, to this day, no idea how she got out.

A darkness enters her face as though she's also recalling our first meeting. I can see the veins in her neck, her chest rising and falling. Yes, she's petrified alright. Since then, we've only been in proximity at the public inquiry and at *The Alder Centre,* and there's always been someone else nearby. She's got no colleagues or panic buttons here.

"In hindsight," I continue, "I'm glad that the intended outcome I initially had for you didn't come to pass. When I think of all we could have missed out on. It clearly wasn't meant to be. But now..."

"Daniel will be back any minute. He's only gone to the shop, you know. You need to leave. Now." Suzannah tries to get to her feet.

"Stay right there." She drops back to the mat at my raised voice. I lower it again. I've never been a shouter. "Ah, yes, Daniel. Tell me - what the fuck does he have that I haven't?"

She frowns beneath my gaze. "What are you on about?"

"Oh, come on Suzannah." I laugh. "You're nothing but a cock tease. You knew how I felt about you all along. Right back when you waited at court to give me your business card. And you can't lie. If I'd kept coming to *The Alder Centre,* you wouldn't have been able to resist me for much longer. It was written all over you."

All these years, I've had an image of her inside my head. I've built her into something she really isn't anymore. Her hair is scragged back and her stretch marks are visible above the waist line of her leggings. *It's not yours.* She reminds me of how shitty Eva used to look. And not just when she was pregnant. She looked constantly shitty. *Get rid of her.*

"You need to leave," she repeats, sounding as though she's trying to keep her voice level. But I can hear the wobble in it. Her eyes scan the room again and she slides back towards the wall. "I mean it Will. If you go now, I'll give you time to get away."

Yeah right. However, I'm intrigued by her use of my name and the way she says it. *Will.* Familiar. She's more connected to me than she'll admit. "I'm going nowhere just yet. I haven't come all this way for nothing."

She rests her arm in a protective gesture as I take two more steps towards her. Bad move. *It's not yours. It's not yours.*

"So, whose is the kid then?"

"Why do you want to know?"

"It's his, isn't it? After everything he did to me..."

By now, she's edged as far as she can go. Her back's fully against the wall and I notice she's trying to edge to the left towards the desk where the mobile phone is. As I make a grab for it, she hauls herself up. I've got to it before she's even got to her feet.

"If you're talking about Daniel, he only did what was right."

"He gave evidence at my trial Suzannah." I drop the phone into my coat pocket. It might come in useful whilst I'm here, then I'll probably have to throw it away. "Evidence against me. Remember? So did you."

"Of course we did." We're eye to eye, and she looks directly at me. "I'm not scared of you Will." It's a defiant look, not unlike something I'd have seen on Heidi's face once. Heidi. It's because of these bastards that she's had to grow up without me, and it's time for them to pay.

"Well, you should be scared. Anyway, I expect I was good for business, wasn't I? After I got sent down."

"Like I said, Daniel won't be long." She looks towards the door and for a moment, I think she's going to bolt for it. I move myself back so I'm blocking any chance she has of an exit. She must sense this is *it* for her.

"Good. As I've one or two things to get straight with him too. He set me up. In more ways than one."

"He did what he had to do."

"Bullshit. I got the blame for that mother and daughter. He set it up. He hired someone, didn't he? And I'm going to make sure he regrets it."

"No one will believe you Will."

So my hunches were right. They *did* set me up. I glance towards the back of the cabin, spotting a rack of dumbbells and a set of barbell weights. Perfect. *Get rid of her. Get rid of her.*

She follows my gaze, any remaining colour she had draining from her face. "Please don't hurt me Will. I'm begging you."

"Give me one reason why I shouldn't. If it wasn't for you. And him."

"You did enough damage to me all those years ago. It took ages to get over the nightmares. You needed help Will, and we made sure you got it, that's all."

Tears are pouring from her eyes, which makes me despise her even more. Once I respected her. To say I'm disappointed at what she's become doesn't begin to cover it. "You mean you had me locked up? You ruined everything." *Get rid of her.*

"You needed to be locked up. So you couldn't hurt any more women. I know there's something decent somewhere inside you, but there's also something very dark. Very wrong. Something that needed treating. And still does, by the looks of you."

"Sit down. Who the hell do you think you are, judging me?"

"Don't you want to be free one day?" She slides down the wall into a crouch. "To have another chance? If you hurt me now, you'll never have a chance of parole in the future. You'll be locked up until you die."

Either she hasn't heard about the other women in the news over the last few days, or she's playing dumb. But she's lit a fire with her words – when people comment about what might or might not be inside me, when they claim to know me, no, I can't take it. I don't want people to know me. She'll be saying she can hear the voices next.

"What do you know about what's inside me?" Our eyes lock as she becomes my mother.

Get out, my mother would have said. *There's something about you. Something nasty, deep inside. Something that makes my skin crawl.*

Suzannah's shoulders have slumped somewhat. My silence appears to have calmed her. She's clearly waiting to see what I'll do next. *Get rid of her. It's not yours.*

"Please Will." There are beads of sweat on her upper lip and she draws her legs towards her and wraps her arms around her knees. "You can go now. Before Daniel gets back. I truly won't tell anyone you've been here."

"Do you really think I'm going to fall for that?" I wipe the spittle from my mouth and my fists clench at my sides. I can't believe she thinks I'm just going to leave.

"If not for me, do it for my baby. He deserves to be born. He's innocent in all this."

He. It's a boy. I should have had a son. Hell, I should have had a son with her. If I'd had my way.

"Please, Will."

"Are you sure the kid's even Hamer's?"

It's not yours. It's not yours. I think of the kid Tina aborted. Then the promise of trying for one with Eva, which she cruelly snatched away. Then of Harry. I never even knew of him until

Alysha told me a year ago. Witches. Women. The lot of them. *Get rid of her. It's not yours.*

"Of course it's Daniel's."

"It should have been mine. You should have been mine." By now, our feet are touching. She shrinks back. Somehow this angers me more. I'm so used to her being kick-ass, confident. She wraps her other arm over her belly and presses herself even more into the wall.

"It's because of you I lost the chance to bring my kids up." My voice is a snarl. I hardly recognise it. "So why should you get to keep that one?" I point at her belly. She looks like she's about to drop at any moment. I'd be doing the kid a favour to end its life before it starts. Imagine having Daniel Hamer as a father. Daniel, with his tweed jackets and odd socks. Daniel, the conniving, lying, two-faced...

"Help! Somebody help me." Shit. She's found her voice. *Get rid of her.*

I yank her feet so she slides forwards on the wooden floor, yowling as she lands squarely on her back. As she recoils, I dart across to the weighted bar, grabbing it from the floor as though it's a feather. As I dash back to her, she's trying to get up. I push her back down with the flat of my foot. *Get rid of her. Get rid of her.*

"No!" She wheezes as I land on her belly. *It's not yours. It's not yours. It's not yours.* I haven't been near a pregnant belly since Heidi. Repulsive. Suzannah twists this way and that, doing all she can to throw me off before finally succumbing to the pressure I'm exerting.

As I force the bar down onto her neck, pressing down with all my might, she gurgles. Her stomach contracts between my legs so I force my weight onto it even harder. Harder. Harder. I press with all my might, my body weight onto her belly and the bar onto her neck. Harder. Harder.

Eventually she stops thrashing around. I watch as her eyes

bulge and her face turns purple, the veins in her neck protruding from all sides.

Her body stiffens. She's going. Harder. Harder.

She's on her way. My breath slows with hers as the fight begins to leave us both.

Suddenly, I'm yanked backwards.

I'm thrown to the ground with such force that all breath is forced from me. He's back. Dan the man. Here to fight for what he believes to be his. Only he's too late. I dodge the heavy vase that hurtles my way as he rushes towards Suzannah. It narrowly misses my head and crashes to the floor. As he bends forward and grips the bar across her neck, I leap on his back from behind, bringing him and the bar backwards.

I grunt as the weight forces me down again. He turns and grabs for the bar, but he's not quick enough. We're writhing around like pigs in mud. Suzannah's as still as the midnight river. She hasn't moved since Daniel arrived.

I need to end this. Here and now. This is the difference between me going on from here, or everything grinding to a deadening halt.

I slide a couple of inches along the wooden floor on my stomach, stretching my arm out for one of the hand weights, then groan as Daniel sticks the boot into my side.

Suddenly, he's up, back on his feet, brandishing the barbell aloft with a crazed look in his eyes.

But he's not quick enough. In a split second, I'm back on my feet too.

"Come on then," he says through gritted teeth as sweat slips down the sides of his head. We circle each other for a moment, both panting like dogs.

Eventually, I lunge at him with the weight. He holds the bar up to shield himself. So I come at him again from the other side. And again. He runs at me, but I'm too agile for him. I dodge to the side and this time I get a lucky hit. He howls as blood spurts down his face. The bar and its weights come crashing down onto his foot.

He yells out just as I bring the weight crashing down onto his head, smashing it into his skull. The sound of metal against bone makes me feel sick. I'm used to violence, but not at this level, and not in this way. But then I feel the elation of what I'm doing.

Twice more and finally, he's out cold.

He's my first male victim. It's taken years for me to leverage what they did to bring me down, back at them, but finally, my own kind of justice is done.

I stand back and look from Suzannah to Daniel, before pulling out Suzannah's phone and capturing the scene on camera. In the past, I always enjoyed being able to revisit images of my work. I sometimes got access to the morgue and got my photos that way. These more recent images will be more enjoyable for as long as I get to keep hold of this phone.

Noticing the sink in the corner, I fill a glass with water and gulp it down like I've not drunk for a week. Then, cold water splashed onto my face and over my hands goes some way to wash away the blood splatters from stoving Daniel's head in. It's no worse than some of the remains I used to see in road traffic accidents.

As my breath slows, I move around the room, twisting the cords that close all the blinds, before feeling in my pocket to make sure I've still got Suzannah's phone and the key for the Fiesta. The key to this building is in the back of the door, so I lock it behind me.

As I make my way past their cars on the drive towards the road, I notice the rear registration plate on the Fiesta has been wiped. Shit. I look up and down the street. There's no one to be seen, but I can't risk it. With the plates visible, the car will be intercepted as soon as I get near a main road.

But I need to get out of here. The police could be here in a matter of minutes now. As I contemplate returning to the cabin for Daniel's car key to drive his, I hear sirens in the distance. There's only one thing I can do.

Run.

15

ALYSHA

"Where are you going?" Eva eyes me with suspicion as I point my toes into my trainers. I've had four missed calls whilst I've been sitting here. From a number I don't recognise. I don't know that it's Uncle Will for certain, but it must be. No one else would be this persistent. Or they'd leave a message.

"I need to get some air," I reply, probably with too much friendliness in my voice. Eva's used to me being more hostile. "These walls are closing in on me. I'll just be in the back garden."

"As long as you don't go any further." She frowns. "And don't go anywhere near those reporters."

"This is the stuff of nightmares," Grandma says as I rise from the sofa and head towards the door. "As if Will Potts is still out there. Even I'm feeling claustrophobic, and I only arrived here yesterday."

I pace the garden, my trainers quickly becoming sodden from the wet grass, as I wait for the phone to ring again. I should have put a coat on too – it's freezing out here. It probably feels colder because I've been in the house for so long. Sat around, doing sod all.

He's rung four times, that's if it is him, so surely, he'll ring again. If I go back into the house and shoot out once more to take a call, they'll all be asking questions. And my phone calls are my business. I've allowed my stupid family to control my life more than enough lately.

Standing on tiptoes to peer over the gate, I watch the group of reporters for a few moments, still hanging around in the cul-de-sac. Their job must be as boring as Adele's is. All they do is shout questions that don't get answered to anyone who comes or goes from the house. I duck down before any of them spot me. Not that they can do much. As Auntie Eva has said, if any of them come into the garden, we can do them for trespassing.

Heidi's been a right miserable cow today. Now that we live together in the flat, we don't get on as well as we used to. We just do each other's heads in. As soon as I've passed my course and been made permanent at the salon, I might get my own place. Maybe with some of my friends. Heidi acts so badly done to, like she's got the weight of the world on her shoulders. She was crying in the kitchen earlier and *my* grandma was comforting her. Sometimes I think she does it just to get attention. At least she's still got her mum. Not like me. I've always had a mother-shaped hole in my life. It's irritated me when Auntie Eva's tried to fill it in the past. But she could never come close and stopped trying years ago, which pissed me off even more.

I glance up to see Harry watching me from his bedroom window. He's frowning, as if to say, what are you doing? As I wave at him, my phone rings. My stomach twists with nerves.

"Is that you Alysha?"

"Yeah. Sorry I couldn't answer before. I was in front of everyone." This must be weird for him to hear – after all *everyone* is actually his family too.

"No one can hear you now, can they?"

"No, but I can't talk for long. I'm in the garden and one of them might come out." I glance up at Harry. He's still there, watching me.

"OK, right. Look. I need you to do me a favour."

"What favour?" The nerves bubble up even more inside me. Or maybe excitement. Uncle Will wants me to help him.

"I need to get hold of a car. Soon. Sooner than soon."

He sounds out of breath like he's been running.

"Yes. But..." The bubbles inside my stomach feel like they're exploding. I hope he's not going to ask for my car.

"You got a car for your birthday, didn't you?"

Shit. He is. I picture it, parked down the road from when I couldn't get it through the reporters the other day. My baby. I've never been so happy as I was when I woke on my seventeenth birthday. Dad had even stuck a big, red bow on it.

"I need to get out of Alderton. As soon as I can."

"You're in Alderton?"

"Yeah. And the car I'm driving's been spotted. So, it's marked now."

"How did you get hold of a car anyway?"

"It doesn't matter. What matters is that I've been seen coming out of somewhere and they've taken the number. The police will be crawling all over it by now."

"Who's seen you?"

"How should I know?" Uncle Will's voice is full of irritation. I'm probably asking too many questions. "That's the thing. I'd parked up for a few minutes and when I returned to the car, someone had wiped the number plate clean."

"What do you mean, wiped clean?"

"God. You can tell your dad's a copper." There's the slightest trace of amusement in his voice, which makes me relax slightly. "You're as bad as he is."

"And my uncle." I smile, remembering the days when he'd

call home on his breaks in one of the patrol cars. I'd be around at their house, playing with Heidi.

"The registration was unreadable before. I'd made sure I caked it in mud. Anyway, I've had to abandon the car where it is and make a run for it."

"I don't think…" Maybe he doesn't want my car. It sounds more like he might want me to pick him up. I could get into real trouble here. Speaking to him on the phone is one thing. What he's asking of me is something else altogether.

"You're my only chance Alysha. I'm on foot now. And I'm not going to get very far without your help, am I?"

"I don't know."

"There's literally no one else I can ask. You know that."

"It's just…"

"Alysha. I've been telling myself I can count on you. As I've always said, you should have really been my daughter instead of my niece."

He's never said that out loud to me before. "But… I don't know how I can get out of the house. Auntie Eva and Grandma are barely taking their eyes off us. Any of us. Not for a minute. It's a miracle I've been able to get out into the garden."

"I slept outside last night, you know. I'm freezing cold and starving hungry. You've got to help me Alysha."

Although part of me is pleased about having this secret of possibly helping him, the other part of me is warning that Dad will kill me. Then I think of everything Grandma has told me about my mum. She was daring and risk-taking. If she wanted to do something, she wouldn't let anything stop her. I want to be like her. I am like her.

Uncle Will goes quiet for a moment and I realise I probably shouldn't have mentioned Auntie Eva just now. Or *all of us*. The family he is no longer part of. It will bring Heidi and Harry into his mind. It must be awful having a daughter he hasn't seen for years, and a son he's never met.

"Are you still there?" I say.

"They could catch me and send me back to prison at any moment." His voice softens. "And I'd love to see you. You know that, don't you? Don't you want to see me before that happens – before I'm sent back?"

I do want to see him. My mind races with excuses I could make to get out of the house. I haven't seen Uncle Will for so long, but can still picture him. Eyes which crinkle at the corners when he speaks. Strong arms which used to throw us around the room. Him sitting by the pool when he took us to Florida. I can hardly believe this other side of him, and what he's supposed to have done. But clearly, I bring out his best side – and I've only ever felt safe when I'm with him, never like I'm at risk. He's not dangerous at all, not to me anyway. As a kid, I loved spending time round at their house. When Auntie Eva was just my auntie and not trying to muscle in with my dad. But even in those days, it was always Uncle Will that had the edge.

"If I can get out of here, where will you be?"

"That's my girl!" His voice changes completely. "To be honest, I can't believe how grown up you sound. Where did my little niece go? I can't wait to see you again."

"I can't wait to see you too." Suddenly I feel like a shy, young girl and my heart hammers inside my chest. "I don't know Alderton very well, so I'd need a post code to find you." What am I getting into here? But I've just about decided that I'm going to help him. After all, if I don't, who will? However, I'm absolutely terrified about it.

"What are you on about? You used to live in Alderton."

"I know. But I was only eight when we moved house." I remember it like it was yesterday. Dad had, by then, got together with Auntie Eva, and was following her here to Filey. At first, we were going to get our own house, just me and him, but then they went and got married, and we all had to live together as one big weirdo family. No one asked me what I wanted, which at the time was to be near Grandma, my Auntie Claire, and my school friends. I didn't want to leave Alderton. I even tried to get left behind, to live with Auntie Claire or Grandma, but Dad wouldn't let me.

"Can you set off now?"

I hear a scratch of what sounds like waterproof fabric against concrete. He must be hiding somewhere. Of course, he's going to be hiding somewhere. He's hardly going to be taking a stroll down the high street.

"Where exactly are you? I've got sat nav on my phone." I'm really doing this. Oh no. What am I doing?

"We need to be careful. I can't just meet you out in the open." He falls silent for a moment. "I know. We could meet at my sister's house."

"Auntie Claire's? But..."

"I'm her brother when all is said and done."

He must have forgotten what Auntie Claire's like. No way will she just invite him in whilst he's on the run. "I don't think..."

He cuts me off again. "She didn't want anyone to know, but we've been in contact over the last couple of years. Between you and me, I reckon she's mellowed. Especially with all the therapy I've been having."

"I didn't know you were speaking to each other." Suddenly I feel jealous. I want to be the one who helps him. Not Auntie Claire. Then I remember. "She won't even be there. She stays with her boyfriend at the weekend."

"Bloody hell. If she's not there, that scuppers that one. OK, so where then?"

I think for a moment. My breath is coming in sharp gasps. "Actually, Dad should have a key to her house. He's had it since..." My voice trails off. Auntie Claire has told me she feels better with Dad having a key since she was attacked. I'm probably best not bringing that up.

"It'll be on our key hooks in the kitchen," I continue. I'm going to be mincemeat for this, but someone's got to help him. What if it's true though – what's been on the news? "Uncle Will..." I feel almost guilty asking him. It feels really strange when I talk to him now – like I'm really six again. "They're saying on the news that it was you who's killed two more women in the last couple of days. It wasn't, was it?"

"Of course it wasn't." His voice sounds strangled and shaky. I hope he's not mad at me for asking him. "They're looking for the wrong man Alysha. It's easy to pin it on me, isn't it? But like I've told you before, all that sort of thing is well and truly behind me now."

That's good enough for me. "There's no door on Auntie Claire's shed," I tell him. "The wind in the last storm blew it off, and she hasn't fixed it yet."

"Does she still have a gate at the back?"

I can hear in Uncle Will's voice that he's cold. He must be dying to get indoors somewhere. To have a warm drink. Something to eat. I can't help but feel sorry for him.

"The police might be watching her house, so if I can get around the back..."

"Yes, I think so."

"If I can't get near because it's being watched, then I'll ring you back. Keep your phone handy, will you?"

"Yeah. I'll let you know when I'm getting near."

Feeling very important, I stride back into the house, although I'm not sure how I'm going to pull this off. "Who were you on the phone to?" Auntie Eva stuffs her arms into her coat and zips it up without looking at me.

"No one. Only work." As if she's watching me on my phone. Talk about an invasion of privacy.

"On a Sunday?" She peers at me more closely. I hope I'm

not blushing. I always do when I'm lying. And she knows me better than I'd like her to.

"They were just asking if I'd be back at work tomorrow."

"But you don't work on a Monday." She tips her head to one side and crosses her arms. I feel like a specimen under her microscope.

"I meant Tuesday," I say quickly, bending to adjust my shoe so she can't see my face. "Where are you going anyway?"

"I'm having to call out to the supermarket," she replies. "I've tried and tried to get a delivery slot, but there's nothing going. We're running low on everything."

"Shall I go for you?" Wow. It's one way of getting out of here.

"What's up with you?" Auntie Eva eyes me even more suspiciously as she wraps a scarf around her neck. "This has got to be the first time you've ever offered to do anything useful."

"I'm bored, that's all." Good answer.

"No - you'd better stay here. So we know where you are." She swipes her keys from the hallway table. "I thought I'd take advantage of Brenda being here to keep an eye on you all."

"Erm, how old are we? Me and Heidi? Do we need keeping an eye on?"

"I know – but still. Anyway, a fat lot of use Brenda is. She's fallen asleep in front of the fire." Eva shakes her head. "Keep your ear out for the boys, will you? They're on that bloody games thing again and I haven't got the energy to suggest they do anything else."

"What about Heidi?"

"She's about to get in the shower."

Perfect. Grandma's well known for falling asleep everywhere at any time. *Just resting my eyes*, she'll say, if anyone tries to disturb her. *Or I wasn't asleep. I could hear everything that was going on.* Still, if she's asleep, and Auntie Eva's off out then...

· · ·

As the door bangs after her, I stand in the still of the hallway, listening. All I can hear is the sound of my own ragged breath. I'm as scared as hell, but I can hardly back out now. I've agreed. He's waiting for me.

Harry and Isaac are occupied upstairs and the shower's going, so Heidi must have got in already. Adele rang in sick this morning, so Dad says they're trying to sort someone else out. Another useless Family Liaison Officer. Adele probably couldn't face another long day of boredom. And I can hear Grandma snoring above the TV, which means she's well away. This is going to be easier than I thought. *What's meant to be always finds a way.* Another one of Grandma's sayings.

When Dad made me come home early from the salon the other day, I refused to leave my car and get into his, so he followed me back from there. No way was I leaving my gorgeous Fiat in the grotty car park behind the salon. It might have got broken into or nicked. It's parked outside one of the neighbours' houses as there's no room on the drive here. Not that I'd want to try driving a car through all those reporters. I glance out of the window at them, then head towards the kitchen. Hopefully, I'll be able to get past them without too much hassle.

The key to Auntie Claire's house is where I thought it would be. I add it to my keyring, then glance around the kitchen for some food. Uncle Will said he was hungry, and Auntie Claire never has anything in apart from fruit and salad stuff. There's hardly anything in here either. No wonder Auntie Eva has had to go shopping. I find a breakfast bar and a packet of crisps in the back of a cupboard and drop those into my bag before sliding my coat from the back of the chair.

After clicking the back door shut behind me, I walk towards the crowd of reporters, attempting to look as confident as possible. They shouldn't be saying that it's Uncle Will who's killed those women. I've heard with my own ears that it isn't. He wouldn't lie to me. I just hope nobody's looking out of the window at this moment. Especially Heidi, if she's heard the door. She'd come chasing after me. I think Harry would as well, having already spotted me on the phone earlier. He'd better not say anything about it.

"Any news on your dad yet?" someone shouts as I pass them. They must think I'm Heidi, though we're nothing like each other. Uncle Will used to say we could be sisters. Maybe as kids, but we couldn't be more different nowadays. In looks as well as personality. I wish they'd shut up. I don't want Harry or Isaac to hear them and let Grandma or Heidi know.

"Are you sure you feel safe going out?" a woman's voice shrieks out. Avoiding eye contact with anyone, I stride towards my car, starting it up quickly and waiting until I've got around the corner before I set up my sat nav.

I've never driven to Alderton on my own. Dad always drives if we're going to see Auntie Claire, or occasionally Grandma picks me up. Although she's even less confident driving on the A64, than I am. It's the slip roads coming on and off that scare me. Usually, I only use the car to get to work and to go shopping or whatever. But today, I haven't got a lot of choice.

The sat nav's saying fifty minutes. I text the number that Uncle Will rang me from to let him know I'll be there just after one o'clock. Butterflies flap in my stomach as I get the delivered message. I wonder where he's got the mobile from and hope it's not from one of the dead men in the van. Although if it was, surely it would have been tracked by now. I've seen it on the TV all the time. It's always mobile phones that lead the police to a person. Uncle Will's in the wrong for all sorts of things, from what he did all those years ago, to escaping from the accident he was involved in. But no matter how much I tell myself what could have happened, or what should be the case, there's something inside me that doesn't want him to get caught. Especially before I've been able to see him. I really do want to see him. As I keep telling Dad, I'm old enough to make my own mind up now.

As I leave Filey, my phone beeps on the dashboard. I pull into a layby to read the message, hoping it's not Heidi or Grandma, realising I've gone out.

> In the shed at Auntie Claire's. No reporters or police as far as I can see but don't bring a car in front of the house. Park as close as you can round the back.

My stomach lurches. I'm not sure whether it's with fear or excitement. Probably both. I'm going to see Uncle Will again after all this time, and on the outside too. I thought I'd eventually get to see him in prison but not like this. What's happening here is the stuff of films. It'll certainly give me something to talk about at the salon other than holiday destinations, or, at this time of year, *have you started your Christmas shopping yet?* Yawn.

I wonder how long it will be before anyone at Dad's notices I've gone. Auntie Eva will be gone for a couple of hours at the supermarket. Dad always moans about how long she takes when she's shopping. Harry and Isaac aren't likely to notice I'm not there; not once they're on that games console. In any case, they tend to follow Heidi around rather than me, and as long as Grandma stays asleep, I'll be fine. If it's anyone, it'll be Heidi who will notice I've gone. But even then, she might just think I've broken the 'rules' and sneaked out for a walk. It's not as though I left my car where she might see that it's gone. With any luck, by the time anyone realises I've left, I'll be at Auntie Claire's house with Uncle Will.

The journey passes by quickly. Probably because I need to concentrate so hard on my driving whilst also following the sat nav. It's the longest drive I've done since passing my test. Not as many tourists drive to and from Filey in the winter, so it's a clear run, as Dad would say. Filey's packed in the summer but becomes a ghost town at this time of year. It's so depressing. Driving back to Alderton feels like driving home, even though I've now spent more years in Filey than I did in Alderton. It *is* driving home.

As I turn off the A64, onto the bypass, there are police cars at every turn. They must be looking for Uncle Will. As I pause at a roundabout, I twist my neck towards the rumble overhead. I wonder if that's the police too. Dad's told me it costs over a thousand pounds to get the helicopter up, so they only do it when it's something big. Uncle Will must be something big.

I smile to myself. *You don't know where he is, but I do.* It's a very important feeling.

I leave my car at the park, which is a couple of streets away from Auntie Claire's - the same house she's always lived in. She too, thought about moving after Mum was killed and she was attacked. But in the end, she stayed. Auntie Claire apparently had some awful injuries which she recovered from, but left her with some memory problems. Dad told me she decided to stay in her familiar surroundings where she could feel more comfortable in the same routine. Even her furniture is in the same place it's been in for years. He also told me she's had a ton of counselling, and in any case, her attacker, Ingham is dead, so she's safe now. I'm glad he's dead. I wouldn't feel safe knowing the man who killed my mother was still hanging around. Especially when I'm told that I look so much like her.

16

WILL

I CAN HARDLY BELIEVE that my sister's house isn't being patrolled. I only hope Claire doesn't come back before Alysha gets here. Claire wouldn't just turf me out, but I don't think she'd keep quiet for me either. Sister or not. Although she's definitely softened towards me over the last couple of years. Paying lip service throughout all that prison therapy has been worth it. Claire was getting to the point where she might have even considered visiting me. It would have been good to have had a visit from someone who was actually family.

Over the years, my only letters and visitors have been from obsessive women who've fancied their chances. They've turned up with their plunging necklines, their bangles, and their red lipstick – everything I detest. After the initial pleasantries, there's been very little else to say. Though, I guess visiting me gave them something meaty to talk about. And it got me off the ward. It turns out a reformed villain is a bit of a turn on for some. Only as it happens, I'm not as reformed as anyone thought I was. Including myself.

At least the wind's off me in this shed. I've found a battered deckchair and wedged it in the corner behind the lawnmower.

The smell of wood combined with teak oil, petrol and compost reminds me of childhood. For once, it's not an awful memory. It's a memory of Dean and I turning our garden shed into a den. In the days before Mum started kicking me out all the time. Dean's smiling face inside my mind becomes Mum's, and I close my eyes to shut her out. She might be dead, but it seems she'll never leave me be. Whereas, I'd give anything to have my brother back.

I look out of the window at my sister's house. With its colourful blinds and hanging baskets, it's achingly familiar. It may be my last stop if Mark or Eva realise Alysha has cleared off. There was no one else who would have been willing to help me. Or gullible enough. She was certainly easy to talk around. It seems the groundwork I put in worked. And if it leads to me getting to see Heidi and Harry, the risk of being caught will have been worth it. Especially to meet Harry for the first time.

I've got a plan up my sleeve to make it happen once Alysha gets here. Harry deserves to meet his dad. His *real* dad. It's not his fault they have probably been lying to him for all these years. Heidi is less easy to forgive. She knowingly rejected me. Since she turned eighteen, I've been sending visiting orders here, to Claire's that just named Heidi on them. Prior to that, I'd have to name either Mark or Eva as well to accompany her. But neither of them have visited me – not even once.

No one can change the fact that they're my kids. Not even Eva who's clearly done everything in her power to poison Heidi against me. She's got a lot to answer for.

I might not have got to Eva yet, but she's coming to the top of my agenda. At least I've settled some other scores. Seeing my kids, however that turns out, will get to Eva in itself. I'm not ready to be picked up and sent back to prison yet, but any extra shit the prison authorities throw my way is something I'm prepared to live with. It's a price worth paying for what I've achieved since I escaped from that van.

Killing has almost become second nature. Like it's what I was put on this earth to do. My purpose. I remember the first time I ever killed fourteen years ago. The woman had been leaving The Yorkshire Arms on her own, steaming drunk. She could barely walk. The same wave of revulsion washes over me now as it did then, as I remember her. Two women had left the pub a short time after her and tried to get her back to her feet. She must have persuaded them she was alright as they eventually left her sitting on a bench. I watched as she tried to lie down on it, even though it was a freezing cold night. Then she began throwing up. I could hear her retching from my hiding place. I listened as she left a tearful message to someone, saying if she didn't have them, she might as well drive her car into the nearest wall. They were the words that did it for me.

Dean's face had flashed into my mind. The only person in the world, other than Heidi back then, who had loved me just for who I was. Until a drunk driver snuffed him out. I wasn't going to stand back and let this woman inflict her drink fuelled-misery on anyone else. I'd suddenly realised my purpose in life and the voices were urging me on. It was as though they were right with me, whispering into my ears. And as the months passed, they became louder, and more insistent.

My role wasn't just ridding the roads of drink drivers in my capacity as a traffic cop – the task extended into every fibre of my being. I've always hated drunk women. The way they slur, the glassy eyes, the rolls of fat over their waistbands, lipstick marks on glasses and red wine moustaches. My mother often had one of those when I was a kid.

The woman outside the Yorkshire Arms had been the first drunk I'd cleansed the streets of, outside of my police work. Her sins washed clean in the river. She'd been way too drunk to fight me off, though she'd given it her best shot. She didn't even scream before she hit the water.

I always worked under the cover of darkness and in the

winter, when death would be quick. I didn't want to cause unnecessary suffering – just to serve my purpose. It's only since I escaped last week that my endings have turned into something far uglier. I'm not proud of myself, but I've only done what I've had to do to evade being caught. Which is why I'm puzzled by the pleasure that coursed through my veins when I surveyed my handiwork after I finished Hamer off.

I stare at the shed wall. A hosepipe neatly coiled and hanging from a hook, pots of paint stacked neatly on a shelf. Claire must have painted the house. I'm hoping it will almost be the same in there. With my unstable and chaotic life, it would be reassuring for something, no matter how small, to have stayed the same.

I flick the photos open on Suzannah's phone. I'll keep this phone for a couple more hours, at least until Alysha gets here. Then I'll get rid of it. Looking at the colour of her face on the photo and the amount of blood pooled around Hamer, I'm certain that neither of them will have survived our altercation. He's the first man I've ended. Though after what he did to me to set me up, he's had it coming. He used everything he knew about me to lure me back to that river all those years ago. Then he tricked me into saying things I'd never planned to say. Things I didn't want to say. But I always knew at least one of them would get their comeuppance for it eventually. Then it hits me why I felt elated at Hamer's demise, *revenge*, and not just towards drunken women for ruining my life.

I was only expecting to come face to face with Suzannah today. Instead, I got two for the price of one. Though it wasn't a pretty scene that I left behind. My only regret is that I should've probably made sure they were definitely dead. One brief final check would have been all that was needed.

Instead, I panicked, just desperate to get out of there and away. I only hope their bodies don't get found straightaway, being that it all happened at the rear of their house. Any door-to-door enquiries will initially focus on knocking at the front doors. I remember the drill. It could be days before the back of the house is checked, unless someone reports their absence in the meantime.

Suzannah's face, as it once was, swims into my mind. The slim, attractive version of twelve years ago, not the pudgy and lined version of today. The moment I noticed her enormous pregnant belly, the voices started. *It's not yours. It's not yours.* But it should have been.

I hold my breath as a gate behind the shed rattles. "Uncle Will?" Alysha's here. She's really here. I always knew she had balls, that one. Like her mother had.

I poke my head out from my hiding place. "Have you found the key?" I'm knackered after my earlier exertions with Suzannah and Hamer. And I really need food and a clean-up before I meet my kids.

She nods and I follow this grown-up version of the little girl from the shed, towards the back door of my sister's house. There's a light on in next door's kitchen, but so far, so good. No one appears to have seen me. Up to now, I've been invincible. Perhaps I can keep going after all.

My breath catches as Alysha turns the key and swings the door open into my sister's kitchen. All is nearly the same as it was. Heat rushes to my eyes. There's something about the smell and feel of the house that makes me want to blub. Washing powder and warmth. This is the first sense of any kind of family I've had in years. I'm standing with my niece in my sister's kitchen.

Life's shit. Totally shit. I've been under control of the voices for as long as I can remember, and I want them to leave me alone. Alysha locks the door behind us, and I turn to face her for the first time in twelve years, blinking as she becomes

Lauren. Shit. I wasn't prepared for this. She steps towards me and something in her face suggests she wants a hug, but I can't. I just can't go near her.

"You're the bloody spit of your mother." I turn away and fill a glass of water. I can't bear to look at her. Not that I could truly bear to look at her when she was a kid either. I only saw Lauren. I still only see Lauren. The woman who sneered at me and rejected me. Thought she was a cut above. I couldn't even evoke a fearful reaction in her like I could in the others. Apart from the one time. However, I try not to think about that. It throws up too much turmoil when I allow my mind to return there.

"Aren't you going to hug me?" There's a wounded edge to Alysha's voice as it cuts into my thoughts. It's just as well – my mind was heading into dangerous territory.

In person Alysha sounds more like Lauren than she did on the phone. I scrunch my voice against the voices, which are just a whisper right now, but I know they'll become louder. They always do. *Get rid of her.* I want to shout back at them. *Of course I can't get rid of her. She's what will lead me to my kids.* And she's my niece. I don't want to get rid of her. I knew this would be the case one day. Years ago, I was always troubled that she and Heidi would inevitably grow from being little girls into young women.

I stiffly accept her hug, then step back and away. Other than the people I've ended in the last few days, it's been a long time since I've been in physical contact with anyone. Hugs are an alien concept. I open Claire's fridge door – part distraction, part hunger. There's bugger all in here. I don't know how she survives.

"Uncle Will. You've got blood on you. Are you alright?"

As if she's only just noticed the splatters from when I caved Daniel's head in. Suddenly I feel nauseous. I don't know if it's the thought of the blood on me or because I need food.

"Yeah. It's probably just from when I was hiding. There was some broken glass, so I must have caught myself." I look at her. She seems to buy it, though she's still frowning. "I'll have a sandwich, then I'll get a wash."

"I've brought you something." She pulls some crisps and some kind of bar from her bag and looks at me so earnestly that heat rushes to my eyes again. I'm not used to someone being nice to me.

Maybe this boyfriend of my sister's might have left some clothes here so I can get a change. I might even have a shave since they're circulating e-fits of me with a beard. I find some bread in the bread bin and start buttering it. It's been years since I've made myself a sandwich. The ones I've eaten have always been pre-packed and brought from the outside. At least that way, they weren't likely to have been tampered with. The whole time I've been locked up, I've been classified as a VP, a vulnerable prisoner. I'm up there with the lowest of the low. Therefore, I'm deemed to need protection for my own good.

I was heading for the VP wing at Suffolk and had heard the food there was even more likely to be messed with. It was mostly prepared by inmates on normal location. But I'll probably have to face it eventually. Part of me can't believe I'm still ducking and diving. The police have got far more sophisticated technology than they had when I was in the force twelve years ago, and even with that, I'm still evading them. It's almost amusing.

Before I leave the kitchen, I slide the knife I've sliced onion and cucumber with into the pocket of my jacket. A little extra insurance.

Alysha's in the lounge, tilting the blinds, darkening the room. "There's police all over the place out there," she says, turning to face me. "You know, when I was driving through Alderton."

"Have you noticed any round here?" I ask her between

mouthfuls of crisps. "I heard sirens when I was waiting for you, but it wasn't a good idea to be peering out of where I was hiding."

She shakes her head. "I've closed the blinds in case the neighbours can see in. They might know that Auntie Claire isn't here at weekends."

"Where's your car?" If plan A doesn't look like a go-er, I might need her to take me to Filey instead.

"At the park - only around the corner."

"It's just that I might need you to drive me."

She nods, but looks really uncertain.

"Have you definitely locked the door? Here, I mean?"

She nods again.

Can't you speak all of a sudden? I feel like yelling. Or shaking her. Nodding her head like a performing dog. It's not even her I want to see. Especially now. Thank God the voices have quietened. But I need Alysha. I would struggle to get any further without her. Fury rises at the prospect of being so reliant on a female. Particularly one who's the spit of Lauren. "I'll have that key, if you don't mind."

"Why?"

"Then I know where it is." I hold my hand out.

She plucks the key from her pocket and drops it in my hand.

I swallow the last of my sandwich. "Tell me where everyone is."

"How do you mean?"

"At home." Misery wraps itself around me. If they catch me, prison will probably be my home for the rest of my life. What I'd give to go back in time.

"Dad's at work. When I left, Auntie Eva went shopping at the same time. But she could be back any minute. And Grandma was asleep." She makes a gap in the blinds and looks out, much to my increasing irritation.

"Come away from the window," I tell her. "Now."

A hurt expression passes over her face, but she does as she's told.

"What about Heidi? And Harry?" It's strange saying his name out loud. I like the sound of it though. Since I found out about him, I've often wondered what he looks like and what he's been told. If anything. "Does he know about me?"

"He does now. They told him the other day."

"They've only just told him?"

"He couldn't understand why they were keeping him off school."

Bitch. As if Eva kept the truth from him. I've seen other prisoners in the hospital be allowed closed visits with their kids. Women who prevent their kids from seeing their fathers, like Eva has, want stringing up. It's child abuse. I glare at Alysha. "Sit down, will you? You're making me nervous, pacing around like that."

She drops onto the edge of the sofa. She's certainly more obedient than her mother was. Maybe Plan A will pan out quite easily.

"You were telling me where everyone is? Heidi and Harry?"

"They're all at home. Heidi was in the shower when I left. Harry was playing on the games console with Isaac."

I don't want to hear about him. "Right. OK. Here's what I need you to do. Are you listening?"

She nods. Again.

"You've got your phone with you right? Of course you have. You sent me a message, didn't you?"

With that, I remember I should get rid of the one I took from Suzannah. I slide it from my pocket and take it out of its case. I turn it this way and that, wondering how to get to the battery.

"What are you looking for Uncle Will?" I wish she wouldn't call me that. She's practically a grown woman. *Uncle Will.* I'll let it lie for now though. Until she's done what I need her to do.

"First, I want to get the battery out of this thing. And to get rid of the sim so it can't be traced. Phones can't have changed that much whilst I've been inside."

"Do you want me to do it?" She holds her hands out.

With shaking fingers, she pushes her earring from her ear and pokes it into the side of the phone, sliding out a piece of plastic before handing it all back to me. I'll get rid of it as soon as we move on from here.

"Next, I want you to ring Heidi. From your phone." This is it. Plan A.

"And say what? I can't exactly tell her where I am."

"Do the two of you still get on?" An image of them together in pink when we were at the airport flashes back. That was a rare happy day where I felt like a normal human being. In the two weeks I was away with my wife, daughter and niece, the voices completely left me alone. I probably didn't sit still for long enough for them to find me.

"Not quite as well as we used to, but we live together now, so…"

"Will she keep quiet if you tell her where you are?"

Alysha bites her bottom lip in the same way Lauren used to do when she was thinking about something. "She won't keep quiet about you, no way. She'll go mental with me."

Something inside me darkens. Eva turned my own daughter against me more than I could have ever thought possible. But I'm not only angry with Eva. Heidi's a grown-up now. Old enough to know her own mind and do what she wants. How dare she reject me after all I did for her? "I'm not asking you to tell her about me. Not yet. It's up to me to make her listen when she gets here."

"What do you mean, *gets here?*" Alysha sits up straighter and tucks her hair behind an ear.

"You're going to let her know where you are, at Auntie Claire's, and tell her you can't get your car to start."

"She'll just tell me to get the rescue service out."

"Then you tell her you cancelled your policy. You couldn't afford it. And that you're scared your dad will know that you've gone out if she doesn't help you." The words *your dad* stick in my throat. "Tell her your car broke down near to Claire's so you've walked the rest of the way. All she needs to know is that you need picking up from here."

"She'll want to know what I was doing in Alderton in the first place."

"Say you needed to get out, to get away. You'd had enough of being told what to do by everyone." I've got an answer for everything. Sitting in that shed gave me plenty of thinking time.

"She'll believe that." Alysha's face breaks into a faint smile.

"To really make sure she sets off to help you, tell her you're not feeling too well." If my daughter is the same as I remember her, she was always a sucker for a sob story. The only person she evidently doesn't feel sorry for is her own father. My hackles rise again. "When you speak to her, make her swear she won't tell anyone where she's going. And I don't care how you do it, but make sure she brings Harry with her." I put my aversion to looking at Alysha to one side and watch for a reaction from her.

Her face falls. "I can't do that. She won't be able to bring him. No way."

I sit beside her on the sofa, wrapping my fingers around her upper arm, perhaps a little too firmly. Fear crosses her face. "You're hurting me, Uncle Will."

I relax my grip and force a smile. "You can swing it for me Alysha. I've got every faith in you."

"Please let my arm go."

I relax my grip completely and move to the other chair, facing her. "I'll be right here, whilst you make the call."

17

ALYSHA

"WHAT THE HELL are you doing there?"

"Like I said. It was walking distance from where I broke down."

"You shouldn't even be out of the house, let alone in Alderton."

"I know. I just wanted to go for a drive."

"As if you've broken down. That car is practically new."

Heidi's right. It is. I'm not even sure if it's still under warranty. I think quickly. "It's something electrical, I think. There were some strange lights on the dashboard." I glance at Uncle Will who nods his approval. I can't get this wrong. He's not taking his eyes off me. And I'd be lying if I didn't admit to being a bit scared of him, now I'm here with him.

"You've got breakdown cover, haven't you?"

"I cancelled it."

"Too busy spending your money on nights out, I bet."

"Cut the lectures Heidi. Are you going to help me or what?" Uncle Will's glaring at me. Maybe that wasn't the right thing to say to her. He'll be able to hear her voice in the silence of the house. It must be well weird for him after all these years.

"I didn't even realise you'd gone anywhere. You must have sneaked out. Did you tell Brenda where you were going?"

Heidi sounds as suspicious as I've ever heard her. I might as well be talking to Auntie Eva. Or Dad.

"Grandma knew I was going for a walk." My voice shakes like it always does when I'm lying. Heidi knows me so well that I'm surprised she hasn't picked up on it. "She just told me to get back before Auntie Eva did. Is she back yet?"

"No. You know what she's like." Heidi half laughs. She won't be laughing soon though. "And Brenda's fast asleep. I don't think she slept too well last night." She sighs now. "So what do you want me to do Alysha? Not that I can do a right lot. I've got the boys here, haven't I?"

Taking a deep breath, I put on my most beseeching voice. "I need you to come and get me. Please."

"From Alderton? For God's sakes Alysha!"

At least she isn't saying no, so I continue. "I'll leave the car where it is for now, if you can just get me back to Filey. I'll worry about it later."

"Uncle Mark will kill you if he finds out where you are. We're not even supposed to leave the house Alysha." Off she goes again. "And I'll probably get killed for helping you."

She's right about Dad. He'd go off his head if he knew I was here. Especially if he were to find out who I'm with. That's an understatement. "That's why I need to get back before anyone notices I've gone. Or before Auntie Claire comes back here."

"Isn't she there with you?"

"No." My voice falters and my face burns. At least Heidi can't see me. "I forgot she wouldn't be here today. Auntie Claire goes to her boyfriend's at the weekend, doesn't she?"

"Haven't you tried ringing her? It might be better if she sorts this out, rather than me driving across."

"No. She'll tell Dad." She would as well.

"Look Alysha. The rest of us have done what we're supposed to. But you always have to be different, don't you?"

"Heidi. Please. You've got to help me out here."

She falls quiet for a moment. "As if I'm going to end up getting in trouble for you."

"I really can't get my car going. My bank card's back at the flat and I'm freezing cold. I'm not feeling too well either," I add at the end, remembering what Uncle Will told me to say.

"Where exactly are you?"

"Standing outside Auntie Claire's house. And my phone's running out of battery. You need to give me an answer – quick Heidi."

"You don't sound like you're outside." It's that tone of voice again. She doesn't believe me. She never does.

"I'm inside her shed if you must know – which doesn't even have a door on it. Come on Heidi. I'd do the same for you." She'll know that's true. Not that Heidi gets into any scrapes. She's too much of a goody two shoes, but I'd always help her out if she did.

"What about Harry and Isaac? What am I supposed to do with them? I'll have to wake Brenda up." Uncle Will is shaking his head and I really don't like the look on his face.

"No! Don't do that. She'll do her nut. And she'll tell Dad. Heidi! Please!"

"Anyway, my car isn't even here – it's back at the flat. I came around with my mum the other night."

"You'll just have to bring Harry and Isaac with you. They'll be glad to get out of that house anyway." I pause, wondering how she can get to her car. Then I remember. "Just use Grandma's, OK? Her keys are on the hallway table. But don't wake her up, whatever you do. She was exhausted. Let her get some sleep."

Uncle Will is nodding his approval again.

"But the boys will tell on you." Heidi's voice rises. "They can never keep a secret. You know what they're like."

"I'll worry about that later. There'll be something I can bribe them with. There always is. Just set off now, will you?" I force a noise as though my teeth are chattering. "I'm bloody freezing here."

"Haven't you got a coat with you?"

"No. I didn't know I was going to break down, did I? I'm not psychic."

"Perhaps one of Auntie Claire's neighbours will let you wait inside."

"I can't. They'd tell her. I just want to get back to Filey. How long will you be?"

"As soon as those two have put their coats and shoes on. So long as Mum doesn't turn up before we set off."

"Just hurry Heidi. Please."

"Hopefully Brenda won't wake up either. I can't believe you've put me in this position. I've spent my life covering your arse Aly..."

"Alright. Alright. I'm sorry. I'll make it up to you, I promise. Text me when you're out of there."

"That's my girl." Uncle Will comes towards me and places his hand on my shoulder. "Let me know when you get that text from her. I'm going to make a drink."

I slump against the cushions as he leaves the room. The enormity of what I'm doing is beginning to hit home. Suddenly I realise I could be in even more trouble than just with Dad, especially for dragging Heidi, Harry and Isaac into this. I could even end up in trouble with DSI Jones too.

Though in a way, it serves everyone in my family right. Auntie Eva hasn't wanted me around ever since she got together with Dad, and even Dad hardly notices I exist most of the time. He's too busy with Isaac and Harry. All I ever seem to do is irritate everyone, which is why they let me move in with Heidi. Grandma had argued with Dad that I was too young to leave home, but they couldn't get rid of me quick enough.

I reach for one of Auntie Claire's magazines and thumb through it, trying to distract myself whilst Uncle Will bangs around the kitchen.

He returns to the room with a mug of something and rips his breakfast bar open. He never asked me if I wanted a drink. I fold my arms across my chest, feeling like a sulky child. I read and re-read the same paragraph in the magazine, taking none of it in. Then I start to feel angry.

I detest the sound of people eating and drinking and have no choice but to sit here and listen to Uncle Will chew and slurp. I search for something to make conversation about, but can't think of anything. He's stopped making conversation with me now. Obviously, he can't be bothered. I'd have thought he'd have wanted to know all about what I've been up to over the years, but since I made the phone call to Heidi, he's barely said two words. This isn't anything like what I expected, and I can't help but feel as though he's used me just to get to Heidi and Harry. This is the story of my life. I'm always second best. At least everyone will sit up and take notice of me when they find out what I've done. Some attention is better than no attention. Grandma is the only person in the world who really cares about me. My life could have been so different if only Mum hadn't died.

I glance up from the magazine. In the light that's shining on him from the hallway, I see he's got more blood on his clothes than I first realised. That's more than just a cut from a bit of glass. Uncle Will might be my uncle, but he's on the run from the police when all is said and done. He's been found guilty of thirteen murders in the past. Guilty. In a court. And here I am, in Auntie Claire's house, completely on my own with him. He even looked at me strangely before. What if he tries to kill me? No, of course he won't. It will all be fine. And Heidi's on her way.

> We've managed to get out of here. I'll be there as quick as I can. You owe me BIG TIME for this.

"She's coming," I tell him.

"Has she said whether she's got Harry with her?"

I nod. "And Isaac as far as I know."

"Good work Alysha." For some reason, he won't look at me anymore. "I'd better get myself cleaned up and presentable then." He sounds almost cheerful now. "Before I meet my kids. You've done well."

I listen to the trickle of the shower and try to still my whirring thoughts. This is all seriously warped. I didn't give myself the chance to think about what I was doing. I can hear Grandma's voice. *Fools rush in where angels fear to tread,* one of her favourite sayings. I might never see Grandma again. Uncle Will might really kill me. This could be my final day on earth. Now that he's got what he wanted me for. But he won't quite have finished with me yet. He'll be relying on me to get the rest of them inside the house. And then he might kill me. Then he might kill them too. And it will be all my fault.

My mind is running away with me. I'm probably being stupid here. He only wants to see Heidi again, and meet Harry, and then he'll take my car away and carry on with being on the run. But maybe I'll never see my car again. And I'll be in the biggest trouble I've ever been in. In my whole life. I'll just have to play dumb. Say I was scared. I can blame Uncle Will. Say he made me. They'll believe me over him.

I can't sit still. I stand and pace the room, picking up Auntie Claire's pictures and putting them down again. It's strange that Uncle Will doesn't seem to have noticed them. He seems as wired as I am, understandable really. The police could turn up here at any time. The closed blinds in the middle of the day might even bring more attention to the house. Especially if the neighbours know Auntie Claire isn't here. Or Heidi might have secretly let someone know where I am. Though I doubt it. I think I can trust her. She won't suspect in a million years who I'm with.

I study a photo of Auntie Claire with her boyfriend, Fraser. He's asked her to marry him several times, but she reckons to be not interested in all that. I miss Auntie Claire. We spent a ton of time together when I was young. At one time, she was like my second mother. But things change. People change. She's closer to Heidi than she is to me these days.

I put the photo back in its place and pick up one of me and Heidi when we were eight and six. That will be how Uncle Will remembers us, before seeing us today, that is. From looking at this picture, I can see why people say Heidi and I have a look of each other, though my hair is blonde and Heidi's is brown. My eyes are blue and Heidi's are brown. My gaze moves to the picture of Harry and Isaac beside it. It's obvious that they're brothers – though they're not proper brothers. On the surface, we could be one big normal family. Except we're not. Far from it.

The shower stops and my heart beats faster. I walk to the kitchen and fill a glass with water. I'll need to listen out for Heidi in a little while. She's expecting me to be keeping warm in the shed so will head straight into the back garden rather than coming to the door when she gets here.

Part of me wants to run for it. I'm scared. I'm starting to

realise that I shouldn't have done this. Right now, I'd do anything to be back at Dad's, curled up on the sofa with Grandma. I close my eyes. Last time Uncle Will saw Heidi, he threw her into the river. She nearly died. Oh God. Maybe I should let Auntie Claire know I'm here. She'll know what to do for the best. She'll go mad with me, but I can't just sit here, waiting to see what's going to happen. I'm going to have to do something.

> Auntie Claire. I'm at your house. My car broke down. Can you come home?

Then I put my phone on silent. If Uncle Will finds out I've texted Auntie Claire, I don't know how he'll react. Though when they see each other again after all these years, maybe they'll be happy I brought them together. That's only if the news reports have definitely got it wrong, and the police really are after the wrong man for the killings over the last few days. And I have to believe that Uncle Will behaved as he did all those years ago because he wasn't well. And now he's had treatment, and he's better. Especially now that I'm here on my own with him.

I stiffen as I hear the top step creak. I've gone from excitement to terror in the last hour. And guilt for the first time in my life. Perhaps I should warn Heidi about what's really going on. Stop her from coming. But then what? What would I do? How would I get away? I should definitely make a run for it. Get out of the window. As if I let him have the key. But then, I could hardly say no. It's not too late if I go right now. Nobody ever needs to know anything, apart from that I needed to get out of Dad's house. That I was going stir crazy and didn't like being told what to do.

I reach for my phone. I've got to sort this out before it's too late. Stop them all from coming here. But before I can do anything, Uncle Will is standing in front of me. Any idea I had of getting out of here has disappeared, for now.

"I'm just going to the loo," I mumble as I try to get past him. The plan now is to message Heidi and send another message to Auntie Claire. I'll stop them from coming, then I'll climb out of a window. Though perhaps I should try to call her. If I flush the loo at the same time, Uncle Will hopefully won't be able to hear me.

"Why are you taking your phone to the bathroom?"

"I'm just, I'm just keeping it handy in case Heidi texts me again. She could get stopped on the way, or Dad might ring her, or something."

"You're lying." He smiles a smile that makes me realise now why Dad calls him evil. "You always were a rubbish liar, Alysha. You've gone as red as your cardigan."

I glance down at it. It is a very red cardigan, and I have a very burning face.

"Leave the phone there." He points towards the hallway table. "And don't be long. I don't want them pulling up outside without you being here to bring them in."

Uncle Will's whole mood has changed since we spoke on the phone this morning. He's gone from telling me I'm more like his daughter than his niece to calling me a liar. I don't know why suddenly he doesn't seem to trust me. I have no choice other than to do as he asks, and put my phone down in the place he's pointing at. Thankfully, he doesn't ask me to unlock it. I haven't deleted the message I've just sent to Auntie Claire, and I'll be in real trouble if he sees that. When I come back downstairs, I'll text them both. Hopefully, I should still have at least ten minutes before they all get here. Time enough to stop them. Uncle Will will be sent back to prison soon enough. No one ever needs to know anything. I'll be in the clear.

· · ·

I stare at Auntie Claire's spotty dressing gown hanging on the door as I sit on the loo. Something so ordinary in such an out-of-the-ordinary situation. The last time I was here was two Christmases ago when I was still living at home. When life was as 'normal' as it's ever been for me. But this situation is all my fault. I don't know what I'm more scared of – what's going to happen next, or what Dad's going to do to me when he finds out where I am. And who I'm with.

My phone is where I left it as I descend the stairs. Thank God. I snatch it up. Uncle Will is doing what I was doing before. Picking up pictures and putting them back down. As I type a text to Heidi, I hear a car crunching the gravel on the drive outside. I peer through the pane of glass in the tiny window in the front door. Too late. It's Grandma's car. Shit. Shit. Shit. Heidi's here already. I wasn't quick enough to stop her. What the hell am I going to do? Then Grandma's voice enters my mind again. *Everything happens for a reason Alysha.*

"She's here." Uncle Will curls his head around the lounge door into the hallway. He actually looks nervous. "You'd better bring her in, hadn't you? And the kids." He takes the key from his pocket and holds it towards me.

I swallow and stride past him to the back door. As I unlock it and tug it open, Heidi's walking past, evidently heading for the shed. I should bolt for it but I'm frozen to the spot.

"I thought you said you were waiting in there." She looks puzzled as she turns back.

"I, erm, found a spare key." No. No. No. What have I done? I glance at him. He could grab me within seconds if I tried to run. Hopefully, he'll just want to meet them and then he'll let us all go. I'll have to keep them near the door.

"Lock up then. We should get back, really. We're probably

going to get caught as it is. As if you've dragged us all over here."

I see Uncle Will move towards me in the corner of my eye. I don't know what to do. I'm scared. He'll be waiting for me to do something here.

"You'd better come in for a minute first," I say to Heidi. What else can I say with him standing there? Though I try to load a 'warning' expression into my face.

"What for? We need to get in the car Alysha."

"Just come in here."

She steps into the kitchen and looks past me to where Uncle Will's standing in the doorway. Blinking fast, it seems to take a few moments before recognition enters her face. This quickly turns to an expression I've never seen before.

"It's... No... It's not..." She turns, poised to bolt in the direction she's just come from. But Uncle Will lurches forward and slams the door shut before she can get back to it.

"Just hold on a moment Heidi. I only wanted to see you." He turns his back against the door and studies her.

She backs into the hallway, terror written all over her face. I feel awful. She'll probably never forgive me for this. And I don't blame her. What I thought was a bit of exciting drama has gone horribly wrong. Dad has always said that I act before I engage my brain.

"You've hardly changed Heidi." Uncle Will's face relaxes into a smile. "You're just as I pictured you."

"Please. Let me out of here. My brothers are in the car. I need-"

"Just come and sit down for a few minutes. It's been twelve years. You owe me that much."

"You tried to kill me Dad. I owe you nothing."

It's strange to hear her call him Dad. After all this time. She's physically shaking now as she stares from him to me. I feel guiltier than I've ever felt in my life. What have I done?

These words keep repeating in my head over and over. *What was I thinking of?*

"You've completely ignored me for twelve years. Of course, you owe me. And I never meant what happened that night. I was just backed into a corner."

She's staring at him, open-mouthed.

"I loved you so much that if they were finishing me off, I was taking you with me."

Still, she doesn't speak but stands, rooted to the spot, shaking her head.

"Take that look off your face Heidi. No matter how much your mother tried to poison you against me, I won't have you looking at me like that."

"Heidi! Auntie Claire!" Harry shouts from the other side of the door.

I close my eyes. This is all my fault. I've put us all in danger. He's still a big bloke. He could do anything to us.

Uncle Will points at Heidi. "Stay right where you are. And don't even think of doing anything stupid." Then he opens the door and stands aside. Harry and Isaac burst in and race over to me.

"I didn't know you were here Alysha." Isaac looks happy to see me. I'm warmed by this – for a nanosecond.

"I thought you were broken down in your car," Harry adds. "Heidi said. How come you're here? Where's Auntie Claire?" He looks into the lounge then back at me.

Uncle Will turns the key where I've left it in the door and returns it to his pocket. Heidi backs further away from him, until she's standing in front of me, Harry and Isaac. He's locked us in. Why has he locked us in? What are we going to do? What is he going to do?

"Who are you?" Harry steps forwards. Heidi puts her hand up as if to stop him from going any further. Being the eldest, she's flown straight into protective mode. That's the sort of person she is. Sometimes, she irritates me, but deep down, she's a good person. Not like me.

"I'm your dad," he replies, smiling at Harry. "Your *real* dad."

Harry's face drops into an expression that veers between bewilderment and terror as he sidles around Heidi so he's behind her.

"Are you the bad man?"

I look at Isaac, all innocent in this. What have I brought him into? If Dad could see us all now, standing in Auntie Claire's hallway like this, I don't know what he'd do. Well actually, I do.

18

WILL

"Who told you I'm a bad man?" I keep the smile plastered on my face as I stare at the kid. He'll be, well, my nephew, I suppose, being Mark's kid. But he's Eva's too. I look from him to my son. My son. All I've ever wanted is a son. And that bitch kept all knowledge of him from me. And me from him. As did my so-called brother. If they were in front of me right now, I wouldn't be responsible for my actions.

"My daddy's a policeman," the kid goes on. "And he shoots bad men with his guns."

"Shut up Isaac." Harry steps back and puts his hand over the kid's mouth. He's definitely a chip off the old block. And he looks so much like me. I wonder if he can see it too. Yet his entire demeanour says he doesn't want to know me. Which makes me sad. And more irritated than I can possibly put into words.

"Why don't we all have a sit down?" I step towards them, whilst gesturing toward the lounge. "Get to know one another better."

Nobody moves. The look of terror on the faces of Heidi and Harry is making me angrier by the minute. Alysha's expression has gone that way too. There's only the kid who seems OK being in here with me.

"If you let us go," Heidi begins, sticking her chin out like her mother would. "We won't tell anyone we've seen you. In fact, you can take Brenda's car. No one will be looking for that. It's right outside." She gestures toward the front door. "We'll give you time to get away." She dangles the key at me. "If you go now, you might be able to get away."

"You'll be on the phone before I get to the end of the street." I look at the key, then back at her. "I don't trust you one iota."

"I don't care." Whether she means it to, her lip curls in apparent disgust towards me.

"How dare you disrespect me like this? I'm your father." I'm literally shaking with anger. Not that I expected her to fall into my arms, but I expected better than this.

"You threw that privilege away a long time ago *Dad*." The way she says the word *dad*, well, I might as well have Eva standing in front of me. "Perhaps you should have said, *I wouldn't trust you as far as I could throw you*. Which wouldn't be as far since I'm not eight anymore."

Alysha has the nerve to snigger at this. Heidi briefly shifts her glare from me to her. *Get rid of her*. Oh no. They're back. I can't handle the voices. Not here. Not now. But they're shouting this time, exactly like they were all those years ago when I threw her into the river. *Get rid of her*. It was ages before anyone even told me she'd survived. It was as though I didn't have a right to know about the welfare of my own daughter. *Get rid of her*.

I waver for a few moments. Should I just take the key and get out of here? Then I look at Harry, clinging to Alysha. I thought he'd be glad to meet me. It's criminal what they've done to him. Child abuse.

Suddenly, there's a screech of brakes and a slamming of doors. We all look at each other. Then a thundering of footsteps, a key turning in the lock of the back door. Another hammering of boots on the drive outside and then...

"Armed police. Get down on the floor."

I dart amongst the huddle of kids, landing in the centre of them before getting hold of the youngest kid in one arm, and Alysha in the other. Heidi and Harry crouch down as they try to crawl away – Heidi's ushering him forward. I stretch my foot out and bring it down on Harry's. He stops moving and looks back at me. It's not the way a son should look at his father.

"I said get down on the floor!"

Both Alysha and the kid are frozen stiff at either side of me. I raise my eyes from Harry's into the eyes of my sister. I see nothing but pure fear, not to mention hatred.

"This is your last chance Potts!" I hear the metal on metal of a gun as I keep my gaze fixed on Claire.

"Auntie Claire. Where's my dad?" Harry raises his head from the floor.

"I'm right here son." Mark steps in front of the other officers, pointing a gun in my direction. "Everything's going to be alright. Just stay really still."

Who the hell does he think he is? What's he even doing here? How did anyone even know I was here? One of this lot has clearly squealed on me. I tighten my grip on those who have now become my human shields. No one's going to open fire when I've got them all in front of me. I can still get out of this. I know I can.

"He's not your fucking son." My voice is a snarl. Like that makes any difference to me now.

"Give me the key to the car," I command Heidi. Without hesitation, she throws it at my feet. I bring Alysha and the kid even closer to either side of me as I bend forward to pick it up.

"Don't move." The bellow of some jumped up officer stops me. "Place your hands on your head and get to the ground."

"Hold fire." Mark commands his colleagues, not taking his eyes off me. "I can handle this."

"Sir." There's a collective sound of guns being lowered. Mark's doesn't move. I never thought I'd be staring down the barrel of a gun wielded by my own brother.

"Let them go Will," he continues. "Then we'll talk."

"Listen to him Will, for God's sake." Tears are rolling down Claire's cheeks. She always was overly dramatic. "I don't want anyone to get hurt, even you."

"What do you mean, *even you?* It's partly your fucking fault everything turned out like this."

Alysha sobs at the side of me as I raise my voice.

"Shut your noise," I yell into her ear. The other one is still frozen solid, not taking his eyes off Mark.

"Things are serious enough," Mark continues from behind his gun. "Don't make them any worse. I don't want to have to take you down. Just let Alysha and Isaac go."

"Any worse." I literally spit the words at him. "How can things be any worse? You took my life from me. You took everything. Even my wife. That's all you've ever done. Him there," I nod towards Harry on the floor. "That's my kid. Not yours."

Harry edges closer to Mark, which makes my blood rise to boiling point. And where have the voices gone? I suddenly seem to be on my own here.

There's a slam of another car door then the sound of heels click-clacking up the drive.

"Stay out there," someone shouts.

I do a double take as Eva appears next to Mark. The woman that was my wife. If I thought my sister looked at me with hatred in her eyes, this is magnified by ten in what I'm seeing from Eva. She moves her attention to Alysha.

"You stupid, stupid little girl." She points at her. "Look what you've done. The two of you deserve one another. Two identical peas in a pod."

"What are you on about?" Alysha's gone from being frozen stiff to shaking like a shitting dog in my grasp. I almost feel sorry for her. Almost. "I'm sorry. Really, I am. I felt sorry for him, that's all. I tried to stop it all, but it was too late."

"You can't fight biology," Eva continues. There's a rustle amongst the men standing behind them as this family drama plays out. If I wasn't Mark Pott's brother, perhaps I'd have been shot by now. Though I think it's more to do with the kids surrounding me. This is supposed to be my family, yet I've only ever been cast out of it time and time again. They've all got as much blood on their hands as I have. If not more. Yet, I'm the scapegoat, like I've always been.

"Enough love." Mark shifts his gaze momentarily to Eva then straight back at me. He raises his gun slightly as though to remind me he's still got it. "This isn't the time."

"This is most definitely the time. Look at the danger she's put my children in."

The situation is almost laughable. I'm standing here, sheltered by my so-called nephew and niece, whilst my brother points a gun at us. Not that he'll have the guts to use it. And my ex-wife is standing there, chelping like an old fish woman. It's a standoff if ever I saw one. However, they don't know about the knife in my pocket. And with the car key at my feet, I can still bolt for it.

"You know the trouble you're in, don't you Alysha." Eva wags a finger at her. "I hope you're going to arrest her." She twists her body towards Mark's colleagues. Who probably used to be my colleagues too.

"Why?" Alysha's voice is even smaller.

"Concealing a dangerous criminal. But then he is your *father*."

19

ALYSHA

UNCLE WILL ALMOST RELEASES his hold on me at Auntie Eva's words. But not completely. As I try to get away, his fingers dig into my flesh. "Get off me." I thrash from left to right, trying to free myself. She's lying. The complete bitch. How can she say Will Potts is my father? What's she on about?

"Keep still," he hisses into my ear. "Or you're really going to get it."

"You've already tried to murder one of your daughters." Auntie Eva actually smiles. "So you might as well have a go at the other."

"Mum!" Heidi shrieks.

She's saying all this to hurt me. But whatever her plan is, it's working. "You're lying."

"I'm not." She folds her arms. I look from her face to Dad's.

Dad lowers the gun slightly, his expression sagging with it. From the way he avoids my eyes, I can tell there's more than a grain of truth in what Auntie Eva just said. She's always been jealous of me, and hasn't liked me since she and Dad got together, but surely she's got this wrong?

"But that would mean..." I twist around, trying to look at

Uncle Will. I want to see his reaction. If she's telling the truth... But he tightens his grip on me even more. What a time for her to come out with something like this.

"Let me go. Take your bloody hands off me." As I struggle in his grasp, Isaac screeches at the other side, and Auntie Eva darts toward him.

"Get off him!" She doesn't say, *get off her*. She probably hopes he'll kill me. I suppose I deserve to die after what I've done today.

"Get over here," one officer yells from behind Dad. He's talking to me.

I'm shoved from behind and I stumble forward into Heidi. He's let me go. But in one movement, he's flicked a kitchen knife from his pocket with the hand which held me. I'm unable to get my breath as he presses the knife against Isaac's throat. Isaac's eyes roll back in his head. The blade reflects under his chin. His teeth are gritted, and he's as still as a monument.

"Do something Uncle Mark," Heidi cries out.

"Please Will." Auntie Eva drops to her knees before them both. "Let him go." She holds her hand out. "Take me instead. Please don't hurt him. He's five years old, for God's sake." I've never heard her beg like this before. No matter what she's just said about me, she doesn't deserve to have her son held at knifepoint.

The room is silent apart from Isaac now sobbing in fear as he's turned to face the side wall.

"Shut the fuck up." Uncle Will drags him backwards and closer to the front door, keeping him against his body the whole time. Why has nobody shot him yet? They're supposed to be trained to target. Isaac only comes up to his ribs. Surely they could shoot him in the leg or his head. But in a split second, perhaps anything can happen, and one wrong move could get Isaac killed.

"Where's the key to this door?" He jerks his head towards

Auntie Claire who wipes at her tears and points at a rack on the wall.

"Well, move it then."

I don't know how he thinks he's going to get out of here. There will be police crawling all over the street. I guess he's intending to continue using Isaac as a human shield, but even then, he's not going to get very far. They'll shoot him before he can get anywhere near Grandma's car.

All this is my fault. I should have told someone the moment Uncle Will got in touch. I can't believe I'm still calling him Uncle. He's nothing to me, not anymore, and yet Auntie Eva says he could be my dad. And Dad didn't deny it either.

Tears burn the backs of my eyes. This isn't the time for dragging family skeletons out of the cupboard. It's a time for making sure no one gets hurt. Which isn't likely with several firearms police in front of us.

Someone's going to die here.

Auntie Claire is trembling as she lifts a key off a hook on the wall. I can't imagine what's going through her mind. It's the first time in twelve years that she's set eyes on her brother. She will probably have nothing to do with me after this. She's been full of criticism about me over the last couple of years already. Probably because of Heidi constantly telling tales about me.

"Get it fucking open then." Uncle Will gestures at Auntie Claire, then at the door, crouching behind Isaac as he continues to grasp him with one hand and point the knife at his throat with his other. If anything happens to Isaac, I'm pretty sure I'll be without a family. Forever.

"Now." He yells, making me jump. "If any of you moves a muscle whilst I get out of here, the kid gets it." Momentarily he raises the knife and waves its blade around the room at his assembled audience before bringing it back to Isaac's throat.

A radio crackles and beeps. The only words I catch are *shoot to kill.* I've never seen a dead body, but maybe I'm about to. The question is, whose will it be? If Auntie Eva had her way, it would be mine.

There are five police officers in here, three with guns, and they haven't tried to get Isaac away from him yet. As Auntie Claire fumbles with the key in the lock, DSI Jones appears at the door.

"Bring him in, I don't care how," he bellows.

The icy blast is comforting against my burning face as the door swings open. I glance behind me. There are police officers all over the street, their guns pointing at the house.

"Get back inside," a voice yells from the street, presumably pointing at a neighbour, watching from their doorway.

"But I need to go to work."

"Inside. Now!"

Uncle Will lurches towards the door, his body in a stoop, clearly making himself smaller in order that Isaac's head comes up to his chest.

"Daddy! Help me."

Harry is pressed up against Heidi, covering his eyes as though he can't bear to watch.

Tears are streaming down Heidi's face. "Please, Uncle Mark. Get Isaac away from him."

"I hope you're happy with what you've done." Auntie Eva looks at me with venom in her eyes as she jumps to her feet from where she's been crouched beside Harry. She follows Dad as he rushes through the back door and around the side of the house. "Whatever happens here, it's you that will have to live with yourself."

"I'm sorry. I'm..." I reach out to her.

"Stay away from me. If anything happens to my son because of you."

Uncle Will still has the knife against Isaac's throat as he edges closer to Grandma's car. If he presses any harder, it's going to be all over. This little boy, who I've spent the last five years believing to be my brother, will be dead. But if what Auntie Eva is saying is true, which I don't see how it can be, Isaac is really my cousin.

It's deathly quiet. Seven guns point at Uncle Will from all sides. He still appears to think he can get away. Maybe they should shoot me whilst they're at it. My life certainly feels like it's over.

Dad draws level with Uncle Will and Isaac on the drive. They stare at each other.

"The firearms division chose *you*." Uncle Will laughs. "You're nothing but a coward. You always have been."

"Daddy!"

"You won't shoot me." Uncle Will laughs harder.

Dad raises his gun and closes one eye. The knife against Isaac's throat glints in the sunshine.

"I'm your brother."

"Take him down," DSI Jones yells into the silence.

I don't know what comes first, Isaac's scream or the deafening bang. But there's blood everywhere. Uncle Will lands heavily on top of Isaac.

"Isaac. Oh my God." All at once, we rush over to the bloodied heap on the ground.

"Get back," a loud voice booms.

No one listens.

Auntie Claire and Dad roll Uncle Will from Isaac. His skull lands against the concrete with a crack. His eyes are glassy and blood is seeping from his head.

Isaac isn't moving. Dad's attention is on his neck. There's so much blood, it's difficult to see from where I'm standing where it's all coming from. Has Isaac been cut? His eyes are also glassy. Dad feels his wrist. "It's OK. I think he's just in shock."

"Thank God." Auntie Eva is weeping as she pushes towards them. I'm suddenly reminded this is the second time she's seen one of her children at serious risk of losing their life at the hands of her ex-husband.

"Is it true what you said?" I tug at her arm. "Is he really my dad?" I look from the man lying in a widening pool of blood, back into her face. I'd give anything for her to have made it up to hurt me. I deserved to be hurt.

"I've got nothing to say to you," she replies, her voice icy as she turns her attention back to Isaac.

"Dad? Please!"

"I'll speak to you soon." Dad glances at me as he cradles Isaac in his arms. I'm jealous. Maybe he isn't my dad anymore. He loves Isaac more than me anyway. He loves everyone more than me.

Swirling blue lights reflect onto their faces and I have a sense of not belonging like I've never felt before. Auntie Claire rushes over to Heidi and Harry, gathering them up in a huddle next to me.

It should have been me that was shot dead or stabbed in the neck. Nobody wants me. Maybe they never did. The only person I have left is Grandma. And even she won't want me after this.

Having been so close to it all, I'm splattered in blood. As are Heidi and Harry. The same blood which I fear is running through my veins. Who am I? What will become of me now?

An ambulance screeches around the corner of Auntie Claire's cul-de-sac and police tape is stretched across the edge of her drive. Silence has given way to commotion as neighbours gather outside each other's front doors.

But despite all the noise, I still only hear silence as they pronounce Uncle Will dead at 3.12 pm.

20

ALYSHA

Dad passes me Mum's journal then sits facing me. His face has far more wrinkles than it used to have. Part age, he says, part stress. "We've marked the passages you should look at," he says. "We'll be right here as you read it."

He remains sitting in front of me and squeezes my shoulder. I look down at the swirls of handwriting and try to imagine my mother writing in this book. I can almost see her, blonde and concentrating, an older version of me. There's not a day that passes when I don't wish she was still here.

Dad and Auntie Claire, who is sitting at the side of me, seem calm. They've obviously discussed this moment.

"Ask us anything you need to," Auntie Claire says.

"Exactly how long have you known?" I look up from Mum's journal, still unable to believe they have kept this secret from me. After all, Harry knows where he came from now. But as Dad has already explained, Harry's conception was under entirely different circumstances.

"Since I was helping your dad pack to move house," replies Auntie Claire. "Your mum had clearly meant to get rid of this journal some day. Obviously she'd never suspected that she wouldn't still be around."

"Did Grandma know? Before it all came out, I mean?" She enters my mind, crying and hand wringing. Poor Grandma. As if she hasn't had enough to cope with.

Dad shakes his head. "It was always going to be too much for her."

"We thought she'd suffered enough." Auntie Claire's voice is gentle. "And really, we never wanted you to know either."

"I'm sorry it came out like it did," Dad adds, and I'm reminded of Auntie Eva's venom that awful day last week. Probably the worst day of my life. Yes, I know I deserved it, but part of me is still struggling to forgive her. As Grandma said, *I'm not even eighteen yet. She's supposed to be the adult.*

But one of Grandma's favourite sayings is *what comes around, goes around,* and I guess what I've found out could be my punishment for helping Will Potts, and for putting everyone else in danger.

Dad says I've been extremely lucky not to be prosecuted and instead to have been formally cautioned like the thoughtless, stupid idiot I've been. The media has gone crazy about it all and said I've only got off because I'm the daughter of a senior officer. Hopefully, it'll all die down in time.

"This changes nothing between us." Dad takes my chin between his fingers and tilts my face towards his. "You'll always be my daughter and I love you, no matter what."

Tears fill my eyes as I look from him, back to Mum's journal, feeling her presence for the first time in a long time.

November 15th

I haven't stopped throwing up all morning.

Never, ever am I drinking again. I didn't want to go to that stupid wedding in the first place. I only dragged myself along for Eva, and obviously for Mark's benefit. They both know I've never liked Will. But they both just think it's a clash of personalities, rather than him repeatedly trying to come onto me over the years. Mark would probably kill me for not telling him about it, but he's been through enough with losing his other brother.

I don't want to be responsible for tearing their family any more apart than it already is.

Will cornered me last night, telling me I had to be nice to him now that we're 'family.' His breath was sour in my face, and I felt sick when his spittle landed on my cheek. I told him to keep away from me, and when he didn't come near me again for the rest of the evening, I assumed he'd got the message.

Eva got really drunk, I mean really drunk. I would have done in her shoes - I mean - who'd want to be married to that? She had to be put to bed early. But I wasn't long after her and only too glad to get away.

Mark had been deep in conversation with his police station buddies, so I left him to it. By that point, I was pretty drunk as well. I'm not even sure how I found the right hotel room.

I can't believe I'm even going to write this,

but I have to try. It might help me make sense of it. Writing always helps. Things keep coming back to me and I'm not sure how real they are. Nasty things. I was so drunk that I don't even know if I dreamt it all.

I'd honestly thought it was Mark when I suddenly felt a weight beside me in bed. Then the weight was on top of me. I might have even responded at first, believing it to be Mark. Then suddenly he was boring into me. Sliding up and down. Groaning. Slavering. And even though it was pitch black, I quickly realised the shape in the darkness wasn't Mark.

I tried rolling over, trying to throw him off balance, arching my back, then ripping at his skin. When I tried to scream for help, he slammed a pillow over my face, snarling he'd kill me if I didn't shut it.

That's when I went limp. It's all I could do. Let him get on with it. I felt the heat between my legs as he shuddered on top of me. Eventually the weight lifted. But I was too scared to make a sound.

"There. You've got what you always wanted." It was Will's voice.

I lay, motionless, waiting for him to either hurt me or to leave. Lips were being fastened and shoes were being put on. I listened as he drank the water I must have poured when I came to bed - I don't remember. He told me that one word to anyone would be the last time I'd speak. I waited for the squeak of the door and the echo of his fading footsteps before I could breathe again.

I still keep wondering if it was all a horrendous dream. One of those that's vivid to the point it almost becomes real. I was so drunk that I can't make sense of it.

I didn't go down for breakfast this morning. I told Mark I had a hangover, so he went down without me. Will acted as though nothing had happened when I hugged Eva before we left the hotel. I couldn't look at him.

They're on honeymoon now for two weeks. Hopefully that will be long enough for me to piece it all together. Did Will Potts rape me? Or was I so drunk that I was hallucinating? And if he was on top of me, did I allow it? Did I encourage it?

Oh my God, this is awful.

November 26th

They're back off honeymoon and have just been round to ours. I stayed upstairs for as long as I could, but then Eva came to find me. She was tanned and looked really happy. I couldn't exactly say, your new husband might have raped me on your wedding night, or there again, I was so drunk I might have dreamt it.

If it really happened, Will would say I led him on. And if it didn't happen at all, well, how would that make me look? Totally nuts.

Since that night, I haven't touched a drop of alcohol. I don't trust myself anymore. I just want to put the whole thing behind me and get on with my life. I'd like to suggest to Mark that we move away, but we've both got our work here. And why should I let an arsehole like Will Potts drive me away from my mum, my home and my friends?

And I think the world of Eva. She looked really hurt earlier when I didn't go straight downstairs. So I tried to act normal. And I'm going to keep acting normal. It's all I can do.

There's no real harm done. And it may not have even happened.

Mum's always said I have an overactive imagination.

December 21st

My period is late. I feel sick all the time. I

don't know whether it's a symptom of something I can't bear to contemplate, or whether it's just misery.

I have nightmares and flashbacks about what happened. I wish I could tell someone. Mark keeps asking what's wrong, but I can never tell him. He must never know. I'm so ashamed. This is all my fault.

January 2nd

Some start to the new year this is. I've just done a test, and it's positive.

If it was Mark's baby, I would be over the moon. I don't know if the baby's Mark's or Will's. At least that's what I keep telling myself. Really, I do know. Mark always wears a condom. We agreed to save having a baby for a few years. Focus on our careers and having fun. Fun. What's that?

I'm going to have to convince Mark the condom split. He'll wonder why I said nothing at the time, but I cannot bear the thought of Will being involved after what he must have done to me. I'd hoped my drunken mind was playing tricks, but no, I'm pregnant with Will Potts's baby. If I was to *say anything, I know he'd say I led him on. Or worse. He's capable of anything.*

As I write, I can't stop crying. I should have said something as soon as it happened. I've been such an idiot. I'm so, so scared.

All I can do now is tell Mark the baby is his. He'll be an amazing daddy. I've thought of getting rid of it, but I wouldn't be able to live with myself. I've always wanted to be a mother. And maybe it is Mark's. If I tell myself this for long enough, I'll hopefully begin to believe it. And I'll still love this baby with all of my heart. No matter what. It's not the baby's fault.

One day, when everything has settled down and I've got through this, I'll burn all my journals. I'll have to. No one can ever know the truth. No one. And I'll spend the rest of my life making sure Will Potts never gets near my innocent baby. I'll take this secret to my grave.

I can't read any more. Tears are sliding down my face. For myself and for what happened to my mother. Things will never be the same again. I'll never be the same again. I thought I was born out of love and that Dad was my dad – instead I'm a product of rape and my father is a murderer.

Our 'family' is about as messed up as it gets. Heidi is my cousin, my stepsister, and my half-sister. Harry has become my half-brother and Isaac is no longer my brother at all. My tears turn to full-blown sobs.

"Come here, you." Dad pulls me towards him, and I nestle my face into his jumper, longing for nothing to have changed. Auntie Claire strokes my hand.

But everything has changed. I am Alysha Potts. Daughter of murder victim and serial killer.

And I can't help but feel like a victim too.

21

HEIDI

"Thanks for keeping us informed. No. No way. We don't want his ashes."

Uncle Mark places his phone on the chair arm. No one speaks for a few moments.

"That's it then," he finally says.

"I just wish it had taken place before the new year." I'm not sure how I feel. Peculiar. That's the only word I can use to describe it. Everyone told me I'd feel better after the funeral. That it offers a sense of closure.

Part of me wanted to watch the curtains being drawn around him for the final time and without seeing that, the closure doesn't seem to apply.

"I don't see what difference it makes. Before the new year... after the new year..." Alysha refocuses on her phone. She'd better not be posting on social media about this.

What's just taken place should stay between us for now. She was incredibly meek and mild in the weeks following Will Potts's death but seems to be reverting to her usual bolshy self again. I suppose that's a good thing.

"I think I know what she means." Mum reaches for my

hand. "It would have been good to start this new year with a completely clean slate."

"Two months isn't bad in the scheme of things. Not with all the investigation that's been necessary." Uncle Mark drains the last of his tea. "I think I could do with something stronger. It might settle me down."

"Me too." Auntie Claire stands from her place next to Alysha. "I'll do the honours, shall I?" She's been staying with us since that horrendous day, unable to go on living in her house after what happened there.

"Will Auntie Claire go back to Alderton?" I ask when she's left the room. "Now that the bastard has been burned."

"Heidi!" Mum shakes her head. "Please! Where are the boys? They don't need to hear language like that from you."

"Upstairs," Uncle Mark replies. "Getting their uniforms ready for tomorrow. It's time to get back into a routine. And as for Auntie Claire, you'll have to ask her."

"I doubt it," replies Mum. "She's only been back there for some clothes." Then despite the news we've just had, her face breaks into a smile. "But she's been making noises about moving in with that man of hers."

"I wish she'd move over here." Alysha's voice is definitely back to its familiar whine.

"We're all going to have to get back to normal eventually," Brenda says, glancing up at the rattle of glasses as Auntie Claire returns to the room. "Now that it's all over."

"There's no sign of reporters back out there, is there?" Mum watches Auntie Claire. "Now that he's been cremated."

"No. Don't worry."

"None of them know he's been cremated yet," says Uncle Mark. "Nor do they know where. It's just a shame I didn't get to press the button on the incinerator."

Everyone falls silent. There's not much of an answer to that. I want to say something about Uncle Mark having been the one to pull the trigger that killed Will Potts, but it's the one aspect of that day that's barely been spoken about since it happened. Uncle Mark speaks to Mum. Alysha speaks to Brenda, and I've got Auntie Claire. For now, anyway. And we're all having counselling. Harry and Isaac seem to be OK. Harry's had a load of questions asked of him at school and Isaac initially had a few nightmares. But according to Mum, they've both come through relatively unscathed.

"Are we all having one?" Auntie Claire glugs brandy into Mum's best glasses.

"Isn't this a bit inappropriate Dad?" Alysha raises her gaze from her phone. "Raising a glass to his body being burned?"

"That's not what it is love." Uncle Mark takes a glass from Auntie Claire. "We're raising a glass to surviving everything we've all been through as a family. And to the future we've got ahead. He can't hurt anybody anymore."

"I'll raise a glass to that."

I take two glasses from Auntie Claire and pass one to Alysha. Despite what's come out, I find it very difficult to think of her as my sister. We all know the truth now – it's been agony, and still is, to process, but it's better to know. And nothing's changed between us really – Mum and Uncle Mark spoke to us all around the table and said how important it is that we go on as before.

At least we've got the chance to go on. Which is more than can be said for the new victims of his most recent killing spree. Mum and Uncle Mark went to the funerals of Tina, Suzannah and Daniel.

They didn't find out about the funerals of the hotel receptionist or of the woman he killed in her holiday cottage until after they'd taken place. I'm sure they'd have gone if they had known though. Me and Alysha weren't allowed to any of them. Mum says we've been through enough.

I sip at my brandy, pulling a face as it burns the back of my throat.

"Are you alright Alysha?" Mum looks at her. One good thing that's come out of all this is that their relationship has shifted. Alysha knows how serious her actions were, but Mum accepted she was coerced into it. There's been a lot of talking done over the last few weeks and they're getting on far better.

"Yeah. I just feel weird."

"We all do." Auntie Claire perches on the arm of her chair. "But we've got through everything so far and we're going to live again now."

"I'll drink to that." Uncle Mark raises his glass. "To living again."

Before you go...

Thanks for reading Emergence - I really hope you enjoyed it and will consider leaving me a review on Amazon and/or Goodreads as this makes such a difference in helping other readers find the book.

Join my 'keep in touch' list to receive a free book, and to be kept posted of special offers and new releases.

Find out more about me via www.mariafrankland.co.uk and find out more about my other psychological thrillers by visiting my author page at Amazon.

Emergence is the third and final book in the Dark Water Series. First in the trilogy is Undercurrents, and second in the trilogy is Drowned Voices.

BOOK DISCUSSION GROUP QUESTIONS

1. To what extent do you agree with Eva who says, *they should bring back the death penalty,* regarding someone like Will?
2. Discuss the psychology of how the family of a high-profile criminal might be hounded and vilified when they personally haven't committed an offence.
3. Do you agree with what Heidi says in the early part of the book? *People like him don't change.*
4. What were the reasons Alysha thought she was justified in helping Will?
5. The book mentions how people might accuse Heidi and Harry to be like Will in some way. What are your thoughts on the genetics of mental illness and personality disorders?
6. Will's mother is dead. What role does she still manage to play in Emergence?
7. Do you think a prisoner who has committed crimes of the magnitude Will has, can ever be reformed?
8. How does the loss of childhood manifest in the story?

9. Discuss your thoughts on the huge secret Lauren kept about what Will did to her.
10. To what extent has justice been done in this story?

FRENEMY
PROLOGUE

I step back from the door, peering up at the house. The upstairs is in darkness, but the flickering TV is visible between the cracks of the blind. Is she *hiding* in there? Ignoring the door? She wouldn't have known I'd be calling tonight, so it can't be that.

I lift the flap of the letterbox and peer inside. Nothing. I check up and down the street. Deserted. I brush beads of sweat from my brow before creeping around the side of the house, picking my way through the bins and stepping over plant pots. The gate creaks as I push it open.

Curtains curl out of the open patio doors. As I start in that direction, my attention is diverted to a dark shape at the side of the shed.

It's... She's...

I drop into a crouch beside her. I reach for her hand. As my fingers search her wrist, I see a halo of darkness surrounding her head. Blood. Her hair flutters in the breeze. Her eyes stare back.Dead.

Available via Amazon

.

INTERVIEW WITH THE AUTHOR

Q: Where do your ideas come from?

A: I'm no stranger to turbulent times, and these provide lots of raw material. People, places, situations, experiences – they're all great novel fodder!

Q: Why do you write domestic thrillers?

A: I'm intrigued why people can be most at risk from someone who should love them. Novels are a safe place to explore the worst of toxic relationships.

Q: Does that mean you're a dark person?

A: We thriller writers pour our darkness into stories, so we're the nicest people you could meet – it's those romance writers you should watch...

Q: What do readers say?

A: That I write gripping stories with unexpected twists, about people you could know and situations that could happen to anyone. So beware...

Q: What's the best thing about being a writer?

A: You lovely readers. I read all my reviews, and answer all emails and social media comments. Hearing from readers absolutely makes my day, whether it's via email or through social media.

Q: Who are you and where are you from?

A: A born 'n' bred Yorkshire lass, with two grown up sons and a Sproodle called Molly. (Springer/Poodle!) My 40's have been the best: I've done an MA in Creative Writing, made writing my full time job, and found the happy-ever-after that doesn't exist in my writing - after marrying for the second time just before the pandemic.

Q: Do you have a newsletter I could join?

A: I certainly do. Go to https:www.mariafrankland.co.uk or <u>click here through your eBook</u> to join my awesome community of readers. I'll send you a free novella – 'The Brother in Law.'

facebook.com/writermariafrank

instagram.com/writermaria_f

tiktok.com/@mariafranklandauthor

ACKNOWLEDGMENTS

Thank you, as always, to my amazing husband, Michael, who is my first reader, and is vital with my editing process for each of my novels. His belief in me means more than I can say.

A special acknowledgment goes to my wonderful advance reader team, who have taken the time and trouble to read an advance copy of Emergence and offer feedback on the book.

I will always be grateful to Leeds Trinity University and my MA in Creative Writing Tutors there, Martyn, Amina and Oz. My Masters degree in 2015 was the springboard into being able to write as a profession.

And thanks especially, to you, the reader. Thank you for taking the time to read this story. I really hope you enjoyed it.

Printed in Great Britain
by Amazon